BETTY MILLER

(1910-1965) was born in Cork, the second daughter of Simon and Sara Spiro. In 1920 she travelled with her mother, sister and two brothers to Sweden, where they lived for two years. Thereafter the family settled in London, where she was educated, graduating from University College with a diploma in journalism in 1930.

Betty Miller began writing at the age of seven and her first novel, *The Mere Living* (1933), admired by her early mentor St. John Ervine, was published when she was twenty-two. In the same year she married the physician Emanuel Miller, who specialised in psychiatry, an influence which permeated her seven acute novels. Her second, *Sunday* (1934) was followed by *Portrait of the Bride* (1935), *Farewell Leicester Square* (1941), *A Room in Regent's Park* (1942), *On the Side of the Angels* (1945), and *The Death of the Nightingale* (1949).

She had two children, Jonathan and Sarah, with whom she moved initially to Sussex at the outbreak of War. The Millers returned to London in 1945 and Betty Miller re-established her large circle of friends. These included Stevie Smith, Rosamond Lehmann, Marghanita Laski, Naomi Lewis, Olivia Manning, Eleanor Farjeon, R.D. Smith, Isaiah Berlin, Sir Sydney Cockerell and Montagu Slater.

Her lifelong interest in Robert Browning crystallised with his biography, published in 1952. This established Betty Miller's reputation and she was elected a Fellow of the Royal Society of Literature. Following its success she edited the Letters of Elizabeth Barrett to Miss Mitford and collaborated with Sam Rosenberg on 'Shadow On the Window', a play about the Brownings which was never produced. This was to be her last completed work, although she continued to contribute articles and reviews to *The Times*, the *Times Literary Supplement*, *The Twentieth Century* and the *Cornhill Magazine*, as she had for some years.

In the 1950s Betty Miller began work on a life of Kipling, but by this time her health was deteriorating and she was diagnosed as having Alzheimer's Disease. She died in London in 1965.

ON THE SIDE
OF THE ANGELS

BETTY MILLER

With a New Introduction by
SARAH MILLER

PENGUIN BOOKS – VIRAGO PRESS

PENGUIN BOOKS

Viking Penguin Inc., 40 West 23rd Street,
New York, New York 10010, U.S.A.
Penguin Books Ltd, Harmondsworth,
Middlesex, England
Penguin Books Australia Ltd, Ringwood,
Victoria, Australia
Penguin Books Canada Limited, 2801 John Street,
Markham, Ontario, Canada L3R 1B4
Penguin Books (N.Z.) Ltd, 182–190 Wairau Road,
Auckland 10, New Zealand

First published in Great Britain by Robert Hale 1945
This edition first published in Great Britain by
Virago Press Limited 1985
Published in Penguin Books 1986

ISBN 0 14 016.117 1

Printed in Finland by
Werner Soderström Oy, a member of Finnprint
Set in Baskerville

To
Henry William Spiro
Dear brother: incomparable friend

Missing, presumed killed, in
H.M.S. *Firedrake*

"*The question is this: Is Man an ape or an angel?
I, my lord, am on the side of the angels*"

—Disraeli
Speech at Oxford Diocesan Conference, 1864

INTRODUCTION

"I like your sauciness and your eager young mind and your determination that you will be somebody when you are twenty-two" wrote Irish author and critic St John Ervine to my mother in her eighteenth year. Four years later, Victor Gollancz published her first novel *The Mere Living*, in which she recounted a day in the life of the immigrant Sullivan family from Cork.

If there is a "monologue interieur", there is also a "dialogue exterieur" of the senses with the objective world. An equal combination of *Ulysses* and *The Old Wives Tale* would succeed in giving a reasonably comprehensive portrait of life, I think, but it requires the two. The price of stocks and shares and the stream of consciousness. (*The Mere Living*, 1933)

My mother was born on 8th October 1910 in Cork, the second daughter of Simon and Sara Spiro. Simon had emigrated to Ireland from Siauliai in northern Lithuania some thirty years before and by the time of his marriage had a thriving cigar and jewellery store on Bridge Street. In addition, he was a JP and secretary of the local synagogue, serving a prosperous Litvak community, many of whom were "landsmen" that is, from the same district of Lithuania as himself. He was also a good enough violinist to take his seat at a second desk in the Cork Opera House orchestra during its season. His wife Sara was Swedish born of Polish parents, a branch of the family of the philosopher Henri Bergson. Prior to her marriage, Sara had been a teacher in her native Karlstad. The family was completed by the birth of two sons, Henry and Julian. Then came the Troubles, and as a JP Grandfather was responsible for sentencing many IRA prisoners. The family home on Western Road faced the jail and the scenes enacted there featured thirty years later in my mother's only radio play:

> I lay and watched them and listened half asleep, to the singing and the cheering of the crowd. Every now and then I could hear an echo of insubordination running through the night. There was in the sound something that awoke an uneasy response in the heart of a child, of one subject as are all children to the constant vigilance and restraint of others. The door opened and my Mother came into the room. She went over to the window and pushed it shut. In the quick emphatic way she did it, I could feel how deep was her mistrust not only of the crowd outside, but of all spontaneous and disorderly emotion.

By 1920 the situation became untenable and Grandmother took the children to her family in Sweden for what turned out to be a two-year sojourn, whilst Grandfather remained in Cork despite IRA threats to his life. When Grandmother declined to return to Cork, London was agreed upon as the future family home so that the children could receive an English education, and Betty was sent to St Paul's School. But she contracted scarlet fever and then measles and was sent to convalesce at a Catholic sanatorium and boarding school at Berck Plage, near Boulogne where she stayed for a year.

Charlotte and Simone Richard, sisters who ran a dressmaking business in Paris were friends of the Spiros. Near the end of the war, Charlotte sent Betty a French magazine, which sparked immediate interest. "I greatly admired *Poesie 44*" she wrote to the Richards early in 1945, "What intrigued me most was Sartre's article on someone called Francis Ponge because that's exactly how *I* see things." As a result of her discovery, she wrote an article on Ponge for *Horizon* which was later reprinted in French in the "Hommage à Francis Ponge" edition of the *Nouvelle Revue Francaise* to which Braque and Camus also contributed. After the war, Betty visited the Richards at their flat in the rue de Vaugirard and Ponge came for coffee. Charlotte remembers "he made quite a long speech to explain how he worked . . . Betty was very proud that he would have come specially to see her and he was very proud to see a young writer listening to him so intelligently." At that meeting, Ponge presented Betty with a handwritten copy of his poem "La Cigarette" inscribed "A Mrs Betty Miller en la remercient de son attention and de son exigence à mon regard, en hommage et en souvenir de notre rencontre, à Paris 20 Mai 1948."

When she returned from Berck, my mother joined her sister Dorothy at Notting Hill High School. This was the time when her desire to become a writer became much stronger. She had been writing since the age of seven, making up stories for her siblings and plays for family performance — but now she bought herself a cream-coloured secondhand Olivetti portable for £5.00 and everything that she subsequently wrote was typed at great speed on this machine with her two index fingers.

From school, Betty entered University College London to do a two-year diploma course in journalism, which she obtained in July 1930. It was at this time that she met Montagu Slater — novelist, journalist and later, the librettist of Britten's "Peter Grimes" — and often visited him and his wife Enid at their house on Haverstock Hill. Enid remembers "She would come and talk to us or have a meal and so I got to know her pretty well: she was such a nice intelligent reasonable being. She had always wanted to write and Montagu was writing and she used to bring her writing round for him to see." It would seem then that Montagu was her sole mentor during her writing apprenticeship. However, when her first novel was about to be published, my mother decided to announce it to her old correspondent, St John Ervine, whose response was: "Aren't there enough novelists in the world without you adding to their number? Aren't there far too many women novelists and not enough good cooks? If you had written to tell me that you had burnt your manuscript and made a fine cake, I'd have cheered."

However a week later, having read the book he wrote again: "In spite of these stodgy passages the book made an indelible impression on my mind of an author who has a head on her shoulders and, although she does not yet know how to use it, one day will. I find you more interesting than your novel. What are you going to do with that brain of yours? Make an author of yourself or merely a clever-clever girl novelist. It is a feat for a girl of twenty-two to plan a book in the style you've planned this one, even if you've pinched some of it from Joyce. The technique is immensely interesting. I don't usually invite authors to let me see their books but you can send me your next novel. In the meantime, since you say you can make good currant buns, you can post one to me so that it arrives here on Wednesday." And a few days later: "Thank you for your letter and for the buns. At the moment of dictating, I have eaten two of them. They are very good."

A friend within walking distance at this time was the young Isaiah Berlin: "Betty was a pensive, slightly melancholy girl, with the most beautiful manners I have ever known. She also had a quality which I can only call moral charm, which I found, and still find, the most attractive and moving of human characteristics. We were invited to the same small Notting Hill-West Kensington dances; since neither of us greatly enjoyed dancing, we used to sit in corners, to the distaste of the hostesses and talk mainly about literature. Betty loved Browning even then ... These conversations were among the most delightful and spontaneous that I had with anyone in those days ... I looked forward to these gatherings, provided I could reckon on having an extended conversation with your mother. She used to wander off into long rambling modulations which I found totally absorbing."

The Mere Living was published in February 1933 and three months later Betty became engaged to Emanuel Miller a physician eighteen years her senior who had specialised in psychiatry. Six years before, he had founded the East London Child Guidance Clinic, the first of its kind in the country. For the rest of her life, Betty made much use of my father's professional knowledge in her own work. They married in August 1933 and went to live in a maisonette at 23 Park Crescent, Regent's Park where my father had his consulting room.

Living in on the job in the medical district was an experience that my mother wrote about abrasively in a later novel *A Room in Regent's Park* (1942):

The children born to medical men living in Harley Street, Wimpole Street, Devonshire Place lead, during five days of the week, a very specialised sort of existence. In their own homes, they are treated as a species of contraband: to be smuggled in and out of doors between the exits and entrances of patients . . . unlike most children, they have not the free run of their homes: their routine has to be carefully timed, their conduct governed: not only must they not be heard, but during consulting hours, they must not be seen either. This entails an elaborate system of repression, not the least complicated part of which revolves round the daily passage through the hall of the family perambulator.

In July 1934 my brother Jonathan was born — and in October of the same year, Betty published her second novel *Sunday*. Like its predecessor, it was despatched to Devon for St John Ervine's judgement. "Words intoxicate you . . . other women get decently drunk on gin but you must have lexicons and lexicons before you will consent to fall on the floor in a drunken ecstasy. Now listen to me. You have a high, if hysterical sense of language and a quite extraordinary sensuousness. You do really feel things and, as I have already written, you have brains in your skull. But you overwork your words, and you yield too much to your sensuousness . . . Simplify yourself, girl. I won't ask you to send me your next book, because you might send it, but if you have the brains I think you have and you do as I tell you, I'll buy it."

Her third novel, *Portrait of the Bride*, was published in 1935, followed by *Farewell Leicester Square* (1941) in which my mother informed Gollancz she was tackling "the social and psychological conflicts of a Jew in the modern world". However, Gollancz turned the novel down when it was delivered which was such a shock to my mother that she did not write another for some years. (Six years later Robert Hale accepted the novel and went on to publish Betty's remaining three works of fiction.) Instead, she directed her creative energies to short stories for magazines like

John O London's Weekly and to writing a couple of stage plays, which never saw the light of day.

Two family events took place around this time: her mother Sara was taken ill with abdominal cancer and died aged sixty in May 1936. A month later Betty became pregnant again. I was born the following March and named after Grandmother according to the Ashkenazi custom. Our Nanny at the time, Enid Hogarth, remembers Betty as not wanting to go out much. She didn't like to exert herself, preferring to stay in and write. She was also not very good at running her house, 'I always thought she wasn't used to it. I think she was shy and she was afraid of them — cook and the maid.' Indeed, she had once gone so far as to engage a new young nanny before she had plucked up the courage to give notice to the old nanny. It was not until the day arrived when our new nanny was expected that Betty steeled herself to rush up to the nursery and tell old nanny to pack her bags and go at once. Such a story, while not redounding to my mother's credit to say the least, provides a good illustration of her obsessive fear of people. "I'm frightened of everything and everybody, like Walter Pater" she confided to me years later.

When war was imminent my parents decided to close up their house in St John's Wood where they had moved to only a year before and Betty with Nanny Hogarth took Jonathan and me down to Sussex. My father remained at his work in London to await his call up, which came in 1940 when he was commissioned a major in the RAMC, a War Office posting so that he could assist in the selection of officer material for training. This involved him in moving from camp to camp and once he had joined up, the family was only able to be together by moving around with him. Thus we had half a dozen different homes for the duration of the war.

While we were living at Bishop's Lydeard, near Taunton, my mother became dangerously ill with pneumonia. Fortunately my father was able to obtain some of the first batches of EMB/Penicillin. For the remainder of her life Betty was never very healthy. She would regularly take to her bed with a temperature, a chill or some mysterious virus — and even suffered another attack of pneumonia whilst at work on the Browning biography in the early 50s.

It was my father's work for the War Office which led to the germ of the idea that became *On the Side of the Angels*. Though basically a Freudian, my father was enough of an eclectic to be considered a rebel in orthodox psychiatric circles. He had a particular interest in law and criminology and became Joint Editor of the British Journal of Criminology. While I never heard my parents discussing psychology, I think we can perhaps get a flavour of their talks from the speech of Andrew at the birthday dinner in Chapter 8. Part of the novel was written when we were living in Droitwich and the "church in the field " is St Peter's Church there. But the episode of the German airman's funeral was based on an incident when we had moved to Abbots Langley. And there an enemy plane did indeed fall out of the sky one afternoon and the village women hurried about putting kettles on for cups of tea. For the rest, life in our home went on much the same as it did for others in wartime, save that my mother was always writing. Years later, Betty lent her only copy of the novel to her friend, author John Verney with this note of explanation:

Actually, it is all (but for the Commando Officer) an almost exact picture of the military hospital wherein Emanuel was a Lt Colonel during the war. What fascinated me in all this was the astonishing effect on quite ordinary civilians of army life. No sooner had they donned uniforms than these men (and women too) who in everyday life were respectable God-Fearing citizens became — under the influence of a *very* peculiar C O quite unrecognisable. The book I tell you in confidence, is very close to the reality . . . the C O used to invite women into the Mess. In the book he is portrayed exactly as he was. Luckily no libel action followed: he had sense enough to lie quiet in the circumstances. By the way, Major McRae who appears now and then in the book is based on Adrian Stephen — Virginia's brother, he was an immensely tall man, and the army couldn't find a uniform big enough for him. He was a most civilised and witty person and he and I got on very well together. He had a delightful slow wit — and when telling a story would open wide his blue astonished looking eyes with the most comical effect. One evening at the Officer's Club a lot of Polish officers came in. I said to Adrian "I wonder what they think of Taunton." The blue eyes opened even wider. In his slow way — "Oo-h I don't know" he said at last — "it may be that Taunton is more like Poland than we think."

Although the novel was delivered early in 1944, the paper shortage caused it to be held back for publication until February 1945. One friend and fellow writer who wrote to her about the novel was Rosamond Lehmann: "It is so intelligent and — rare treat — it has a serious moral problem in it. Sometimes too stressing of sensuous impressions . . . is if anything a little overdone for my taste but there is some wonderfully vivid and sensitive writing; and the characters are stereoscopically clear. The men are as good as the women; I envy you being so successful with them."

Whilst at work on *On the Side of the Angels*, Betty suffered a terrible loss. Her brother Henry, on his first voyage out after undergoing training, was reported "missing presumed killed" when HMS Firedrake was torpedoed in the North Atlantic. Hence the novel's dedication to him. Eighteen months later, Betty took Jonathan and me on a seaside holiday in North Wales, very close to where Henry had done his naval training. While we were there a young boy from the village, Dewi, was drowned in a fishing accident. My mother never recovered from the shock of Henry's death — the two had been very close — and withdrew even more into her work.

This was after we had moved yet again — to the village of Abbots Langley, near Watford. Another young writer also living there with her family was Marghanita Laski: "My friendship with Betty was very much a personal one rather than to do with her being a writer. Betty didn't talk to me about her books when she was writing them. She certainly liked to have a picture of herself as a small, timid, incompetent woman needing a great deal of help and protection. And she always pretended that she was highly incompetent   domestically. For instance, one of you children had a birthday and she kept saying she didn't know how she would do the birthday party. But my children were invited and when I went there, she had done a beautiful birthday party with all the food and everything exactly as was required. I was very fond of her and desperately sad that she died so soon."

For her final novel, *The Death of the Nightingale* (1949), my mother chose to return to her Irish roots. We had moved back to our London house, in Queen's Grove, St John's Wood, in July 1945 and my mother was able to renew old friendships and make new ones, especially among her literary colleagues. Many of them were frequent visitors: Olivia Manning and her husband R.D. (Reggie) Smith lived a few doors away and often popped in; Stevie Smith left her "Lion Aunt" in Avondale Road and came for a meal and to sit in the garden with us; Inez Holden, once freed from her UNWRA duties was a regular visitor and later on, Naomi Lewis joined this small select band. And I have golden memories of a day that my mother and I spent at the Meynell home near Pulborough with Viola Meynell and her family and Eleanor Farjeon.

After *The Death of the Nightingale* Betty felt that she had written herself out in fiction and began a series of biographical studies of the Victorians for magazines such as *Horizon*, *The Cornhill Magazine* and *The Twentieth Century*. It was during this period that her lifelong interest in Robert Browning and his poetry surfaced again and, after an initial article in *The Cornhill*, John (Jock) Murray asked her to undertake a life of the poet. She was well into her book when in the autumn of 1950 Grandfather Simon died at the age of eighty-eight. The first three parts of the book were delivered "in folders lent to me by my son, the title 'The Invertebrates' does not refer to the Brownings" on 30th January 1952 and three days later came a handwritten note from Jock Murray, "This is an unprofessional note but I am spending the weekend in Tennyson's house with 'Browning'. I have read 150 pages and cannot go to bed. This must sound like the beginning of a 'fan' letter — just what it is, for I cannot resist expressing my admiration for your skill and mastery not only in detail but in the selection and the structure . . . for me at least you have bridged the poet and his poetry."

Jock Murray says of that period: "It was fascinating working with her because she had a wonderful tolerance of other people's views but an iron will at a certain level and one learnt as one learns with all authors at what level you can hope to go on persuading and when there's a point at which they're utterly determined. You could sense immediately the moment when she was not prepared to compromise or to change. I loved working with her and of course, the good thing was that as soon as you discovered why she felt so strongly it could go like a dream. It [the Browning] was a remarkable achievement and it was for her a marvellous subject. It seemed to stimulate her strength as a writer and her extraordinary ability to select and order details from a mass of research material so that events seemed inevitable and characters became alive. It was a magical book."

Six months before publication, Jock made the travel arrangements for my mother to visit Freya Stark and see the Browning house at Asolo. "Not being like my hostess of an intrepid nature, or disposed to live dangerously, the news of the *through train* is, I assure you, immensely reassuring." After publication, Freya Stark wrote to Betty: "You have written a splendid book — I am full of admiration and delight over it. Everything about it is good — the delicacy of observation and also of language, a perfect choice of adjectives and of the incidents which you illustrate — you must be very pleased because it really is an achievement . . . It made me suddenly realise that in this difficult year I too was faced, as I suppose so many of us are, with RB's choice: to cling to one's own truth or to accept the bourgeois as you call it (and I have often thought the bourgeois just is the living for values that are other people's and not one's own). But it seems to me that you put your finger on the central problem of life."

The Browning biography produced two offshoots: Jock asked my mother to edit a volume of hitherto unpublished letters from Elizabeth Barrett to Miss Mitford and then a friend of her brother's, the American writer Sam Rosenberg, asked her to collaborate with him on a play centred round the effect on the Browning's marriage of the meeting with Daniel Home, "Sludge the Medium", during their visit to London in the summer of 1855. This play, like its 1930s predecessors remains unproduced, but is of interest for making the death of Elizabeth's brother Edward, drowned at sea during a family holiday at Torquay, the catalyst which prompts Elizabeth Barrett Browning's obsessive interest in Home's spiritualist powers.

Sam Rosenberg recalls "Betty and I had a very sort of formal collaboration, always with a writer friend of hers as chaperone in the next room. Sometimes we sat in Regent's Park. She was extremely modest, almost pathologically so, and blushed brightly when praised for her superb essays, reviews, novels. Nobody ever wrote more brilliant and original essays than Betty. I use them as a model, in part, for my own investigative essays. No one could dramatise ideas as brilliantly. I will always be very proud that Betty thought enough of me to collaborate on our play. It was for me a great experience to have that prolonged contact with such a formidable intellect."

Shadow on the Window — the play Betty wrote with Sam — was, apart from occasional articles and reviews for the quarterly magazines and *The Times Literary Supplement*, her last completed work. In the late 50s she began a life of Kipling — but by 1960 her health was deteriorating. She wrote to the Richards in Paris "Getting old is never amusing and I'm surprised to find myself in a state of melancholy for the first — and I hope for the last — time in my life. My memory keeps failing all the time, which makes me sad . . . I can't even complete my Kipling, which is three parts finished. This scares me."

My mother went into University College Hospital for tests — and when they were completed we knew that she was suffering from Alzheimers's Disease. She went very rapidly downhill and died on 24th November 1965, a month after her fifty-fifth birthday.

Whenever I think of my mother, I see her at the dining-room

table of our house in Queen's Grove, typing rapidly on her battered Olivetti portable or, pen poised over her manuscript, rubbing her nose with a spare finger while she polished a sentence — or a paragraph until she was satisfied with it. Then as soon as my father's key was heard in the door, typewriter, manuscript, reference books and all were at once swept off the table and hidden away out of sight.

In the late 1940s a niece of my father's came to stay with us and asked Betty's advice on how to become a writer, the response was: you should get married as soon as possible and have children. You have to conform with the outside world, do all the rituals of domesticity of being a wife and mother — but keep the true faith to yourself and hide every trace of it. In other words, my mother advised Renie to become a "Marrano" — the Jews of fifteenth-century Spain forced to convert, or face death or exile, but who while outwardly conforming, went on secretly practising Judaism.

Isaiah Berlin writes: "She was indeed withdrawn and as you say fearful. Her skin was very thin, perhaps she had no skin at all ... her nerve endings seemed to be very exposed ... I met Betty not long before she died — at the Wallace Collection and talked with her at length about her work. She seemed to me to be unchanged: gentle, acutely sensitive, receptive, infinitely truthful and accurate, with a quality difficult to describe which the Germans call *Innerlichkeit* — inner light which shone through everything she said like remote but steady candlelight ... she was far more troubled than when I had seen her before and wandered a little and seemed wan and worn out. I liked and admired her very much. I wish I could see her again."

Sarah Miller, London, 1985

CHAPTER ONE

AFTERNOON

A T that hour of the afternoon the house, it seemed, was empty. Nothing stirred: the long windows yawned, creeper was motionless on the walls. On the wide veranda the canvas flagged in an unoccupied deck-chair, next to it, an open work-basket revealed its lining of strawberry-red satin pierced through with fine scin-tillating needles. A child's tin engine, a sandal with a broken latch lay as they had been left, on the dusty wooden boards. Somewhere in the silent garden a bee rattled suddenly inside the bell of a flower, and then was still. Trained upon the desiccated ramp of the veranda was an aged rose-tree: the roses it bore, drooping low, pressed forward to nuzzle with bland curled lips the sensitive air.

The child in his cot thought of the roses: he thought of the lips of the big horse, rose-soft, in his palm. He lay between sleeping and waking, the innocent nostrils lifted, eyelids dewed with moisture. The drawn blind made a novel twilight in his room. He breathed lightly, in and out, a quiet rhythm. Now he was in the meadow again, the hedge was full of the sweet lisping kissing sound of birds; he saw the white-haired dandelions smoking in the breeze. The birds broke from the hedge with quick-clipping wings. What had frightened them? Confused, his eyes opened and shut. He sucked his thumb with an avid, senseless movement.

There was a sound from the next room. The door opened and his mother came across the floor. Bending

over him, she let down the side of the cot with a familiar
click. "Been asleep?" she regarded him absently. He
scrambled up in his short vest, she ran a hand over the
small ivory-cold buttocks. "Come, then" she helped
him into his suit. "Hurry—they'll soon be here." At
once he wriggled away from her as if her presence, the
vague eyes, the deep soft chin, oppressed him. She
followed a moment later, carrying the baby in the
crook of her arm; miniature feet dangling in the splayed
gesture of the very young, a rosy-purple in colour.
She went through the empty living-room, out on to
the veranda and then down two shallow steps into the
garden. The pram was in the shade of a sycamore-tree:
she laid the baby down on its side: sunlight stencilled
an elusive pattern upon the white pillow, the sleeping
face. That'll do, she thought, turning the pram a little.
She went back to the veranda, to her deck-chair. The
striped canvas tautened under her weight. For a little
while she did nothing, staring before her while a small
breeze lifted the hair on her broad troubled forehead.
Then with an automatic gesture she reached out for the
work-basket at her side and began to darn a pair of
khaki socks.

At the same hour of the afternoon Linfield itself
appeared deserted. The small High Street, from the Blue
Trout Hotel at one end to the squat grey church tower
at the other, lazed undisturbed in the sunlight. A dog,
dusty paws outspread, lay with its nippled belly upon the
hot stone of the pavement: in its ear flies whined and
danced. Facing each other window-panes gaped, vac-
uous: a plait of horse-dung lay newly minted in the big
cobbled square. Lower down the street one or two of the
small shop-fronts had put forth striped sun-blinds: doors
stood latched back, inviting coolness. There were no
customers. In the cotton-smelling gloom of Twain's,

drapers, a pale-fingered girl knitted steadily, framed among cards of hair-slides, of boiling elastic: unreproved, a large ginger cat slept between tins of soup on the grocer's counter next door. In Darwin's shop the lettuces, picked that morning, were wilting in their crate; on a flat wicker cradle lined with sky-blue tissue paper, the tomatoes had a bloated appearance. Mr Darwin himself, in his faded drill overall, unheeding, sat and read of births and deaths and police-court proceedings in the local paper, while above his head a suspended fly-paper hissed with unavailing fury, like a kettle on the boil.

The acidulated whistling of the train, drifting before it along heat-glazed rails, reached the village. Thrilling in vacant ears, it acted as a sudden stimulant: simultaneously heads were raised, eyes sought the mantelpiece clock, the watch, limpet of metal, on the heated wrist: what, the train already? It was time, then, to throw off the afternoon sloth, to seek again the direction, purpose, relinquished during these hours of inertia. Papers, parcels, passengers, would be arriving; an impulse from the outside world, a series of demands to be met and countered. The whistle, a summons, ricocheted through the village, vibrating upon the grey stone walls it passed away and was extinguished in the wooded slopes beyond. But it left in its wake a widening furrow of activity. Linfield was awake again.

Those within the carriage saw the familiar fields rotate past: the sheep raising bleached inquisitive faces. A waft of country sweetness blew in at the lowered window, displacing the closeness of plush. The train was slowing down: a counter-impulse perceptibly checking the onward-sliding wheels. "Linfield!" cried a voice outside; "Linfield!" Claudia stood up. "Excuse me," she said. They withdrew their legs to enable her to pass: examined with open interest, now that she was about to leave them, the personality she deployed as she arose. The young airman put forth a blue arm and opened the heavy door. "Thank you" she gave him her smile and stepped down onto the small gravel of the platform. A wayward breeze, swelling, waltzing slowly, mailed her silk dress between her legs for a moment, sighed fondly about her neck. She wore a round-brimmed straw hat: the sunlight, sieved through its interstices, printed itself in tiny motes all over her face as if she wore a veil of light.

Honor, sewing on the veranda, heard the whistle of the train. She lifted her head. There's Claudia now, she thought, she'll be here in five minutes. In her mind, as she spoke, she saw her sister crossing the small railway bridge, coming up the long white-powdered road from the station. "Peter," she said automatically, speaking to him as one speaks to a child, with a part of her attention only, her real self withheld, "stop banging on that thing." Her needle flagged, the khaki sock, the skein of wool lay in her lap: her small bright-beaked scissors. She waited: presently she would hear Claudia's footsteps in the lane, the turning of the broad white gate on its hinges. Claudia would appear, gloved, powdered, crisp still from her contact with the outside world she would bring with her its tokens: newspapers from Cirencester, a woman's journal, cigarettes, sweets perhaps for Peter. At once the day which as it unwound for her insolitude seemed at times to sag unendurably, would tauten again; she would know the rhythm, the sense of continuity lost to her, she felt, during the undifferentiated hours given over to the company of children. Now Colin himself would soon be here: dismounting at the gate, wheeling his bicycle along the short gravelled drive, his face under the peaked cap withdrawn-looking, tired, as he frequently was after the long day at hospital. Yes, what was it——? The voice went on. ". . . Please.

Mummy? ... Please? ... Please, Mummy? ..." Peter
was tugging at her arm, wanting her attention, wanting
something, attacking her with his desire. Languidly she
considered him. She saw the pallid face, the short upper
lip. He looked, at that moment, exactly like Colin. She
turned to him then, and without answering, sombre,
suddenly, she looked into his face with a concentration
that startled him.

The bedroom window was open. Dark green, gripping
the stucco with tenacious veins, the ivy nodded and
stirred: a gust of warm air came sighing across the sill.
Claudia leaned over the china basin: almond-smelling
soap mottled her skin, pricking freshly: she sluiced it off,
pressing the cool water out of her sponge. "Oof—that's
better." Blind, she reached for a towel and buried her
face in it. Rubbing her arms briskly. "Well—how've
things been?" she asked.

"With me——? Just as usual." Honor, sitting on the bed,
watched her sister, expectant, like a child trusting to a
stronger personality to give entertainment, direction.

"Colin back?" Claudia asked. She tucked the towel
away in its rack under the basin and came forward. The
air was cool on her newly washed skin, brief knickers
revealed her legs, the cross-hatching of hairs on the dark,
keen-muscled thighs.

"No, not yet. He'll be late, probably. He's on Boards
this afternoon."

"Again?" Claudia spoke lightly. Honor lowered her
eyes. She chose not to question the malice in that comment. At once she spoke of something else. "That new
officer we see about the village——" she began. Quickly,
Claudia looked up: "Yes, him—— What about him?"

"He's a Commando. A Commando Captain."

"Is he?" Claudia said with interest. "How do you
know?"

"Colin told me. He's met him. He comes up to the hospital sometimes. And besides, the green beret——" She watched her sister pull a clean cotton dress over her head, seeing the mossy armpits, nervous shoulders. Claudia adjusted the dress to her flat neat figure, then pulled a leather belt firmly about her waist and buckled it. There was a finality in the gesture, as if she insulated herself, thereby, from the external world, proclaimed herself inviolate. Honor thought: I was like that once. Before the babies, before Colin. . . . She has yet to learn. . . . Aloud she said "You're getting thinner than ever. You don't eat enough."

"You know how it is. Rushing about after those hefty girls——" Claudia hung away the silk dress in the wardrobe: stooped to discard her shoes and put on a pair of coloured sandals. Visibly, item by item, she stripped from her the personality of her working hours: the disguise of "Miss Abbott," assistant mistress at Waverley Park Girls' School: a disguise that must defy speculation and impose the fiction of its wholeness upon the adolescent mind. Claudia had been teaching for six years now: quite consciously she had perfected, out of her distrust of the bright, incalculable eyes that watched her, an elaborate system of defence in depth, a system that had the advantage of covering her every move and the disadvantage of leaving her, at times, in some doubt as to where camouflage ended and the field of her own spontaneous nature began. She went to the dressing-table, set at an angle to the wall, and began to comb her dark hair, turning the soft fibre of it back upon her finger, lifting it with a few deft insertions of hairpins into a roll off her small domed forehead. I'm pale, she thought: the heat—— Or am I worrying about Andrew? She paused, as if surprised, and looked searchingly at her own image. Worried? Was there, then, something to worry about? . . .

Honor stiffened suddenly. She lifted a hand. "Hush," she said sharply "Isn't that the baby crying?"

They listened, movement suspended. "No, it is not," Claudia said, finally. "You have a mania about hearing babies crying——" Raising her swansdown puff she leaned towards the mirror with that oddly groping, near-sighted, gesture of hers, of which she herself was unconscious. She shook the puff lightly: dust-soft, powder mantled the skin of her face. "If ever I'm a mother——" she said.

"But I do hear him," Honor said, defensively "I can hear him when no one else in the house can—it's not imagination, always——"

Mounted on shields of polished wood, the masks of foxes, slim-nosed, exchanged glances out of their dusty eyeballs. Beneath, the banister rail fell away: worn blue carpet lined the stairs. The two sisters descended. Across the flagged hall, hooked back on its brass latch, the front door, standing open, revealed a bright greenish oblong of the outside world. On the oak chest in the corner a brass jug held overblown garden flowers that spilled a soiling pollen at the slightest touch: gathered more than a week ago upon one of those sudden impulses of Honor's when, after days without a flower in the house, she would similarly fill every vase she could lay hands on, the flowers stood now, in their diminished and weed-smelling water, disregarded, pursuing unhindered by arbitrary attempts at grooming, the rhythm of their decay. Honor sighed faintly: the responsibility, after all, was hers. To-morrow (let them stand one more day, what harm) she would gather up the friable leaves, the slimy stalks, spill the dark water down the sink and then, the empty pots set back in place, regain a certain stealthy peace of mind. . . .

At that precise moment "The flowers, Honor——" Claudia began.

"To-morrow," Honor said quickly.

"Don't forget, then."

"No."

They descended. The leather heels of their sandals rattled momentarily on the uncarpeted floor. Bare, under short sleeves, the arms of the two sisters were similarly cool as, involuntarily, their elbows touched. Honor bethought herself: she turned aside. "Just a moment—I'll tell her——" She opened the baize-covered door opposite the living-room: light fell on a stone passage, on to yellow-washed walls. Summoning the voice of authority "We'll have tea now, Edith, please," she said.

"And the Captain?——"

"He won't be back."

"Very good, 'm." In the narrow kitchenette (a butler's pantry, this, before Honor's landlords, the Hadley-Stuarts, had separated and let off as a war-time expedient a portion of their large Victorian house) Edith sat in a round wicker arm-chair and dispassionately read yesterday's newspaper. Taking cognizance of opinions already assimilated or discarded by her employers, she sat, head lowered, while a foot away from her, lid purposefully knocking, the electric kettle hissed forth steam unheeded. Honor glanced at the latter then averted her gaze: gently she closed the passage door behind her. But not soon enough. She heard the severe click of her sister's tongue. "You saw?" Claudia said.

"What?" Honor was evasive.

"You know very well—the kettle."

"Oh, that," Honor said. She shrugged those sloping unagressive shoulders of hers. "After all," she said, "one can't—can one—expect perfection——"

Claudia frowned. "It's not that." Her eyebrows were rigid and prominent, a sudden contraction in her nature

made visible. "I can't stand *stupidity*.... Just sitting
there, doing nothing, letting it boil away, for hours
probably——"

"Oh, Claudia, dear!" Unexpectedly, Honor laughed.
She passed an arm round her sister's waist and pulled
her to her: one of her infrequent caresses in which was
expressed the latent fullness of her affection as well as,
surprisingly from her, a sort of pity. For people will
only fret so sorely and incessantly over mere details, when
it is not the detail itself but something else, deeper, un-
acknowledged, that is amiss. She looked for a moment
searchingly into Claudia's face aware, at the same time,
that she was incompetent to read it. "Come along and
have some tea," she said. "We'll all feel better——"

She opened the door. What was now the living-room
for Honor and her family, had at one time been the
Hadley-Stuart drawing-room. Tall French windows
opened onto the veranda and the light from the garden, filtered through the big acacia tree, wavered
greenish on faded *moiré*-silk wall-paper, kindled a green
response in the long gilt-laced mirrors hanging on their
discoloured cords. It flashed blindly off the glazed panels
of a tall satinwood cabinet, in which, insulated from the
climate of daily existence, an assortment of objects—
Japanese coffee sets; filigree silver bonbonnières; a flimsy
fan starred with sequins; a yellowed spray of lily-of-the-
valley off a wedding-cake—lay on velvet-lined shelves
with the haphazard air of things divorced from their true
context in time, preserved in the immunity conferred on
them by their total lack of contemporary meaning.

Honor advanced into the room stooping, mechanically,
to pick the baby's celluloid rattle off the floor. "Peter—
go to Edith. Ask her to wash your hands." Blue and
pink, the bauble rattled lightly in her fingers. "And
don't forget to peepee...." Tea was laid, already, on

the oval table in the centre of the room. One of the
Hadley-Stuarts' table-cloths (*rent includes plate and linen*),
massive as a bedspread with its crocheted lace borders,
lay unfurled; the rose-patterned plates in a ring about it,
attended by rickety bone tea-knives. Gathered to the top
of the table where Honor sat, an array of tea-cups
waited in their saucers, ears all tweaked in the same
direction. Claudia looked the table over indifferently: the
usual brown bread and butter; honey, camphor-white
in its glass jar; yesterday's swiss roll. She pulled out a
chair and sat down. "I meant to bring you some biscuits,"
she said "but there was such a queue——"

"Did you meet Andrew?"

"No," Claudia said. She frowned slightly.

Edith pushed the door open with her knee, and came
in carrying the teapot and hot-water jug: she set them
down: battered silver, with a silver flower perched on the
lid of each. Honor poured boiled water into a cup, she
picked up a teaspoon. "See if baby will take some of
that," she said to Edith "he may be thirsty."

"He don't care for the spoon, 'm."

"Never mind. He has to get used to it."

Edith went out through the veranda, cup in hand.
Honor looked round. "Now, where's that child gone?
Peter!" He came in, his fair hair teased fine by Edith's
comb. Newly washed, his palms were damp and rosy. He
saw Claudia: at once he stopped in his tracks. "Did you
bring me anything?" he demanded.

"No—not *every* day, you know——" She noted with
regret that he still wore the suit he had worn all the
week, stained in front with blackcurrant juice. Honor
reached out for him and lifted him into his place: there
was a square of mackintosh under his plate and mug.
Deftly, she tied a bib round his sunburnt neck, cut him
a honey sandwich.

"Now eat, and be good, for a change."

"Mummy—I don't like boiled milk." He was smelling at his mug with distaste.

"I can't help that. Daddy said we must boil it." Honor poured out tea. "They tested the milk at the hospital," she explained to Claudia. "Colin says there's *Bacillus abortus*, or something, in it." Claudia reached out and received her cup. Before she could set it down she caught Peter's eyes, fixed on her steadily in an act of unqualified observation. Instinctively she looked away. Other people's eyes, she always felt, were a distorting mirror: she wondered for a moment what she looked like in those of of the child: seeing herself, unwillingly, as Peter very well might at that moment (she forced herself to smile at him), oversize, grotesque, a meaningless grimace spread from ear to ear—— "Eat your tea," she said severely, breaking off diplomatic relations with him. He sighed and did so but not before he had picked apart his sandwich to smell surreptitiously at the honey inside it. . . .

Honor, both elbows on the table, the cup upheld between circling hands, sipped slowly, absently. Moist with heat, her hair lay lax and gentle on her forehead. Her eyes gazed over the edge of her cup with a wide, unfocused look. She was off. Away, Claudia recognized, in one of her "moods": trances of absent-mindedness, profound, absorbing, in which she lived some life other than the life she lived at the surface, inexplicable by its terms, and from which nothing could effectively rouse her but a baby's cry or Colin's step in the hall. . . . Claudia moved impatiently: she did not like to see Honor thus. How she's let herself go lately, she thought, looking at the broadened waist, the mature elbows and she used to be so good-looking, she thought, remembering her sister as she used to be in the old days, at their home in Worthing, before Colin—Dr. Carmichael as he then was— started visiting the house: drawing up in his spick-and-span car, coming across the crazy-paving in his pin-

striped trousers, his black-bound hat in his hand, exposing
the fair, prim, youthful head. . . . He'd had it all his own
way with Honor from the start. It was as if Honor were
hypnotized by something in the fair clipped features, in
the manner, jaunty and yet somehow overbearing: the
little bantam cock, Claudia thought contemptuously,
irritated even now by the affectations she remembered:
the spruceness, the dapper turn-out, the jocose way,
always the same, of greeting people. . . . The fuss he made
in those days if his shirts weren't just so, the time he
spent choosing his socks and ties. . . . And Honor sitting
back with a sort of complacency, accepting everything,
uncritical audience to all this male pirouetting. One
couldn't seem to rouse her to any sort of consciousness of
her real position. . . .

Claudia pushed her cup away from her; in the well of
it tea, cold already, was marbled with stale milk. On
the other side of the table Peter, whose plate was littered
with uneaten bread-crusts, was unwinding the jam-
stained coils of his swiss-roll. Claudia saw the gummy
childish fingers at work, she made a grimace of distaste.
"Peter, don't." The blue eyes looked guardedly at her.
She leaned across the table and cut the cake up with
her bread-knife while he preserved the silence of complete
outrage. That done, she sighed and forgot him: her eyes
went to the other end of the drawing-room where a glass
door, kept locked, led into the Hadley-Stuart conservatory. Through the bevelled panels of the door she
looked into the long chapel of glass in which, in a green
and consecrated stillness, tier upon tier, the petals of
flowers burned like candle-flame. The conservatory, forbidden to the tenants, was a source of fascination to them
all: a place of seclusion in which in a moist and special-
ized climate, all the year round flowers bloomed out
of season; a privileged constellation; the fleshly tinted
stars hanging in a mist of fern. Mr Hadley-Stuart,

however, was no longer to be seen, in the panama hat of his retired days, gazing fixedly into the faces of this floral harem that he maintained for his own interest and benefit since the new aerodrome established itself four miles west of Linfield, followed by the military hospital in the village itself, the Hadley-Stuarts, affirming their emotional distance from a war fought to ensure conditions they did not desire to see established, had retired to a hotel in a coastal reception area where, according to the advertisements, air-raid sirens ceased from troubling and the war-weary, adequately Vi-sprung, were at rest: and where, too, artificially sustained like the flowers they had left behind them in an atmosphere of service and central-heating, the Hadley-Stuarts found themselves with a fair measure of success able to pursue an existence no less independent of actual conditions, of the treacherous climate prevailing in the external world.

"Peter—fetch me the matches," Claudia said abruptly. He obeyed, and stood at her elbow to watch in open fascination as she struck a match and then, accurately, inserted the end of her cigarette into that eyehole of flame.... "Thank you," Claudia said: leaning back, she drew on her cigarette, absorbing the newly kindled smoke with a conscious hunger. Peter looked across at his mother. "May I go and play, now?" he asked.

"Say, *please*." Automatically, Honor exacted the toll.

"*Please*." He gave it, no less indifferent. Standing by her chair he bowed his head while she unfastened the bib on the nape of his neck where fair hair was, momentarily, feather-warm against her fingers.... She withdrew the bib: "Say, thank you." "Thank you!" Free now, he disappeared with the purposeful swiftness of the child who knows that at any moment an arbitrary word from the adult world can frustrate his most cherished design. They heard his feet drumming lightly on the veranda, the ensuing rattle as he dragged some heavy object over the floor with him. Then nothing more, he was in the garden already, running noiselessly upon grass. A sudden silence fell upon the room. It acted on the senses like an enlarging glass: details assumed a new imminence: the sound the clock made, twinkling steadily from the tall marble mantelpiece, the crochet-laden cloth sagging from the table: on the table itself the cups, cold now to the touch, a tea-knife lying awry upon a crumb-freckled plate. The sisters did not speak. Above them a green light came and went waveringly in the untrue depths of the old mirror. Caught up in the still-ness of the room neither of them moved. Claudia held her cigarette bracketed in forgetful fingers: eyes fixed, she watched the long grey ash emerge from its chrysalis of paper. All the while, unknown to her, her face was framed in an expression of profound uneasiness. She was thinking of Andrew Peirse. Of an afternoon, as they had spent it, in the fields beyond his house. "Claudia," he had said to her "not so fast, Claudia: just a minute, wait for me——"

CHAPTER TWO

NO COAT TO PUT ON

"CLAUDIA—not so fast, Claudia——"
It was the second time he had said it that after-noon. She put her hand on the top rung of the stile and waited, a little surprised, until he came up the slope behind her and stood at her side. Together they leant upon the silver-dry wood of the stile, looking over, not speaking. There was an oatfield beyond, unripe as yet,

greeny-blue in colour, the beads of grain hanging, frail
and graceful. A breeze came running down from the
further slope and submerged itself among the oats:
Claudia listened with a delicious tickling of the senses
to the sound it made: the susurration, the prolonged
stirring: a carillon whispered forth on innumerable
paper bells. . . .

"Listen," she said, involuntarily. "The breeze——"

"The breeze?" He stood, as always when she had
incautiously called his attention to something that she
had perceived, with an air, attentive and yet remote:
politely acknowledging her vision which, he permitted
her to understand, he had no intention of sharing. This
was not new, of course. From the beginning she had
accepted this in him: that beyond a certain point there
must be no intrusion. He had achieved, out of the elements
of his own nature, a specific balance, and would accept
nothing from the outside world that might give a new,
undue emphasis to that composition. In the last resort
she respected him for it. It was, for her, an education in
restraint, to a woman, not without value. . . . She said
nothing therefore, looking at the field before her. White
butterflies palpitated under the sunlight, a coarse vege-
table smell came out of the earth. At her elbow was his
elbow: the sleeve rolled back from the gaunt, vein-laced
arm that the sun could not brown.

"We'll go on." She climbed over the stile, steadying
her hand in his and he came after, swinging his long legs
easily across. He walked before her along the narrow
footpath where the dust was milled, fine as flour. A pair
of grey flannels, which had the shrunken appearance of
clothes that have been put away, unused for months,
hung from his unemphatic hips. The white shirt, too, was
unfamiliar after so much khaki. He walked before her,
whistling abstractedly, looking down at the dust on his
sandals.

The oats gave place to corn: firm, plaited heads, swaying faintly on the taut-sprung stems. Another stile: and then the earth underfoot rose suddenly. They came out onto grazing land: they were half-way up the long hill at the back of Honeybourne. Between closely knit hedges the grass was deep, now: buttercups twinkled, the thistles were strong and crenellated. Unperturbed by their presence, a cow gazed at them, jaws slowly revolving: now and again, spasmodic, it switched its flank with a dung-stained tail. It was very quiet. The hum of a car passing along the white road below, became perceptible only to die away again. Remote, sunk in a downy horizon, the double note of a cuckoo pulsed gently, persistently, like an artery.

The young man seemed to hesitate. Pausing, he stood, suddenly irresolute, looking about him at a scene familiar to his earliest days. Claudia screwed up her eyes against the bright light, then, remembering crows-feet, took out her sun-glasses: at once, and the effect was not wholly disagreeable, the world seemed to fade, to recede from her in some degree. . . . She heard Andrew sigh: "I wonder what sort of a summer we shall have," he said. Something in his tone caught her attention. She saw that he was not referring to the war. Nor, indeed, to the climate. A sudden uneasiness took her. She tried to speak lightly. "You'll be back with your unit, I suppose——"

"That, as it happens, is most unlikely."

She was startled by the detachment in his voice. "Unlikely—why?"

Andrew did not look at her. "You'll know," he said "in good time."

She said sharply "I should prefer to know now."

Andrew did not reply. He looked intently down the long slope of the hill. Puzzled, she turned: she saw, as she imagined, what he did: in the shallow valley beneath,

at a point directly opposite them, the house and grounds
of Honeybourne laid out clearly under the bright afternoon sunlight. Preoccupied, he let it appear, with this
view (the pattern of his own existence exposed, laid out
like a chess board) he continued to look down seeing
his home, the roof under which he had been born.
Claudia standing at his side saw something else : the
house that would one day be hers. They stood together
on the hillside looking down on Honeybourne, the
engaged couple, and looking, discovered each something
different; intrinsically opposed : since it was his past
Andrew Peirse cherished in that house : the future, on the
contrary, that Claudia discerned within its boundaries.

"Andrew," Claudia said "You haven't answered my
question."

"I told you. All in good time." He looked at her with
a disquieting good humour. "Let's continue our walk,"
he said.

She said, apprehensive : "Something is wrong, I know
it is——"

For a moment Andrew hesitated. Then he turned his
head from her. "There's a tree-trunk at the top of the
hill," he said, "let's go and sit down there." Without
further ado he began to climb the long grassy slope. In
silence, knowing that she must wait her moment, she
regained her place at his side. They climbed, not talking
or touching : hands swinging loose at their sides. Gradually Honeybourne fell away from them, dwindled and
then disappeared. The day had grown hotter : unclouded
sunlight fell upon them : she could feel it pinning her
dress between her shoulder-blades; murmuring, bee-
warm, in her ear. Everywhere, in the grass that absolved
their footsteps of sound, dandelions glared : the yellow
manes bristled up at them. In hedge after hedge, upon
the spurred branches of hawthorn trees, the white,
confetti-like flowers gave forth a bridal sweetness. . . .

"Damn it," Andrew said. "There it goes. Racing away——" She turned her head sharply. Andrew was standing, his left wrist cradled attentively between thumb and forefinger. Head inclined, he studied at the same time the watch on his other wrist. "About 120 to the minute, then——"

"Oh," Claudia said. She took a step towards him, brows contracting. "Now, Andrew, you really musn't. Taking your own pulse all the time, like that—it's, it's——"

"Sheer hypochondria. I quite agree."

"Very well," she said. "It is." There was anger in her tone. "Darling, it's not good enough. You're not an invalid, now. You've got to forget all that. Your sick leave will soon be up——"

He looked at her with a queer triumphant expression in his face. "That's where you're wrong," he said. "It won't."

"I don't understand you." Something tightened inside her: a new defensive reaction. Now, what? What is he trying on? "You mean——?"

"I mean that I'm on sick leave for good."

There was a pause. She said quietly "Andrew—what are you talking about?"

Quickly, he looked away from her, down the valley. Then with a visible effort, as if recollecting himself, he turned about, facing her, and spoke briskly. "Well, you may as well have it now, as later. I'm being boarded out of the army, Claudia."

"You're what?" She stared, incredulous.

"Boarded out of the army."

"Boarded out——? You?"

He raised his fair sloping brows. "Does it come as such a surprise? I thought you more or less understood——"

"No," she said "I didn't. I didn't understand—I still don't. You mean?—Just because of that pneumonia you had? Because of *that*? Why, you're better already.

You're well again——" She stopped suddenly. There was a silence between them. "Aren't you?" she said in a small voice.

"Yes, I'm better," he said. "To all intents and purposes I'm well again. At the same time, it's left me with a little souvenir—for keeps, I gather——"

"What do you mean?" she asked; afraid.

He looked swiftly across at her. Her eyes were fixed on his. He said, with an expression shame-faced and yet curiously obstinate, as if what he now had to acknowledge was not weakness but a source of secret strength "The strain affected my heart. It left me with a groggy heart. I'll have to be careful in future, that's all."

"It affected your heart——" Claudia repeated the words mechanically. She was conscious of having received a blow, the nature, the destructive effects of which she would only discover later. Now she could merely repeat his words emptily.

"Yes it sometimes does, I gather, after a bad bout. The M.O. more or less warned me—I didn't believe him, at the time. But now——"

"But are they *sure*——?" Resist, disbelieve, keep it somehow at arm's length, as long as possible.

"Oh yes, there's no possible doubt I'm afraid. They left nothing to chance, they're very thorough once they get going." He smiled at her. "Looked me up and down, tapped me under and over. . . . And they didn't like what they found. Not a bit, they didn't. Under proof, you know. Damaged goods. They don't go in for salvage sales, for remnants, in the army, why should they? So they've boarded me out, returned me to civil life, C.O.D." He looked across at her. "And here I am, *mens sana in corpore* C3. At your service, Claudia, bowler hat and all. . . ."

Claudia said nothing. After a glimpse at her face, he too fell silent. He turned from her frowning. One could not accept humiliation: allow oneself to be reduced by mere compassion. There were moreover, for him at least, certain compensations in this new position though none that could be acknowledged. In certain circumstances illness, like a strategic withdrawal, a falling back on prepared positions, offers undeniable advantages to those who know their own resources to be limited. . . .

The tree trunk had lain on this hill for many years. Opening crocodile jaws, the crusted bark gaped, exposing the wood naked as bone. Generations of insects had peppered it with holes, lonely men and lovers had carved initials on it, patiently, day in, day out, the changing airs had seasoned it. Andrew now added without even heeding that he did, another feature, a mark that would endure: with the point of his knife, he stabbed the squeaking-dry wood earnestly, his fist clenched upon the bone handle of his knife. Claudia sat watching him. All the while, she could feel the bark, sun-warm, against the back of her legs, against her open palms; and she sat silent at his side, taking a small distinct comfort out of the body of the tree, inert but friendly. Andrew continued to stab with his knife: she watched the small blade flash and darken. All at once she sighed deeply, sharply. It was as if something surged up out of her own nature, demanding expression. "All day," she said, "I felt all day — that there was something wrong between us——"

He answered her without looking up. It seemed that they were merely continuing a conversation: that the silence had been a part of what they now said. "I thought you'd guessed. That you knew all along. Your intuition——"

"Ah, yes," she said quickly: "I knew *something* was wrong. But not that." And suddenly it presented itself to her all over again. "Not that!" she repeated and this time, despite herself, grief and dismay broke out, dis-ordered in her voice. No disguising it.... She turned her head away.

He was suddenly very still and attentive. She kept her face averted from him. There was a long pause. Across the valley, a cuckoo flashed its note on and off in light-hearted code. He spoke at last. "Well," he said. "Now that you do know—what exactly are you going to do about it?"

Taken by surprise, she turned her face back to him. "I thought you said that there was nothing that could be done about it!"

"As far as I'm concerned, yes." He paused, the knife suspended in his hand. Deliberately: "But that needn't necessarily involve you," he said. And he returned to his self-imposed task, hacking away briskly at the tree, avoiding her eyes.

"I don't think I understand you, Andrew."

Unexpectedly, then, he grinned at her. "A little slow in the uptake to-day, aren't you, dear?" And he said banteringly, intent, overtly, on his knife, on the wound he was conscientiously inflicting on the tree: "Come, come. You get my drift I feel sure. No nice normal girl wants to be tied for life to a crock."

"Perhaps I'm not a nice normal girl." She, too, spoke lightly. At the same time, she had a sense of suffocation. *Oh*, she thought. So that's it. Now I *see* what's happened to him: I see the extent of the damage.... A spring gone. The pride, the self-confidence.... Either that, or else (almost at once, another explanation occurred to her) he's protecting not me, not himself—but his own in-validism. That, in future, perhaps is to be the dominant thing.... Her heart sank steeply. She looked at him for a moment in a panic, as if the Andrew she knew (the precise and reticent young man) had vanished, and in his place sat this incalculable stranger, whose acquain-

tance she would have to make, slowly, warily. . . . In the
sudden silence, *cuckoo*, *cuckoo*, came the call across the
valley. They both heard it. The sunlight poured down
unabated, warm as a caress on her cheek, upon her bare
arm kindling the fine hair-tips to a brassy fire. Noticing
this (she was ashamed, suddenly, reminded of the dark
hairs on her body) she pulled at her sleeve, trying to
cover her arm.

Andrew turned to her. "Well?" he demanded.

She looked up, resolutely meeting his gaze. "Well?"
she countered, at the same time summoning (as before
a class) her powers of composure: a calm out-going
energy that met and resisted what he was trying to force
upon her.

"Have you considered your verdict?" he said; not
altogether playfully.

"My verdict?" She raised her eyebrows. "Why should
I? Nothing has changed between us."

"No, no," he exclaimed, irritable. "Not that gambit,
please!"

She was startled. "It's not a gambit. I mean it. Nothing
essential has changed between us."

"Are you quite sure of that?" he said quickly.
Defending—her—? himself—? or this new status he had
acquired, and perhaps hoped to maintain? . . . No, no,
that was incredible. No use believing that. She rallied.
She found it in herself to look gaily across at him to say
in a manner familiar to their happier hours, affectionate,
cynical "Come, come, darling! . . . What do you think
attracted me to you in the first place—your athletic
powers——?"

That miscarried. "Yes," he said. "I agree—that does
sound ridiculous."

"Not ridiculous—you misunderstand me——"

"It's immaterial." He cut her short. There was still
something he wished to convey. "The point is that,

whatever you saw in me, you didn't bargain for this state of affairs—any more than I did, for that matter." He contemplated the blade of his knife. "Fair exchange is no robbery, they say. But if we marry, now, it won't be fair exchange—and I don't feel inclined to rob you, Claudia."

If we marry, now. He said that. . . . Take no notice. Smile. "Come off it Andrew, please. Please!" She saw his fair brows contract: wrong, she thought unhappily, too crisp, too breezy, he hates that in me. . . . What *can* I say then? She turned to him in a sort of desperation and for the first time reached out and touched him. She laid her hand on his thin forearm, feeling under her palm (he himself did not move) the involuntary recoil of the muscle, and said gently, simply "Andrew, believe me. What you've told me makes no difference to me. None at all. Only don't—oh, Andrew don't!—don't let it make a difference to *you*."

He sat very still for a moment. Then he moved, and it seemed accidentally lifted his arm so that her hand fell from it. She did not attempt to replace it. He turned to her then with his smile: a smile that revealed nothing; that was a disguise. Recognizing it she knew that her efforts were unavailing, that for the moment at least she would not be able to get contact with him. Defeated, she smiled back. "What's amusing you?" she said.

"I was just thinking—apart from everything else, you're going to miss the purely military side aren't you?"

"What do you mean?"

"I mean that you enjoyed walking out with a soldier— own up—you got a kick out of that didn't you? It's going to be rather a come-down, appearing on the arm of a civilian."

"Really, Andrew—as if I——"

He flashed a shrewd look at her, and began to laugh. "Ah, ah—got you there." And he added the unexpected, schoolboy taunt "Don't blush!"

"I'm not blushing," she retorted indignantly at which he laughed again. "All the same," he said, "it gets you under the skin—confess. You see, I haven't forgotten what you once told me at the beginning of the war."

"What I told you——?"

"Yes when you were a child don't you remember? How thrilled you used to be when your father came into the nursery in uniform—how you used to polish his buttons for him, try on his Sam Browne belt—— And later on, how you read all the war books you could get hold of, saw every war picture—and felt cheated, because you'd only been a child in the Great War and not a woman. You felt *cheated*, you actually said—remember?"

"Yes I remember," she said, obscurely vexed, "at the same time, I wasn't altogether serious—surely you can see——"

He was not listening to her. "Women love war," he said. "It's a known fact. They esteem it very highly if a man kills himself for their sake, don't they? In the same spirit, what could be more gratifying than a mass slaughter, a never-ending series of gallant suicides——?"

"I fail to see what all this is leading up to."

"Simply this. I want you to realize that when you agreed to marry me, you did so largely because I was in fancy dress. In uniform. . . ." He paused. "You became engaged to the soldier, Claudia; not to me."

"That's absurd," she said; and now the tell-tale blood was hot on her cheekbones. "We'd known each other so long—all these years, it was more or less an understood thing——"

"Perfectly true," he said. "Nevertheless—it was the sight of khaki that did it in the end—the brass buttons, the tin hat, the revolver—the paraphernalia of power——"

"Nonsense. All that's completely superficial——"

He shot her a sharp look. "Ah, but is it? You like to believe so we all do. But you've got to have a war to show where people's real values lie. A war turns us inside out, shows the lining: pacifists become war-mongers, intellectuals worship the man with the tommy-gun. All very good for us, Claudia: very good indeed. Gives us a chance to discover the lie we were all living, during the so-called peace years."

"I don't believe that it was a lie——"

"You don't?" He turned his head and looked at her with a curious smile. "Well—we'll see," he said. "We'll see. . . ."

On the way home (down the hill, again, towards Honeybourne, where the polished tea-trolley, where the silver kettle, where old Mrs. Peirse at her embroidery-frame, awaited them) he began to whistle a tune. She recognized it: an old nursery rhyme. He whistled it, over and over again and presently, in the same monotonous, abstracted way, began to hum the words between his teeth:

> "Oh, soldier, soldier, will you marry me,
> With your musket, fife and drum?
> Oh, no, sweet maid, I cannot marry you,
> For I have no coat to put on."

CHAPTER THREE

ENCOUNTER

THE door opened. It was Edith, come to clear away the tea things. She stopped short "Oh, I'm sorry, mum; I thought you had finished." Tray in hand, she prepared to back out again. At the same time, her opaque eyes, going from one face to another, questioned the nature of the silence she had interrupted. They looked at her across the disordered tea-table: the young married woman and her sister: and for all the dissimilarity between them, the kinship, some innate physical basis, was at that moment apparent: that which in the last resort set them apart from other people. It was Honor who spoke first. With an effort she recollected herself; separated herself (but never entirely) from that inner vision which held her. "It's all right Edith, we had finished. You can clear."

Edith came forward. Claudia rose, as she did so, casually, she strolled over to the mantelpiece with her cigarette, and tilted the cap of ash off into a glass ash-tray. Edith set the tray down on the table and began to clear; stacking up the plates, nesting one teacup within the other. Claudia, watching from the fireplace, saw the maltreated shoes ground down at the heel, the bleached sweat-ring under each armpit, and looked away, oppressed by these evidences of physical stress in someone she could not bring herself to like. There was something about Edith. . . . Claudia could never understand how Honor let her handle the children.

Unaware, Honor said, now—Edith pausing, the tray against her hip to listen—"Edith, leave the washing-up. Keep an eye on the children, will you? I want to go out."

"Very good, mum." Edith was pleased: she liked to be left alone with Peter and the baby. Unsupervised by employers, by adults, she became alive, boisterous even, to an extent that would have astonished the former, who met only a self-effacing, self-concealing apathy (and could not be expected to recognize in the hiss of a furiously boiling kettle an emotional safety-valve, a vicarious expression of resentment and contempt).

Claudia waited until the door shut behind Edith and her laden tray. The room relieved of her presence "Where are you going?" she asked.

Honor looked about her restlessly. "I don't know. . . .
I've been stuck here all day." She avoided Claudia's eye.
"I thought I'd just take a stroll. Go down the road and
meet Colin, perhaps. . . . Care to come?" She glanced at
her sister.

"If you like." (I know why you want me, of course. An
ally, a buffer, in case Colin shows himself none too
pleased at the encounter. . . .) Claudia shrugged her
shoulders. "I'll get my cardigan," she said.

They took the short cut through the churchyard. In
the late afternoon the church stood, four-square, a
flawless sky annealed to the grave stone. The shadow of
it, cast negligently to one side, lay over the gentle mounds;
the sunken scalloped tombstones. This was the oldest
part of the churchyard: in contrast the recent graves by
the railings were china-white and staring. Yew-trees,
newly clipped, sharpened the air with a rasp of sap:
behind looped railings, granite chips lay clean and arid.
Everywhere a geometric clarity prevailed. There was
not a leaf, not a blade of grass, out of place. Claudia,
walking on the crisp raked gravel looked about her with
pleasure appreciating the pattern that death maintained
within these precincts. How orderly, how correct (thought
the young schoolmistress) and how easy to impose order
once the unruly spark had gone. . . .

Honor threading her way between the graves looked
carelessly at them. The hem of her dress had come un-
stitched, and she had fastened it up with a safety-pin:
the strands of her hair, escaping from the casual knot at
the back floated from her temples like airy question-
marks. Under the striped cotton dress her breasts were
turgid: it was nearly time for the baby's next feed. Feeling
within her the familiar tingling in breast and armpits
she gave a deep sigh, an expression at once of desire and
frustration: it seemed to her that she was filled with the

very substance of her love for Colin, swelling, burning
her veins: a love, a necessity of her whole being, that
neither his children, nor in the last resort Colin himself,
could fully assuage.

They passed through the lichgate and came out into
the High Street. Honor hesitated, looking both ways.
Finding the scene before her blank, empty of the slim
khaki form she had expected to discern among the passers-
by, she stood, suddenly at a loss, uncertain what to do
next. Claudia, too, looked about her. "He may still be
at the Hospital——"

"Don't you believe it," Honor said in a strident voice.
"The C.O.'s carried him off for a drink somewhere."
Claudia turned her head sharply. Once or twice lately,
she had heard that uncharacteristic discord in her sister's
voice; recognizing it now, she searched Honor's face.
Honor looked away: she did not want to be seen. There
was a pause. Then Claudia said, and because she felt that
she might be trespassing her voice was detached, casual:
"You know, Honor—if I may say so—I don't think you
make quite enough allowances for Colin, these days——"

Honor turned her head. "What do you mean?" she
said quickly.

"Well," Claudia began ("Come on, walk on," she
interjected: together they made their way along the small
stone pavement), "I hold no brief for Colin, heaven
knows—but circumstances do alter cases. . . . You must
make allowances, for instance, for the effect that the army
has had on him—is *bound* to have, on one of his type——"

"Oh," Honor said, and she was now visibly scornful,
glad to refute another's interpretation of a matter which
she felt concerned her alone "I don't know that being
in the army— After all, it's not as if Colin——"

"Yes, yes," Claudia agreed quickly "we know Colin's
no Commando—not even an ordinary combatant soldier.
But even so—it has its effect—it's bound to have—a lot

of men, away from their wives many of them living together under those circumstances——"

"What are you trying to say?" Honor asked evenly.

"Simply that the war has given Colin and plenty of people like him a heaven-sent opportunity of living as they've always wanted to live and never quite dared to——"

There was a pause. Honor said coldly: "If you say that, it's because you misjudge him. I'm not surprised. You always have."

"*I* misjudge him?" Claudia exclaimed. And she added, impelled now to express the truth as she saw it, despite Honor's overt resistance "You don't believe that the pre-war Colin was the real one—was the whole story— do you?—the natty little small-town doctor, lifting his hat to the old ladies——?"

Honor was silent. They walked on. The silence grew. Claudia gave a quick glance at her sister's face. She was a little sorry, now, that she had expressed herself so unguardedly. She had meant to help Honor. But it might well be that a fool's paradise was a better proposition than no paradise at all: one should not interfere. It is true that the temptation, at times—Honor was so complacent, so unsuspecting——

They came to the end of the High Street where the Blue Trout Hotel dominated a wide paved square. Cars were already drawn up here: civilian and military, the latter camouflaged in the now familiar McKnight Kauffer designs. Through the long windows of the lounge, as they approached, they could see the residents in brass-studded arm-chairs, knitting or brooding over the pages of last week's *Sporting and Dramatic.* "Excuse me——" a Polish flight-sergeant with a hard-bitten face, a characteristic wash-leather complexion, stepped briskly in front of them on his way to the bar: at the other side of the entrance hall this; and already crowded: they could hear as they approached, amid the hum of voices, of laughter, the preliminary pips of the six o'clock news. "This is the Home and Forces programme——" Honor appeared to hesitate. Claudia gripped her arm. "Come on," she said fiercely: "you can't hang about outside, even if you think he *is* there——"

They turned down a side street. The neat stone houses faced each other along the pavement diminutive window-sashes painted white, lace curtains parted to reveal a neutral triangle of the room within. There was a softness in the air, a hint of the dusk to come. Cats that had slept through the afternoon hours, waking, arched long elastic backs, unfurled their thornlike claws in anticipation of the evening. Pausing astride his bicycle a young orderly from the hospital greeted a girl at the window above: she leaned on the sill, one bare elbow at either side of her, looking down at him smiling. "See you at the dance," she said. Honor and Claudia approached: the orderly, recognizing Captain Carmichael's wife, saluted; dutiful. Honor sighed: a moment later she said, unexpectedly "This isn't a war for mothers with children. . . . It's all right for young girls—they can go into the Waaf, or make munitions—*do* something—but the married women get the rough end of it. Trailing round in furnished houses, resented by the locals, snubbed by the trades-people—and on top of it all, cold-shouldered, seeing their husbands only on sufferance——"

"On sufferance——?"

"Well, you know the C.O. He hates wives being around. He'd make the whole unit live in the mess, if he could."

Claudia said indifferently, "It's only natural, I suppose."

"What is?" Honor demanded.

Claudia flashed her an ambiguous glance. "The C.O., my dear, doesn't like rivals," she said. . . .

Through the grey ring of the bridge glided the slow
Cotswold waters. As they went they pulled languidly on
weeds that, reluctant with long weeping hair, forswore
the wooing current. Above on the bridge itself, all day
long old men and children, an enchantment in their
faces, hung watching the fluid serial of events. Sometimes a trout would dawn and vanish, sometimes, infinitely mysterious, a submerged can could be seen, its
new-grown fur trembling in the current. Everywhere
between the banks, cressy weeds floated; the frailest leaf
and hair lucidly imprinted in water. Honor stopped. She
looked apprehensively at an evacuee boy lying flat on
his stomach over the parapet of the bridge. Careful, her
heart ejaculated. . . . As if he had heard that unspoken
warning, the boy turned and stared at her with slaty
eyes resentful of the desire to protect him. Confused by
his hostility she looked away.

"Shall we turn back?" Claudia asked, indifferently.
Honor laid her hand against the stone of the bridge:
in it the warmth of that day's sunshine was still registered.
"If you like," she said. She gave a quiet sigh.

At that moment "Aha!" Claudia exclaimed. Triumph-
antly, she pointed. "What do you think of that?" she
said. Honor turned her head. Along the main road, where
a row of telegraph-poles with white china florets looked
like giant hyacinths, came a group of men in khaki. They
walked at a leisurely pace, talking together, the smallest
on the far side, leading a bicycle by the handle-bars.
"There they are, now," Claudia said. "And coming from
the hospital, too, like good boys. . . ." She grinned. "It
seems we misjudged them."

"Oh," Honor said "but—look—look who's——"
Her voice seemed to retract in her throat: it was extinguished. Foolishly (for of course it was mere foolishness,
Colin always said so), every sense in her body seemed to
shrink. She looked about her, as if seeking a way of

retreat, some cover that would mitigate the enormity of her presence on the bridge at that moment.

Claudia too had seen. The gold braid, the tabs: more unmistakable, the characteristic stooping gait. "The C.O.——" she said in a startled voice.

"Yes. . . ."

Claudia gave her sharp boyish whistle. "What a bore. Shall we run for it?"

"No, we can't. Not now. They've seen us."

"Well—don't let him get you down." Nevertheless, Claudia was aware of a certain discomfort. The influence Colonel Mayne exerted seemed to precede him. The two women, standing there in his path as if—(too late, they realized what sort of a picture they must present)—in complacent challenge, felt quite clearly his displeasure reach out and touch them.

The group came nearer. "Oh," Honor said despairingly "and Colin—Colin will be so——" She did not finish.

There was no help for it. At the right moment, the two parties became aware of each other: the appropriate air of surprise, of gratification, was duly simulated. They approached: they met. Face to face ʰey stood, forming a single group, now. "Good evening!" A leather-gloved hand flew to the peak of a braided cap: the Colonel's pale eyes, his fine domed eyeballs, turned on Honor beneath the grizzled smudge of a moustache, his spare lips drew back in that reserved almost mincing smile of his. "We meet again, it seems."

"Yes." Honor admitted the fact. Having done so she could find nothing more to add. As always, she was frozen by this false cordiality of his this deliberate simulacrum of warmth which he extended towards her, and forced her to accept. At the same time she could not repudiate it there was that in his face which made it impossible for her to remove her gaze from his.

Colonel Mayne smiled down at her, the peak of his cap shielding his high straight forehead. "Come to take your husband away from us—rescue him from his bad companions, eh?" he said. Honor's colour came up, flooding her face and neck. "No—no." She denied it, a little incoherently. "We—that is, Claudia and I—we were just out for a walk, and we thought——" He took no notice. As if she had not spoken, he turned to the young man at his side. "Keeps you in order all right, doesn't she Colin?" he said.

"It seems like it, sir." Colin, still grasping the handle-bars of his bike, was smiling in a fixed vexed fashion that both women knew. His eyes, when he looked up, had a queer slant to them: he wished to avoid seeing his wife. Honor understood. she knew that she humiliated him by her presence. Standing there before him, she became aware, in a moment of burning shame, of her own femininity: the fullness, the slipshod contours, of all that was inchoate, ununiformed about her: of that which was capable of giving offence, of making her innately un-acceptable to the men before her. She grew suddenly pale and moved a little closer to Claudia.

The Colonel continued to smile his tight-drawn smile. "And how is the growing family?" he asked. It was more like an accusation than an enquiry. A pointed reminder of that which debarred her from the world he himself was privileged to inhabit, and into which he sought in turn to draw the new-comer, Colin: a male world, with-out loyalties outside the rigid artifact of military life, which, claiming them, afforded in return such far-reaching protection both from disturbing elements within themselves and, equally treacherous, those at large in the undisciplined civilian world. "——Baby putting on weight, eh?—doing all the right things?" He did not however wait for her answer. Turning abruptly: "Let me see," he said: "I don't know if you have met Neil, have you?——" He beckoned to the tall, dark man in a green beret who had all the while been standing in the background, watching and listening to what went on. "Captain Herriot," Mayne said: "this is Colin's wife—Mrs. Carmichael—and his sister-in-law, Miss Abbott."

"How do you do."

"How do you do."

Claudia looked curiously at the stranger. "We've seen you about the village," she said. "You're not by any chance a sort of out-patient, are you?"

Captain Herriot laughed. "No. I'm at Linfield Manor —at the W.O.S.B."

"What's that?" Claudia said. "All these initials——"

"The War Office Selection Board." He moved inadvertently: she saw the Commando flash on his sleeve: she looked at him with interest and respect. So did Honor who, smiling, spoke to him for the first time. "You're the only Commando soldier I've seen in the flesh," she said.

"Really? There are lots of us about——"

"Usually I only see them on news-reels——"

The Colonel turned to Claudia. His usual question: "Well, how's school?" came out so automatically that neither he nor she gave any attention to its answer. Under lethargic lids, his eyes ran over her with a certain amount of curiosity. As regards Claudia and Colonel Mayne, there had early been established a state of armed neutrality, the terms and limitations of which existed undefined between them. She was not married to one of his officers. On the other hand, she lived in the neighbourhood, she came to all the hospital dances and functions: she was a potential source of unrest. In consequence he was both hostile and at the same time, curiously jealous: at times ignoring her altogether, at others paying her marked court: inspired in the latter case, perhaps, to forestall or simulate the reactions of his own junior officers.

He continued to observe her now, taking toll of the dusky skin, the undeveloped breasts, the manner in which she chose to wear her clothes, very much as he might assess the nature and quality of an enemy's equipment: at the same time, and this was perhaps for him something in the way of a personal triumph, it was obvious that his eye could rest on that spare boyish form of hers without the agony of embarrassment that Honor's physical maturity instantly aroused in him. "Where have you been hiding? I don't seem to have seen you around lately," he said.

"I work for my living, you know."

He ignored this. "We missed you at the Sisters' party," he said. His tone demanded of her either an explanation or an apology. She smiled at him determined to give neither. "Did you?" she said. Deliberately she resisted this, an outstanding feature of his: an unaccountable possessiveness which caused him to seek out and compel the presence by his side of people whom it might be supposed that he had reason to fear or dislike. Claudia in this respect was one of his chief victims: a privilege she shared with the bewildered C.O. of the newly established War Office Selection Board at Linfield Manor. He looked reproachfully at her. "It was a good party, you know."

"I'm sure it was."

There was a marked pause. "No doubt you had other, more important matters to attend to," he said. And at that, in spite of herself, Claudia laughed. Capitulating suddenly, she told him what he wanted to know: (with whom she had been: for what reason she had chosen to betray him by her absence). "I had every intention of coming as a matter of fact." She looked at him with candid eyes. "But I had to go to Honeybourne, to see Andrew——"

"Andrew?" Mayne pounced instantly. "But you could

have brought him along. Why didn't you?" The Colonel
had no interest whatever in Andrew Peirse: absent, on
the other hand, he became a sinister factor, potentially
subversive. Colonel Mayne could not rest until he had
assured himself of allegiance on all fronts.

"Oh, we would have come," Claudia explained. "Only,
it turned out rather foggy that evening and he has to be
so careful, you know——"

"Careful, what do you mean, careful? He's a good
driver, isn't he?" Colonel Mayne had apparently forgotten the petrol restrictions.

"No, no," Claudia corrected him: "it's not that. His
chest—since his illness—you remember——"

"Ah, yes," Mayne said: "that unfortunate business,
yes." His voice changed from one moment to the next,
he had lost every trace of interest in the matter: he
retreated from her, withheld himself in a sudden rigidity,
as if he feared that she might be about to sponge on his
reserves of emotion, of sympathy. He could accomplish
a *volte-face* of this sort with a suddenness that was utterly
disconcerting, even to those who knew him well, leaving
them wondering wherein they had offended, or in what
manner they were ever to reinstate themselves in what
had seemed, up to that moment, the closest favour and
intimacy. Without further ado, he turned from her to the
rest of the group thereby withering the mild conversation
that had sprung up among them. Sharply "Well,
Colin——?"

"Sir!"

"What's it to be? Are you coming along with us for
that drink, or——" he paused imperceptibly, he turned
towards Honor, the smile of false jocularity lit his face
again: "——or is your wife going to carry you off single-
handed to attend to your domestic duties?"

This provoked a simultaneous reaction. "I don't think,
sir, that my domestic duties——"

"Of course not! Colin needn't——" Honor's anxious disclaimer collided with her husband's, silencing them both.

Under the peak of his cap, Colonel Mayne's eyes darted from one to the other. Abruptly he intervened, shaking a leather-gloved finger reprovingly at Colin. "Now, now," he said "none of that!" And he went on, speaking now in a new, unnaturally bright voice, like that of a clumsy actor which unwittingly sets the teeth on edge by its falsity. "You want to get back to see that infant of yours bathed, I'm sure. And the other one— that amusing little boy, young Michael—it *is* Michael, isn't it?—oh, Peter, yes, of course, Peter—a most intelligent child. Quite remarkable. He'll want his bed-time story, won't he? Mustn't disappoint him, you know." On he went: his manner was affable, even paternal: nevertheless, every member of the group was aware of an acute discomfort. They stood about him, smiling vaguely, avoiding each other's eyes: bound together out of their very loyalty to the man in a common shame, wishing only that he would cease, say no more in this vein, that he would spare them all the humiliation they endured on his account.

From the bridge, all the while, from pavement corners, through curtained window-panes, the villagers watched and listened. The C.O. himself, wasn't it . . . ? What now . . . ? What was going on this time . . . ? The military hospital of which Colonel Mayne was the commanding officer formed a unit of its own within the larger unit of the village itself. With a fixed curiosity, with a certain suspended resentment, the village observed every movement and attitude of this alien body that it found itself constrained to harbour.

Under the cap with its scrolled-serpent badge, Colin Carmichael's face looked ghostly, consumed with an inexplicable fatigue. He said nothing: his eyes were fixed on the far end of the road where, in close conversation with the attentive Herriot, Colonel Mayne was to be seen walking away briskly in the direction of the Blue Trout Hotel. He looked after them without speaking. Above everything else in the world he wanted at that moment to be with Mayne, walking along at his side. Not cast out, as he now was, left to his own devices but of the group again, accepted, inspired by Mayne's will, warmed by the sun of Mayne's favour. He watched the two men, their backs turned to him, disappear round the bend in the road. Claudia, glancing casually at him at that moment was startled: it was a long time since she had seen such an expression of open frustration on the face of an adult. She looked uneasily at Honor wishing to protect her from the sight.

Honor however had noticed nothing. She was glad to see Mayne go, to feel herself released from the thrall of ineffectiveness that his presence laid upon her. She took a deep breath. Incautious in her relief "Ouf—and that's the last of them," she said.

Colin gave her an unfriendly glance. "Need you be quite so triumphant about it?" he asked. She flushed, "If that's the way you feel—you should have gone with them," she said. "Why didn't you?"

"You made it plain enough at the time that you wanted me elsewhere."

"Well, I happen to be your wife. I suppose I have *some* right to your company——"

Claudia, walking along between them, became increasingly uneasy. Leave it, she wanted to say, hush, no more at the moment, leave it. . . . It was too late. Colin turned with anger in his face. "What you seem very conveniently to forget," he said, "is the fact that Mayne happens to be my C.O. I've told you before—I'm not my

own master. My time isn't my own, even. I'm at Mayne's
entire disposal, I've got to take Mayne's orders whether
I like it or not——"

"I know that—I know you have!" She hastened to
say it, to justify herself. Nevertheless, her face did not
clear. There was another element in the situation; something she did not know how to put into words . the fact
that it was not so much the allegiance given to the
commanding officer that she resented, as that given to
the man. How to say that . . . ?

Colin prepared to play a very dog-eared trump-card.
"There's another thing you seem to forget," he said.
"Not only am I under Mayne's orders, but I happen to be
in his power too. If he takes a dislike to me he can get me
transferred, sent to some God-forsaken spot, or even——"
he paused momentarily, they all knew what was coming:
"——get me posted, sent overseas; India, Libya, Africa,
anywhere."

"Colin, don't—please don't *talk* about it!" At once
Honor became agitated. This was something that she
could not bear to envisage: the sword of Damocles suspended so prominently over the heads of the junior
medical officers. A weapon set swaying, from time to
time, by a seemingly wanton fillip from the C.O.
"Gentlemen, I advise you to enter into no permanent
commitments in this neighbourhood " or "Now then—
who's ready to take his course in tropical medicine?"
Smiling blandly, the while, at the attentive, uneasy faces
before him. . . . Added to which, it was a subject of open
conversation in the village, that a certain dour, if wholly
conscientious Scottish officer with whom Mayne had
failed to establish a sympathetic relationship, was now
kicking his heels in a base hospital somewhere in Irak. . . .
The mere recollection filled Honor with panic. Anything,
but that . . .! Let Colin spend all his evenings in the mess,

in hotel bars from Cirencester to Oxford; let him follow
Mayne day and night in his restless odysseys about the
countryside; anything, anything to avert that possibility.
She would no longer interfere: appeasement at all costs,
consistent, unshamed, would be her programme. . . .
Honor had no friends she did not read or go to the pictures. Colin was the lynch-pin around which all her
thought, her emotions, her smallest daily actions revolved.
She alone knew the disorganization that would ensue if
that system were disturbed in any way.

Claudia, oppressed by the silence between husband and
wife, essayed a diversion. She turned to Colin. "Who is
this man, this Herriot?" she asked. "The Colonel seems to
be seeing a lot of him lately, doesn't he?"

Colin said in a surly voice "Yes, he's Mayne's white-
headed boy at the moment. It's Neil this and Neil that—
I can't think why. A most commonplace individual. Used
to be a motor-salesman, or something."

"What's he doing at Linfield Manor?"

"He's the new M.T.O."

"More initials," Claudia complained.

"Military Testing Officer. He's useful to them I
suppose because he's seen a lot of active service, been on
most of the big raids, and so forth."

"How thrilling," Claudia said.

"Oh, he's quite the little tin god," Colin said bitterly.
"Personally I can't think what Mayne and everyone else
sees in him. He's a queer person. Quite disreputable in
some ways."

Claudia smiled, not without malice. "I expect that's
why Mayne likes him. It makes a change from the staid
company of the R.A.M.C."

"Staid——?" Colin rose to it at once his small new-
grown moustache seemed to bristle as he scented out
potential insult to a non-combatant corps. "Let me tell
you——"

"Joke," Claudia said wearily "forget it. . . . We all know the R.A.M.C. are as dare-devil as the next man."

"Colin," Honor interposed: all the while she had been pursuing her own train of thought, she had not heard a word of what was being said "Colin, isn't it about time you asked Colonel Mayne in to dinner, again? It's ages since he's been round to us in the evening."

"Well, it's up to you, isn't it?" Colin's voice was grudging. "The Lawrences ask him often enough. He was there again last night."

"He was?" A pang of anxiety, of jealousy, on Colin's behalf: this must be rectified, the balance righted in Colin's favour. "Well, don't forget. Ask him any day this week—except Thursday—that's Edith's half day."

"Can you give him anything decent to eat? That stew you had last time——"

"I'll get a chicken! That'll be all right, won't it? And you'll have to see if you can get some more drinks——"

"Why not get a brass band and a posse of negro slaves?" Claudia broke in, irritable. The way we all revolve around that man, dance to his tune, she thought. It's absurd, it's rather horrifying. No one should have that effect on other people. Power corrupts just as they say it does. It's either a chastening fire or it's a cancer, eating all. Look at this hospital. The feuds, the petty jealousies. Surely none of these people would behave like this in ordinary civil life. What is it that this situation has brought out in us all? . . .

CHAPTER FOUR

DANGER

A HEAVY repp curtain hung in front of the door. Its effect was to trap the light, intercept incoming patrons, and afford those already in possession of the bar a moment of pleasurable expectancy as they waited glass in hand to see what the beating and bulging would this time bring forth: who, as one newly born, would come blinking and dazzled into the world of light from the unmeasured darkness beyond. Rita Stafford on her stool behind the counter would look up from her knitting to discover which of her satellites had come to join the evening's court; hailing or assessing each new-comer without for a moment interrupting her activity with the knitting needles, the progress of this all-wool Penelope's Web (her husband, Harry Stafford, was a prisoner of war) that, in the guise of an unending sequence of war comforts, permitted the grass-widow to maintain with all the appearance of receptivity and warmth an unbroken detachment in the midst of the courtiers nightly gathered about her. Rita Stafford, now in her early forties, was petite and emaciated. Her hair, dressed above her brows in a ceremonial scaffolding of rolls and curls, had to this purpose been as rigorously doctored, treated, teased and tortured as the *coiffure* of some primitive African belle. Her talk, almost as rapid as her knitting and no less perhaps a defensive measure, was full of superlatives, of dated Air Force slang. It was obvious nevertheless that the men liked to listen to her: she had an unquenchable fund of reminiscence and small talk, the mere banality of which could not inhibit a character so positive: she told her anecdotes at top speed, assuming each role in turn, as the tale demanded, grimacing and smiling or drawing her brows down in doleful caricature, while the men she addressed watched her, glass suspended, a little open-mouthed as in childhood days they might have watched the incomprehensibly animated figures in a Punch and Judy booth.

The curtain billowed and swelled. "Hallo, hallo, hallo," Mrs. Stafford called out to Colin. In a different tone, "Hallo, my dear," she said to Honor. She smiled, revealing teeth that sloped unexpectedly inwards. "How have you been keeping?" At the same time she threw at Colin, on other occasions somewhat a favourite of hers, a glance that was accusing, almost resentful. Rita was always solicitious towards married women: ready at once, in the presence of one she fancied wronged, to ally herself with her in a solidarity that, ostensibly protective, was in fact hostile, unforgiving and curiously destructive in intent. She leaned a chicken-thin elbow on the counter. "We've not seen you here lately," she said. "Have you been poorly?" Her glittering eyes, snared under crayon eyebrows, looked insinuatingly up into Honor's face.

Honor was a little taken aback. "I'm quite all right," she said. She stood there in the unaccustomed warmth of the bar wearing her old tweed coat that had sheltered two pregnancies, and blushing a little from the interest that she, as a new-comer, excited momentarily in those present. "I can't always get away—the baby——" she explained. Rita nodded, knowing it all. "Say what you like—it ties you down.... Now I remember...." But Colin intervened. "Come along—let's get a table," he said to Honor. He took her under the elbow with a husbandly touch his purpose merely to steer. "There, by the fireplace." He sat her down at a copper-topped table, before a laden ash-tray that said "Haig." Standing over her "What'll you have?" he said, indifferent, since after so many years, she could make no decision capable of surprising him "the usual?" She nodded and he went away back to the bar to engage with Rita in the facetious bickering that, simulating, as it did, sexual intent, in fact absolved both parties of any obligation in that respect: his fair, undeveloped, almost noseless face gleaming under the unshaded light; his hair, treated with a *fixative* in pre-war days specially imported for him from France, standing out stiffly (and this certainly would have mortified him: his own being betraying him when his back was turned) from the base of his skull, like that of some small, inquisitive crested bird.

Honor sat under the cases of speckled fish, under the signed photographs of fishermen and boxers, friends of Harry Stafford's, smiling the indeterminate smile of one who, in the midst of company, sits alone. She made the gestures; unbuttoning her coat, crossing her legs a last resort (he was leaning over the counter holding Rita's bare arm) searching conscientiously in her bag for something that did not exist. Presently he came back to her, threading his way with exaggerated care "Whoa—careful!" a glass in each hand. "Here you are, *madame*," he said. He looked alert and animated. He set the glasses down on the dimpled surface of the table. Pulling out a chair "What's keeping our Claudia?" he enquired.

"She's gone to phone. There was some talk of Andrew coming over, if he could. . . ."

"Do him good," Colin said at once. He lifted a brimming glass, and cautiously advanced his lips to the edge of it. "Sits indoors and mopes too much. Introspective. All the same, these intellectuals." His tone, setting him at an infinite distance from the tribe, forbade any reminder of the unbroken series of scholastic successes that had taken him from prep. school right up to his early hospital days. These were to be discounted, even disavowed (the shameful row of leather-bound books in his mother's bookcase: the hours of concentrated work hunched over pen and paper) whereas, as Honor herself had noticed of late, to the fact that he had once (in the only match he ever played in) broken an arm on the rugger field, he was ready to accord the utmost publicity, appearing to attach to that once fractured humerus of his a significance so disproportionate as to be almost mystical. He looked across at her "Aren't you drinking?" He held up his glass. "Cheer-oh," he said.

The curtain at the door billowed sharply. A new-comer about to emerge from the caul. All turned their heads. Interest rose to a peak: who would it be? Claudia Abbott appeared, displacing by her presence the figure imagination had waited upon. They looked at her with a sort of resentment: a suspended unloving interest. She came forward into the brightly lit room: an outsider still, a separateness upon her. Lips accurately painted, her hair modelled to a formula, she looked self-possessed, civilized, and a little irritable.

"There she is," Colin set his glass down and waved. "Doesn't seem too pleased. Has she been having a tiff with him?" There was a wink in his voice. Honor did not reply. Claudia came towards them, making her way between the tables. "Did you speak to Andrew?" Honor asked. Claudia shook her head. Leaning across the table she dropped two coppers into Honor's hand. "Returned with thanks," she said.

"What's the matter?" Honor held the pennies in her open palm.

"Couldn't get through." Claudia sat down, putting her morocco leather handbag, her glasses, newspaper, on the table before her. "Line's gone dead, or something." A familiar anxiety took possession of Honor. "Do you think there's been an alert——?" she asked: her thoughts fled sharply to the children, asleep and unprotected by her presence, which, in itself could not protect them. "I thought I heard planes, earlier in the evening. . . ." But Claudia shook her head. "No, no. Something wrong with the line, that's all." Determinedly, she settled herself back in her chair. "He'll turn up, I expect. He knows where we are." The faint look of irritation remained between her eyes.

Colin rose. "What will you drink?" he asked. Deferential, he hung over her: "gin and lime, whisky, Pimm's Number One——?" Colin was always gallant to his womenfolk in company: setting up between him and them a formality calculated to neutralize in the eyes of others what might be an offensive reminder of the real intimacy of the relationship.

Claudia cut him short. "Beer, please," she said briskly. He went back to the bar. ("You again?": indefatigable, Rita resumed her role. "Yes—me again": he, too, kept it up). She set aside a half-completed Balaclava helmet, and bent to carry out his order: as she did so, he turned casually to take a look about the room. They were not very busy yet. One or two local farmers and shopkeepers, a portly R.A.F. officer, whose laden sleeve merely emphasized the absence of wings over the breast-pocket, little Smith the Registrar from the hospital, sitting quietly up in a corner with one of the plainer Sisters. . . . He waved, not too cordially, at Smitty and Sister Fry, fearful that they would ask him to come over and join them. And his eyes went, restless, to the clock over the door. It was early yet: they would fill up, surely. . . . ? All the while he was on the alert for voices outside; the sound of a car pulling up; the promise of new-comers. In the hope of such he endured, as others in that room also endured: sitting, glass in hand, before the smiling face of friend or lover, fretted, inwardly, by expectation, by the long fang of boredom or disappointment. There are those who come to public places such as this in the role of spectator; who, limited in private life by their own inability to express what is in them are impelled, from time to time (as a man will visit a prostitute, and with equal distrust) to seek out their own opposite number: the actor, as it were:

the individual, distinct in any crowd, around whose
personality the occasion will crystallize out, whose very
appearance before a word is spoken sets a stillness upon
the room, the man whose presence alone (simply in the
turn of a head, the gesture of a hand) promises release,
fulfilment, in his own person, of the unacted desires of
others. . .

Without any warning, the repp curtain over the door
was pulled brusquely to one side.

The man standing in the doorway screwed up his eyes
against what was to him, coming in out of the darkness
beyond, the sudden brilliance of the room. Then he raised
his hand and drew off a beret, exposing the dark face, a
forehead that was unexpectedly high and jutting. Unaware
of the sudden stillness which had descended upon the
room, he looked about him, turned his head this way and
that. He found what he wanted: briskly, and with the
aloofness of a gesture often rehearsed, he sent his beret
skimming through the air to settle on the upturned prong
of a brass hat-stand in the corner. He came forward, then,
looking about him with an air jovial and expectant,
smoothing, one large hand outspread, the swarthy hair
off his brow.

". . . Well—look who's here!" A ringing cry from
Rita Stafford. Colin, about to cross the room, stopped
short, glass in hand. He turned. "You?" he said. His
colour, his expression changed: in his confusion he all but
betrayed himself: "I thought you were with——" He
caught himself up in time. He stood there uncertain,
biting at his frail moustache, while Captain Herriot
looked down at him from his great height and grinned;
the amiable, fatuous-looking, wholly deceptive grin that,
exposing his long teeth, made him look like the classic
French caricature of the Englishman abroad. Indulgently
he slapped Colin on the back. "We meet again, eh?":

at the same time, he looked about him, waving a hand to those he knew "Greetings, all!" Espying Sister Fry, dovecoated, in her corner (and congenitally unable to distinguish between one Sister and the next, although he had danced with most of them, and even fondled a few starched forms in the blue-lit corridors of Linfield Park) he blew her a kiss, that was meant for the species rather than for the individual; a distinction not wholly apparent to Sister Fry, who, in consequence of that simple gesture, lost the thread of the story she had been confiding to her companion: resuming it in an altered key, high-pitched and full of strangled giggles, a performance so uncharacteristic of Sister Fry as to evoke a certain bewildered surprise in the simple Major Smith, unaware that he had all in a moment been deposed from a main role to that of supporting player: less, of stooge, of stand-in for the authentic star: a fate he shared with others present, men and women alike, whose companions, sitting at the same table and affecting unabated pleasure in their company, were in fact merely miming a part; under cover of which, all the while, they stealthily bestowed their whole attention on that which was taking place elsewhere in the room.

"What's everybody drinking?" Herriot stood under the hanging light, dark-faced, smiling that toothy smile of his. He wore battle-dress; a baggy blouse which served to emphasize his sparse hips, the line of his long and sinewy legs, gaitered at the ankle, like those of a dancer. With his height, his long dark-moustached face, he had a certain Edwardian elegance that seemed to set him apart from the contemporary mode giving to his assumption of battle-dress a quite unwarranted appearance of travesty, of harlequinade. He turned to the bar. Affably rubbing both hands together. "And how's the Blonde Bombshell, this evening?" he enquired.

Rita prepared to receive his attentions. She fingered

the lie of her curls, the set of the glass beads about her
throat, as if to assure herself that such forces of counter-
attraction as she possessed were in readiness for the assault.
Remembering that attack is the best form of defence, she
laughed, that sudden rattling laugh of hers, that exposed
immature teeth. "You two," she said—she pointed from
him to Colin—"what a pair—absolutely wizard—Mutt
and Jeff isn't in it!"

"Tut, tut." Herriot shook his head. "Rita, love, that
was unworthy of you." Leaning on the polished wood, he
regarded her good-humouredly. But Colin, at his side,
did not smile. He gnawed upon his uneven moustache.
His glance when he looked at Rita was unfriendly. He
hung about Herriot, waiting to intervene, to divert his
attention from this frivolous relationship. The loneliness,
the sense of isolation that the sudden disfavour of Colonel
Mayne had produced in Colin was so great that it brought
him not distress but a measure of low-grade comfort to
find himself in the company of the man who had usurped
that favour. It was as if, through this being who had
access to Mayne, who had perhaps come direct from his
presence that evening, he was permitted to enter into a
certain humble and indirect relationship with Mayne
himself. He seized his opportunity as Herriot lifted up his
glass of whisky and soda. "You'll join us?" he said. "My
wife—we've a table over there——"

"Oh, is your wife here?" Herriot turned his head, a
little vague. Colin fancied he detected in his manner a
certain lack of response to the suggestion and he fabri-
cated quickly, finding out of his own need the necessary
inspiration. "By the *way*," he said: a faint smile lit his
face "I suppose I oughtn't to tell you this, but——"
He lowered his voice, so that, out of curiosity, Herriot
was compelled to bend closer to him: "——my sister-in-
law—she's here too—Claudia—— Well, I don't know
what it is, but it seems you intrigue her rather...."

Fluently, with a singular sense of conviction in what he was saying, he went on to elaborate the suggestion. It was as if, perceiving his inability in his own person to attract Herriot's attention, he held forward an effigy, a decoy, in the person of a young and susceptible woman. He saw the look of surprise, of sudden attention in Herriot's eyes. And a sense of elation filled him, as if he had gained some obscure personal triumph. The wanton sacrifice of Claudia, in this, did not deter him for a moment: his own need was so great that, by comparison, the reality of those about him dwindled until they were mere figments, pawns to be used to the one end alone: a moment of madness that presented itself to him with all the cogency and detachment of sanity itself. "Believe me, old boy, you've made quite an impression, there. And it isn't every one can please Claudia. Don't tell her I told you, of course, but only this evening she was saying to me——"

"Colin's bringing that Commando fellow over to us," Claudia observed.

"I thought he would." Honor was unperturbed. Colin, she knew, did not frequent pubs in order to spend the evening in solitary confinement with his wife. "Is my nose shiny?" Claudia asked her. "No, is mine? . . ." With curiosity the two young women watched the man who was making his way towards them between the tables. Why, Claudia thought, surprised, he's quite old. There were deep hollows under his eyes. Then he moved, the light on his face changed, and she saw that he was, after all, a young man. "Good evening." He was standing over them, glass in hand. The light from the ceiling above glistened on his black hair that grew to a pronounced point in the centre of his forehead. He bowed lightly to Honor, and then his gaze sought Claudia's face. "Good evening," he said again.

"Good evening." Claudia, looking up at him and

smiling with a formal politeness, was puzzled by his manner, by something lingering and ironic in his gaze. It was an expression so unexpected, so unwarranted in a total stranger, that her smile vanished: she looked at him with an air of cool surprise. Colin, at the same time, hovered uneasily in the background, attentive to what was being said fearful that Claudia, by her manner, would repudiate all possible connection with the role attributed to her. "Sit down," he said "don't let's stand about——" Noisily he pulled forth a chair, seated himself as usual in a position commanding the whole of the room. Herriot followed suit. "Do you mind?" he leant across Claudia to set his glass down on the table. Briskly, he pulled out the chair next to hers, and sat himself down beside her.

"So you're Claudia Abbott," he said. His long legs thrust themselves forth, beside hers, underneath the table. Gently, she withdrew her knees from the contact: a manœuvre that did not pass unnoticed. A loud exclamation of concern "Oh, am I in your way? Sorry!" Hastily, he drew back with much shuffling and elaboration, began to readjust his limbs. "It's all right," she said, vexed "it's quite all right. . . ." He subsided. His legs returned to their former position, one knee resting against her calf. She did not move: as far as she was concerned, she made it clear, the contact did not exist. Herriot put one elbow on the edge of the table, leant his cheek on his fist and looked at her, smiling. "I've heard a lot about you," he said.

"Indeed?" The inflection made of the word not a question but a challenge.

"Quite a lot, as it happens. Our mutual friend, Colonel Mayne——"

"Oh, Mayne." And at that she shrugged her shoulders as if to say: you surely don't take *his* estimate seriously. "I don't know him very well, you know."

He raised his eyebrows. "Does any one?" he said. He

reached out to pick up his whisky and soda: she saw his hand: the narrow, cleft palm, the fingers, supple and dark, like those of a native. "Well——" he raised his glass: his eyes, rendered even darker by the curious pigmentation around the lids, looked mockingly into hers "——to us," he said: a moment later, before her frosty stare, he smiled: that long-toothed smile of his, that had the effect of rendering wholly innocuous, ridiculous, even, such intimacy as his own manner had suggested. He tilted back his head and drank.

Colin had been awaiting his moment. He leant forward, now. With an air deceptively casual "And where do you spring from?" he asked.

"I've been dining with Mayne."

"Oh, have you?" Colin busied himself with opening a new packet of cigarettes. "At the mess, I suppose."

"No. Mayne was in one of his moods—wouldn't stay put. We went into Cirencester—or should one say, 'Ciceter'?"

A sharp glow of pain dazzled Colin. He lowered his eyes, so that this should not be apparent to those around the table. "Where did you go——" imperceptibly he paused "to the George?"

Herriot nodded. "You know it?"

"Oh, yes, I know it." Colin raised his head. He looked at Herriot with a veiled, enigmatic glance. Know it? Fool! Fatuous, self-satisfied fool. . . . Just because you wear a Commando flash, because you've seen active service, you think no one but you—— *Know it?* I knew it long before you ever heard of it long before you came here to disturb and unsettle us all: when it was not you or any one else, but Mayne and I alone, who went off evening after evening, to eat and drink in that long hushed room with the row of white-clothed tables, the red-shaded lamp on each. . . . So now he takes you there, does he? What, then, does he say to you, over the white table-cloth, under the rosy-pleated lamp? And later, sunk in velour-padded arm-chairs, sipping, lips pursed, at the stinging hot coffee, cigar-ash creeping slowly from its chrysalis—do you think I don't know it all?—idly, yet without curiosity, watching the people in the lounge come and go, the big swing doors revolve; idly, yes, and without curiosity, since no one now could come in to add to or detract from the sum of that moment's happiness. . . . "Yes, I know the George," he said.

Without warning, with inexplicable force, the room in which they sat was clubbed a resounding blow. The windows chattered in their sockets: on the shelf over the bar the bottles and glasses rang loudly. Every one paused: there was a moment of utter stillness: they sat, glass raised, head turned, caught up in the moment's gesture as in a film still. Equally sudden, the film became animated; heads moved, hands were raised or lowered, the talk, the laughter, broke out again unabated.

Honor looked at the faces around her, bewildered. "Surely—that was a bomb?" she said.

"I imagine so."

Visibly, she lost colour. "But—the sirens haven't gone, have they?"

"Oh, yes," Herriot said. "They went half an hour ago—didn't you hear?"

Without further ado, Honor made as if to rise from the table. "Colin—the children—I must go home——"

"Really, Honor——" Colin looked put out, irritated. His lower lip came forward. "It's always the same," he said. "You know very well, Edith is there—they'll be all right——"

Honor seemed not to have heard him. "I must go," she repeated. She turned, reaching out for her coat. Colin was constrained to make some show of assisting her. He did so, grumbling all the while. "As if it's going to make the slightest difference——" His hands, fumbling for her

coat were leaden, unwilling. "It's utterly ridiculous—
Edith is *perfectly* capable——" Herriot looked across at
him in some surprise. What's biting him, he thought.

Claudia intervened. "We might as well all go," she
said decisively. "There's really not very much point——"
Quickly Colin forestalled her. "Oh, but you can't. What
if Andrew——"

"Andrew isn't likely to come now."

Herriot was listening: his black eyes fixed intently on
Claudia's face. "You were waiting for someone?" he
prompted.

"Yes," Claudia said. She looked coldly back at him.
"My fiancé," she said.

There was a slight pause. "Oh, yes," Herriot said.
"Your fiancé—I see—Yes——"

Claudia turned brusquely away from him: his manner
was beginning to impose a severe strain on her patience.
Resolutely she picked up her handbag. "Let's go then,"
she said.

But now it was Honor who protested. She looked from
one face to the other. "No, no," she said, distressed:
seeing, too late, what she had done. "Please don't—
there's no need for all of you—I can perfectly well go
alone—I've got my torch——"

Claudia cut her short. "Don't talk utter nonsense,
Honor," she said. At her words, she saw Herriot lift his
eyebrows in surprise, and realized too late how peremptory she must have sounded. She flushed. She had not
meant to speak quite like that. But there were times of
late (as frequent in private life as in the class-room) when
something in her, an irritated disciplinarian, attempted
in this fashion to take control, both of her and of the
external situation: thereby displacing a less familiar part
of her own nature: a disturbing, uncharacteristic Claudia:
tender and unstable: wholly, she felt, to be distrusted. . . .

Colin saw them push back their chairs, saw them rise to

their feet. He understood that there was no hope now
of preserving the occasion in its present shape. Already
it was out of control, disintegrating under his eyes. He
must act quickly, improvise anew. He turned to Herriot.
"Why not come along with us?" he said. He forced a
lightness into his voice. "We can continue the session at
home. There's a whole bottle of whisky that's been
scandalously neglected——"

"Thank you," Herriot said, grinning: "I don't mind if
I do. . . ." He did not look at Claudia: instead he turned,
deferential, suddenly, to Honor "That is—if it's not too
much trouble——?"

Honor paused. . . Another late night: rousing a
reluctant Edith to put the kettle on, to take out the
glasses: unguarded laughter waking the children above:
cigarette ash all over the floor: Colin drinking too much;
talking too much: as soon as the front door shut, turning
surly, going up, bleary-eyed, full of inexplicable resentment, to bed. . . "Oh, no. No trouble at all," she said.
"Please do come."

They stepped across the threshold into total darkness.
There was no light anywhere. It was like being suddenly
deprived of oxygen: the senses struggled and failed for
lack of it. Panic-stricken, with the feeling of moving in a
cul-de-sac, they groped their way forward clumsily:
limbs swaddled by the darkness. The brick baffle-wall
protecting the entrance to the Blue Trout, lurched
suddenly up against them. "Damn!" said Colin nursing
a stinging hand, a stubbed toe. They became conscious
of each other, imminent, at large in the dark. Colin's
voice came again, querulous "Honor—where's that
torch? Can't you—here—give it to me——" and then
Herriot's nonchalant "Shine the lamp, Sam. . . "

There was a click: a fan of light was released. In its
beams a part of the kerb, the base of the pillar-box, were

printed on the surrounding darkness like an image projected by a magic lantern. Colin raised the torch: the light swung upwards: they saw each other's faces, bleached and startled, overhanging the darkness. "Hey—turn that down," Herriot said "it's like a ruddy searchlight." "It's got tissue-paper over the bulb," Colin said: argumentative. There was a heavy rumble of guns in the distance. Honor lifted her head, uneasily. "Colin—hurry—let's go, please." She turned, and, "Oh, very well," he hurried after her: together—they were the same height exactly—they walked across the cobbled surface of the square, the light of the torch, controlled by Colin, hopping before them as they went. Claudia, following, felt someone walk up close beside her: before she could turn, a hand groped for her, and then held her firmly by the forearm. "Allow me," Herriot said. She made as if to withdraw from him. "Thank you I can see quite well." He laughed. "You can? Well, in that case you'll have to guide me. I'm as blind as a bat." His fingers tightened confidently on her arm. She did not speak.

Above their heads a searchlight sprang up, wheeling. Like a giant windscreen-wiper, it attempted to erase the darkness. Dwarfed by cloud, it began to smoke and flutter like a torch. A moment later, and another, then yet another sprang up: noiselessly, they fenced; noiselessly met and clashed, tip to tip, until the shining blades were arched above the earth like swords at a bridal procession. The guns had fallen silent: in their place, another sound dawned on the senses: a humming, as of a large top purposefully rotating. . . . "Our fighters up," Herriot said. He walked, head raised expectantly listening. The village was very still: all light, all life withdrawn, ambushed behind sealed doors and windows. The echo of their own footsteps accompanied them obtrusively across the cobbles. They alone, they felt, were abroad with the enemy. . .

There was a flash and a thud: followed in rapid succession by two more: flash, thud: flash, thud. Each time, stricken, the air bucketed like a punch-ball: to quiver slowly back into stillness again. In the ensuing silence, silence, Herriot's voice came to them, with great clarity. "Jettisoned," he said. "He's being chased, as I thought..." Honor cried: "Oh, Colin, where do you think they——?" her voice failed in her throat. Herriot called out cheerfully across the intervening darkness; "You needn't worry," he said. "That was five or six miles away, at the very least."

They walked on, silent now. The darkness, too, maintained an ambiguous silence. Distrusting it they listened uneasily; awaiting the first whisper, pronouncement of danger. Now and then someone said irritably "Sh!" standing still the better to hear; impatient of any sound which might obstruct that sound which the ear awaited... A night bird screeched suddenly. Far away on the horizon, impermanent constellation, a shell-burst twinkled and was extinguished. It was then that they heard it: with sinking hearts, recognized it again: the deep uneven throb of enemy aeroplane engines. "Jerry's overhead..." The comment was automatic: there was no reply. They were listening, curiously absorbed: concerned not to miss a note, a pulsation; as if safety depended on their own awareness of what was going on, of what was about to take place... Throb, throb, throb. Wounded, the night throbbed out its anguish: the waves of pain pulsating across the sky, one after another, one after another... As they listened, their nerves tingled in response. Throb, throb, throb. Plainly, they could feel the night about them festering in its own poison.

Herriot, holding Claudia by the arm, felt suddenly that she was trembling. He was astonished. "Cold?" he asked.

She did not answer for a moment. Then she gave a

small uncertain laugh. "No," she said. She hesitated. "It's that sound. I hate it so. . . "

"*Do* you?" Instantly, he twined his arm round hers and drew her closer to him. "Now why?" he asked, reasonable. "You didn't mind the bombs, just now——"

"Oh, I know," she exclaimed. "That's different. It's quick. . . . But that awful droning, going on and on. . . The *waiting*——"

"Well, it's funny you should say that," he said. "But I rather like that part of it." He found her hand: absently, so it seemed, forced his fingers between hers. "I find it exciting—the gambler's instinct, I suppose." His voice underwent a change: it became withdrawn and dreamy. "To me it *is* like gambling, as a matter of fact. Like watching the croupier's wheel—seeing it spin—hanging on for dear life—and then, suddenly—*Rien ne va plus!*—the fatal little ball—the bomb or the cartridge—shoots into place, and there you are—it's life or death for you or your neighbour, all according to the laws of chance." He laughed. "You see what I mean? It's luxury—a millionaire's game—playing for stakes like that. In peacetime, most of us couldn't afford it. . . "

She sensed the excitement in his voice. Momentarily, it roused her: she felt an answering thrill in her own nerves. At once, she was ashamed: ready to disown her own response. There was something debased in this, she thought. It was wrong to feed on danger: to take to peril as to an aphrodisiac. . .

"A penny for them," Captain Herriot said in her ear. He spoke softly, insinuatingly. She became conscious of his arm, pressed against her side; his strong fingers, wrapped within hers. As if waking up, suddenly, she drew away from him, tried to extricate herself: in fear of that which had got hold of her. . . "What's the matter?" he asked. "You're not going to abandon me, are you? I can't find my way without you, you know."

"Dear me," she said acidly. "A little unenterprising for a Commando soldier, surely?"

"Come, come." Mildly, he reproved her. "You speak as if life, for me, were one long raid."

She paused. "Isn't it. . . ?"

Captain Herriot too paused. Then he gave a small laugh. "I believe," he said, "that you're trying to be nasty to me. I wonder why. . . "

She affected not to hear this. "We'd better hurry," she said "the others are miles ahead, already. They'll be wondering——" The sentence was never finished. "Look out!" she heard: sharply, she turned her head, but before she had time to think or move, Herriot had snatched her: a moment later, she found herself lying flat in the ditch, Herriot's arm flung protectively across her, her right cheek pressed into the cold night grass. At the same moment, she heard it coming: a long rushing whistle that lifted the breath out of her lungs. She lay there in a trance of stillness: freezing, every nerve in her body awaited catastrophe. . . The whistle swelled rapidly: something shot past over their heads: then there was a tremendous roar, the earth bounded under them, and a fountain of sound, of destructive energy, gushed high into the night. And then, equally suddenly, it was all over. It was as if it had never been. There was silence. They felt a queer blankness in the air about them; a sensation as of soap-bubbles bursting gently on the dazed eardrums. . . .

Herriot sat up. He rubbed his elbow; spat a little grit out of his mouth. "Pretty close, that," he observed. He picked up his beret, and brushed it fastidiously with his cuff. "Lucky for us it fell in soft earth." There was no reply from Claudia. He looked quickly at her. "I say— are you all right?"

After a moment, he heard her voice. "Yes," she said. "Yes—I'm all right. . . " "Sorry to have been so unceremonious just now," Herriot said. "But it was a choice of lying in the ditch, or hanging in tatters on one of those elm-trees." Abruptly, he laughed. *"We needs must love the highest when we see it,"* he quoted. "Seems to me, he had something, there. . . Nothing like a little T.N.T., either, for accelerating the process . . . *Excelsior! . . ."*

Claudia said nothing. She seemed not to hear his voice. She was aware of the pervading smell of earth; the grittiness under her palms; the sly, moist touch of grass upon her cheek. She thought of people, lost in the snow, who ask nothing better than to be allowed to sleep, to succumb to the strange fascination of the situation. . . . In a state of delicious reaction from fear, she lay there, feeling that her limbs did not belong to her, that all incentive to action had mysteriously and delightfully vanished.

Herriot bent over her. "We'd better be moving on," he said. "Your sister will be worrying. . . ." Claudia sighed. "Come," he said briskly. He took one of her hands; it was slack, reluctant, in his grasp. "Come," he said again. Seizing both her hands in his, he pulled her, in one movement, to her feet. "There you are," he said. There was a pause. "And where do we go from here. . . ? She did not answer. They stood there, in the middle of the deserted road. Her hands were locked in his. "Claudia. . ." Through the darkness his eyes searched her face for a clue. "Claudia?" She did not answer. Slowly, Herriot drew her towards him. She still said nothing. Gently, then, questioningly, he kissed her. To his surprise, she made no show of resistance. "It's an ill high explosive blows no one any good," he murmured. He kissed her again.

Claudia seemed to awaken suddenly. Sharply, she drew away from him: pulled her hands out of his, one after the other. Without resentment, he released her. He accepted the withdrawal; waited, with a certain amount of curiosity, to see what she would do next.

Without speaking, Claudia stepped back a pace or two.

She buttoned up her jacket, rearranged her hair, tucked her handbag firmly under her left armpit. Her movements were calm and unhurried. Looking up, she caught Herriot's eyes upon her. Carefully, she flicked a blade of grass off the sleeve of her dress. "That was a lucky escape," she said in a detached voice.

In spite of himself, Herriot grinned. "I take it," he said, "that you're referring to the bomb——?"

She gave him a level glance. "What else?" Her voice repudiated the memory, even the possibility, of intimacy. Herriot's brows went up in a steep arc. "So that's the way it is," he said; humorous, resigned.

She looked suspiciously at him. "What do you mean——?"

"I was admiring," he said, "the efficiency of the degaussing system. . . ."

She turned her head sharply. "I *beg* your pardon——?"

He laughed. "Nothing," he said, "nothing. Forget it." They walked down the long road without speaking. In the darkness, Herriot was smiling to himself.

CHAPTER FIVE

AT HONEYBOURNE

THERE was a scratching in the passage outside. The door opened of its own accord, it seemed, and the Pekinese rattled across the parquet on silk-draped legs. Finding the company at table, he stopped and gazed up at them, out of orbs as striped and glossy as a peppermint bullseye.

"Lie down, China," said Mrs Peirse. He raised a

golden forehead to her. His face looked as if it had been compressed, pushed in like the front of a folding camera. "Down," she said. He obeyed. She had that power. Not doubting herself, she did not infect others with doubt: animals, servants, accepted her word: effortlessly, her will prevailed over external circumstance. Dressed in an assortment of purple and mauve cashmere jerseys, she sat there, with her impressive yellow face; her ashen hair neatly crimped; her liver-spotted hands decorated with heavy gold rings. A box of pills, some medicine in a pale blue bottle, standing sentinel by her plate, testified to the frailty of a digestion impaired years before by some obscure illness contracted in the Middle East. Behind the big serving-spoons, the knife and fork rests, the painted cork mats, she sat enthroned in her own chair with its special leather cushion; and from this point of vantage, with Maud in attendance at her shoulder, conducted the tempo of the meal: dispensed and controlled hospitality. ". . . Claudia, a little more?" She raised the silver spoon above the dish. Her tone was interrogative; at the same time, she made it clear, she awaited, not assent but a declining movement of the head. Claudia submitted ". . . No more, thank you," Smiling, she condemned herself to hunger. . . . The baked fillets, in their freckled cheesy sauce, were borne away out of reach. And that was that.

"Elsie has heard that her son is a prisoner of war," said Mrs Peirse.

"She's pleased?" Andrew lent his elbow on the table, and examined his nails.

"Of course—He'd been missing for six months."

"I sometimes think," Claudia said: she hesitated, finding Mrs Peirse's eyes upon her: "in a sense—we're all prisoners of war," she said.

"That's true enough." Mrs Peirse nodded her head. "We don't have much liberty, these days. Filling out

forms for this, filling out forms for that. . . . Prisoners of
war—that's about it."

"As a matter of fact," Andrew intervened "The boot's
on the other foot, if you only knew it. Prisoners of war,
you say—but don't forget the Prisoners of Peace—the
people who've had to live battened down, all their lives,
pretending to conform, pretending to be what they aren't.
And that applies to most of us—— Hence war, in fact.
Call it a general amnesty, if you will——"

Claudia looked at him curiously across the table. "You
seem to like the idea," she said.

"I neither like it nor dislike it. I take things as I find
them."

"You must have a *standpoint*."

He smiled at her. "A vested interest, you mean?"

"All right," she said then "what would *you* do, if you
had the chance? Give up the law—turn criminal?"

"There's no knowing," Andrew said. His glance turned
to the garden: lying, deserted, under the bright noonday
sunshine. "Ever seen a rose-bush that's been neglected?"
he asked. "If you don't keep pruning it, it seizes the first
opportunity of turning itself back into a dog-rose again.
It's queer isn't it how it goes all through nature, this
nostalgia: the longing to revert. . . . Queer, too, after
centuries of grooming, the suckers our own nature throws
off from time to time. . . ."

"Obviously," Claudia said. "Without pruning—there'd
be no civilization."

"True," he said, "and that's where you come in."

"I?"

He gave her a level glance. "You're a schoolmistress,
aren't you?"

For some reason, her colour came up. "And you're a
lawyer——"

"The pot calling the kettle black, my dear!"

"The pot calling the kettle *white*, surely——?"

"Ah yes, far more invidious—I agree——"

Mrs Peirse looked from one to the other. "Are you children quarrelling?" she asked.

"We're not quite sure ourselves, are we, Claudia?"

Maud returned to the room. Six foot to an inch, with a long stringy neck, she looked in her frilly cap and apron more like a female impersonator than a genuine parlourmaid. She brought to the table a dish of pancakes. Of limp yellow suède, mottled from the pan, they were rolled about some sort of cream sauce and served with a mixture of raspberries and red-currants, bottled the previous year by Mrs Dougal the housekeeper. The call-up had not affected Mrs Peirse's staff of elderly women. Nor did rationing make itself felt in a household which grew its own vegetables and fruit, which had a modest farm attached to its own service. Indeed it was true to say (random bombs apart) that Mrs Peirse had succeeded to a very large extent in ignoring the war and evading its conditions. Prompted by the instinct of self-preservation (for which read class-preservation), she had achieved this, not by migrating to California, or insulating herself within the vacuum of hotel life, as her friends the Hadley-Stewarts had done; but by digging herself in; by adhering ever more obstinately, to her own way of life; that is to say, to her own desires and the traditions that reflected those desires. At the same time of course, she was discreet in her intent; indulging in a certain amount of protective cover, even attending village functions in aid of Mrs Churchill's fund for Soviet Russia; visiting evacuee women in their homes; resisting to a certain extent her tradespeople's eagerness to give her preferential treatment over new-comers and evacuees: in the last resort, admitting to the strong-point of Honeybourne itself only those who knew the passwords; who accepted the same standards; who, like herself, aware of living, more and more hard-pressed, in a beleaguered fort, bided their time, waited in patience and with unspoken confidence for the forces of reaction to raise the siege. . .

Maud reorganized the table: subtracted plates, brought new dishes. Talking all the while, they snapped apart the dimpled water-biscuits, lifted small cubes of Cheddar on the pronged knife, discreetly crunched the braids of green-white celery. "Give me a match, Andrew." Mrs Peirse turned to the trolley drawn up at her side, she touched the wick under the Cona. Mauve and spirituous, an iris wavered under the transparent globe. Presently, water bubbled and rose: the coffee was ready. Lifting it off its bracket she poured it, black and tan, into the gilt-scrolled cups. "Claudia, yours. . . . Andrew?" "Thank you, Mother" he put out his hand across the table, and Claudia noticed, with a faint shock, how frail his wrist looked inside the opening of his cuff. He helped himself to coffee-sugar, gently revolving the amber shingle with a toy spoon. His head was lowered: she saw the mauve shadow in each temple; the fair hair, always too fine, now growing visibly sparser. Andrew had his father the late Judge's face: the vague eyes in the well-formed sockets, the haughty nose. But not the legal mouth. Even at this age (he would soon be thirty-five) his lips had the full uncertain modelling that surprises us in the youthful photographs of middle-aged friends. In repose, that is. When he smiled a hitch became apparent; his mouth drew sharply to one side: he smiled with one side of his mouth only, a painful retracted expression, as if part of his nature condemned whatever pleasure or emotion he was compelled, momentarily, to experience.

Mrs Peirse drank her medicine; dolorously raising her eyebrows, pursing her mouth. She set the chalky glass back on the table. "And what are you two going to do with yourselves this afternoon?" she enquired. Mrs Peirse rested after lunch, on doctor's orders, but she could not consign herself to oblivion before acquainting herself, in theory at least, with that which was likely to take place during her absence. "I shouldn't do anything too strenuous," she said. "This weather can be very tiring. . . ." She did not look at either of them as she spoke; she was busy drawing her serviette through its silver ring: nevertheless, Claudia felt that the words were directed at her. She smiled. "Don't worry—we'll be good," she said. There was a certain lilt to her voice. The withered lids quivered: Mrs Peirse glanced quickly at her out of those pale eyes of hers. There was something alert and watchful in her face, calculating, even: as if, looking at her future daughter-in-law, she measured her up, assessing her capacity to fill that role: a certain distrust, too; Mrs Peirse, it seemed, detected in Claudia something which disturbed her; a potential threat to that emotional control which was the basis and governing factor of the temperate life at Honeybourne. Of course, thought Claudia in a sudden flash of illumination: I see it now. She's suspicious of me. Afraid of anarchy. And she's wondering if I'm not, after all, perhaps, a Trojan horse. . .

Claudia sat on the edge of the pond, looking at the flat linoleum leaves of the water-lily. A reflection from the surface of the water trembled continuously across her face: light chasing shadow. Under one of the leaves, a goldfish meditated: now and then unfurling a dreaming tail that, somnolent, seemed to lick and search the yielding water. The garden was silent, caught still in its noonday trance: faintly, from the house, came an intermittent clink, as the plates and forks were washed and stacked up in the long stone scullery. Andrew said, looking into the cloudy water "This pond will have to be cleaned out. It's full of tadpoles."

It was true. The sleek commas were everywhere; nibbling, trembling, wriggling, dimpling the surface of the water. Andrew bent lower to examine them: he was fascinated, and at the same time faintly repulsed. His face, blanched by the strong sunlight, hung over the pond. "Most unpleasant," he said.

"Why?" Claudia asked, surprised.

"I don't know. They remind me of the semolina I used to hate as a child. Jellified—nasty—primitive——"

Claudia laughed. "That's Life," she said, audibly parodying the comment. "You've got to accept it."

"I endure it," Andrew said. "I don't have to accept it." He looked across at her and smiled his one-sided smile. "I'm all against it, really. . . ."

"That's a little unfair, considering the amount of enjoyment you manage to get out of it."

He paused. "Being ill, you know, has done something to that. . . ."

She said quickly: "It can't alter æsthetic appreciation——"

"Oh, yes, it can. . . ." He looked down at the tadpoles. "It's a little difficult to explain, to someone who hasn't been through it." He watched the life flickering within that torpid water. "I found out you see, that when you're ill—ill enough, I mean—the wheels begin to revolve contra-clockwise: negative becomes positive and vice versa. Things that you liked, that seemed desirable—appear hateful, nauseous. I couldn't look at the flowers on my bed-table: the smell of the soap they washed me with nearly made me sick—the smell of starch in the sheets, even. . . ."

"Well?" Claudia said, waiting for him to continue.

"Well—that's all, really. Except that you remember that sort of thing when you're what's called well again. You've had a glimpse back-stage. You know that you're living in a fool's paradise. That it's simply and solely a temperature of 98.6 that maintains the illusion of beauty, and makes the whole bag of tricks tolerable at all."

"Very well," Claudia said. "But that's over and done with. Your temperature is normal now."

He grinned at her. "Sub-normal, darling. Didn't you know. . . ?"

She took a chance. "Don't be so conceited about your disabilities, darling."

There was a pause. He said simply "You're quite right, Claudia. I'm sorry. I hadn't realized I'd reached that stage——"

"What stage?"

"The stage of trying to extract prestige out of my own shortcomings."

This was so unexpected, so like the old Andrew that a sudden wave of longing rose up in her: her eyes filled with tears. Andrew saw this. His expression changed. "Don't," he said, involuntarily. He looked away from her: estranged at once by that betrayal of emotion.

The sky was intensely blue. In the tall trees at the side of the house some rooks alighted, braying. Sunlight flashed like steel on the swarthy feathers. Unwilling to settle, they dipped and circled, came and went, weaving in aerial dance about the maypole of the tree; uttering all the while their plangent, china-flat cackle. Higher still, very high up in the sky, a plane glittered; scarcely moving, no bigger than a pin. Odd, Claudia thought drowsily, to think that there was a human being up there so high in the sky; a man, in a shirt and tie, his hair brushed, bootlaces knotted: fantastic, really. . . . She opened her eyes. She saw Andrew coming across the lawn. He had been to fetch the deck-chairs out of the summer-house. Seeing him drag the unwieldy frames after him across the grass, she had an impulse to go and help him, and then checked it. It was important to them both that she should not appear the stronger of the two. . . . All the while, as she knew, he was baiting her; trying to surprise her into revealing her own strength; trying to prove something conclusive about their relationship. Obstinately she resisted him: protecting them both from his cunning, from this new, curiously destructive obsession of his. He was having difficulty with the deck-chairs. He dropped one, stooped to pick it up again. She did not move.

"There you are, *madame*." He knocked the cross-bar into one of the sockets. "That suit you?" He tossed her a dusty red cushion from the summer-house, and turned to set up his own chair. She watched him. His white shirt ballooned about him, his flannels sagged, he had no waist, no hips; bodily, she thought, amused, he was like Wells's Invisible Man. It was all the more surprising therefore, when he turned towards you to discover, in the gaze of those pale eyes, something so very positive: a sense of authority that made itself felt, at times (as people who had opposed him in the law courts knew) with all the compulsion and directness of physical force itself.

He lowered himself into the chair beside her. The strong sunlight showed up the hollows, the fine under-scorings, in his face. He looked like an ageing *jeune premier*, at the same time older and younger than he actually was. . . .

He settled himself more comfortably: closed his eyes, and linked his fingers across his chest. In the detached voice people use when they cannot see: "What's happened to our local hero, lately? Is he still around?" he asked.

"Who?" Claudia said, startled. She opened her eyes, dispelling the rosy twilight inside her lids.

"The Commando Captain."

She paused. "Oh. . . . Yes . . . him." She glanced quickly at Andrew. "He was at the pub that evening when you didn't come."

"Yes?" His voice was encouraging.

"Colin asked him to come back with us and have a drink," she said.

"Poor Colin. Always the hero-worshipper. I hate to think what his schooldays must have been like."

Claudia hesitated, then made up her mind. "There was a raid on," she said resolutely. "Captain Herriot and I had to shelter in the ditch."

Andrew sat without moving. "That must have been very romantic," he said.

"It was very uncomfortable."

"The position had its compensations, no doubt."

Claudia flushed. Andrew turned to look at her. His eyes were vague no longer, but, as happened to him when he was inwardly moved or excited, a deep burning blue. He looked very handsome. Claudia knew the signs: her heart sank. "You don't have to tell me about it if you don't want to," he said gently.

"There's nothing to tell."

He shrugged his shoulders. "Just as you like," he said indifferently.

"I mean it," She was getting angry.

He did not answer. He had not heard her speak, it seemed. He was looking at the fingers of his right hand, spread out before him. "Since I've been ill—my fingernails have become ridged. Funny, isn't it? Every one of them. Look." He held out his hand towards her. She glanced at it and made no comment. He was displeased at her lack of interest. A silence fell. At last "You don't trust me, do you Andrew?" she said.

"You don't trust *me*, it seems."

"That's not true."

"Then why do you find it so difficult to speak to me?"

"I don't find it difficult——"

"Oh, but you do. I've noticed it again and again, lately. Once upon a time—do you remember?—we used to discuss everything together; but now——"

"One can't forever be dissecting oneself, Andrew!" She spoke quickly, emphatically. He looked at her in surprise. "You've got to have a sense of *proportion*," she said. "What do all these little personal difficulties matter, compared with what's happening in the world around us—compared with a world war——"

"They matter very much," Andrew said, "when you consider that it's precisely the sum and accumulation of all these personal difficulties that makes world war possible."

"That's a very sweeping statement to make. I'm not so sure that I agree——"

He smiled at her. "You're not making the fashionable mistake of supposing that wars are fought for economic reasons alone?"

"These reasons exist."

"So do motor-cars. But they don't get very far without petrol." She was silent, and he went on: "Tell me, Claudia, as a matter of interest. Have you ever seen London, or Bristol, or Coventry, after a blitz? Steel girders twisted, masses of concrete ground to powder. . . . Do you know what the force is, that blasted that concrete; twisted those ten-ton girders like strips of putty? Not T.N.T., Claudia. Something far more terrifying and destructive. Human emotion. It's the force of pent-up human emotion that wrecked Amsterdam, Leningrad, Coventry, Cologne. Why? Because it's compressed, tightly packed down into the shell-case of civilization. Hence our joy in those 'beautiful bombs.' They say it all for us— everything that we've been forbidden to say or think or do. . . ." His hand hung motionless at his side: long and slender, the fingers relaxed. "As a result of our unnatural way of living," he said, "civilization has become so costive that it needs a regular dose of high explosive to achieve a catharsis!"

"You believe, then," Claudia said "that if people were able to solve their own personal difficulties, war wouldn't happen?"

"The explosive power would be less, certainly." He twisted himself round in his chair to look at her. "You're a schoolteacher, Claudia. Teach your children this, *that one man with war inside him creates world war.*"

"One man? Hitler, you mean——"

"I do not! I mean you or me—anyone. We're not fighting something local and external, labelled Fascism—we're wrestling with our own deepest inclinations and desires."

She chose to misunderstand him. "If you're speaking about the Fifth Column——" she began.

He interrupted her. "There's a Fifth Columnist inside every one of us."

"I don't believe that!"

He smiled. "No: you wouldn't. You prefer your devils projected. . . ."

She said hotly, "I think it's a treacherous statement to make."

"It's equally treacherous to ignore it. And damn silly, too; if we want to achieve something, and not go on, sparring blindly, century after century. . . ."

There was a pause. Then Claudia said, in an altered voice "Why are you saying all this to me, Andrew?"

"Because you think you're so civilized and rational. That you've got everything nicely taped——"

"Well?" She challenged him.

"Well—I don't want you to fool yourself—that's all."

Mrs Peirse lay under the quilt in her stockinged feet. Her eyes were shut, but she was not sleeping. Curled up under the downy warmth of the quilt, she clasped a rubber hot-water bottle in her arms: supplement to her own waning warmth. At the other side of the long room the window was half open; she could hear the distant creaking of rooks; the sudden warble and squeal of smaller birds in the shrubbery beside the porch. Once she thought she heard Claudia's voice, and lifting her head off the pillow, she listened attentively. But it was only one of the maids calling out to Foyle, the gardener. She closed her eyes again and lay without moving. Stealthily the sunlight shifted; it deepened; it began to slant towards her across the blue-carpeted floor. She drew her arm up out of the bedclothes and looked at her gold bracelet watch. Another twenty minutes. . . . She lay there, her white hair smudged across the pillow, her tenuous lids twitching upon the wakeful eyeballs. She had not slept, she had not even rested; compelled to retire, she had lain here, as the minutes ticked by, listening, calculating. . . . This always happened when Claudia was in the house. She was uneasy, she knew it, whenever Claudia was about the place. Anything might happen, she felt; unaccountable things: pictures fall, fires break out, as if the girl were some sort of poltergeist. (The threat she envisaged was always something external, to some material part of the house, never to its spiritual foundations, never to herself, the ageing, the soon-to-be-superseded, owner of Honeybourne.) There was of course no tangible reason for this disquiet of hers; none at all: nevertheless there it was; a queer instinct she had: she did not trust those very deep-set eyes, she told herself, that curiously intense glance. . . .

Quite suddenly, she raised herself on the pillow: she discarded the quilt and got up. She did not stop to put on her shoes, even. Noiselessly in her stockinged feet she went across the room. Putting out a hand, she pulled the curtain back very slightly and bent forward to look out. She could see the forecourt of the house; a corner of the lawn. Here they were. . . . They had got the deck-chairs out; the new ones; she saw them lying side by side at a slight angle to each other. Claudia had her skirt raised above her knees, sunning her legs. Andrew lay, inert, one hand hanging to the ground. . . . They were talking.

What were they saying to each other? She stood without moving behind the curtains and watched them for a long time.

CHAPTER SIX

SPORTS DAY

THE big gates of the military hospital were open. Now and then a car swung in from the road; an ambulance, the C.O.'s truck, or a plain saloon with a label stuck in the windscreen. The sentry was on duty: old Mrs Carey, too; drawn up in her basket chair behind the lace-curtained window of the lodge. For some reason, "the military," when they requisitioned Linfield Park, had omitted to displace Mrs Carey from that vantage point; which thus remained, an advanced outpost and accurate source of intelligence to the whole village. She watched the visitors make their way up the drive in twos and threes: men, women and children. Admitted to these precincts for the first time since the establishment of the hospital, they walked along glancing about them as they went; hostile yet full of curiosity; reserving their judgement. The drive was long and austere, planted on either side with laurustinus. At the end was the hospital: a mile away. Originally a lunatic asylum, it had the high barred windows, the many outhouses, towers, bakeries and wash-rooms peculiar to such institutions, as well as the strange forbidding colour of the bricks; as if the spiritual distemper it had housed so long had, like a fungus, succeeded in permeating and discolouring the very walls themselves. In contrast, the grounds were beautiful; and in the days of the lunatics (mysteriously liquidated at a wave of the War Office wand) well kept. Now however, a reserve of coke had been dumped on the superintendent's croquet lawn, and the main rock-garden levelled to make way for a fleet of Nissen huts, erected in great haste to accommodate a proposed increase of personnel, which, six months later, had still failed to materialize.

The patients were strolling about the grounds in their cornflower blue. One or two of them, it was noticeable, looked browned off. They glanced at the visitors with a certain hostility and made no attempt to approach; turning away into the coppice beyond the drive, or lying silent under the chestnut-trees, their caps pulled down over their eyes. These were mostly men who had acquired their injuries accidentally, during the course of their duties at home. They were uneasy in their conspicuous uniform; exposed, thereby ("our brave boys in blue") to a sympathetic admiration which, so far, and through no fault of their own, they had done nothing to earn. The few Libya wounded, on the contrary, and every one of these was very seriously injured, exhibited a serenity and high humour to be found only in those who, physically maimed, are yet whole in their own estimation: hopping about, brown and frail, on their crutches, wheeling themselves in their invalid chairs; watching the civilians approach, invade their domain, with equanimity; confident of their own proved ability to meet the challenge offered to them.

The visitors reached a fork in the drive. One notice said "Out of Bounds" the other, with an arrow, "To the Sports." They followed a gravelled footpath, emerging finally through a screen of privet onto a terrace above a flight of steps: and here they paused for here, at a single glance, the whole of Linfield Park, as well as the nature and scope of the occasion itself, lay exposed before them like a scene witnessed from the gallery of a theatre. There in the background were the barred windows, the crazy turrets, the dark mottled walls of the hospital itself, with cars drawn up in a semicircle before the gleaming mahogany doors of the main entrance. A crescent-shaped lawn; a system of flower-beds bright with Siberian wallflower; and then the ground descended in a series of graduated terraces to an arena, a sort of grassy amphitheatre marked off with ropes; and rose again through a similar sequence of rock-gardens and flower-beds, to a point where a large orange and red marquee, a temporary N.A.A.F.I., had been erected in close proximity to a building reputed, incorrectly, to be the hospital morgue. Against this elaborate back-cloth, vivid in their motley, moved the actors (for such they seemed to the new arrivals, who, distinct as yet from the occasion, had no sense of participation in its general purpose): the blue coats of the patients, the white of the athletes, the khaki of officers and men, the flashing veils and scarlet-lined capes of the Sisters, forming a bright, incoherent pattern; like the component parts of a vast jig-saw puzzle, shuffled and re-shuffled in the effort to find a final and harmonious solution. Muted, through the sunlit air, came the sudden beat of jazz: the Linfield Rhythm Quartette giving their rendering of "Begin the Beguine."

"Where *is* the C.O.? I've not laid eyes on him since lunch time." Megaphone in one hand, a list of events in the other, little Smith looked about him with a distracted air. His plump round chin was bathed in perspiration. Major Smith took his duties seriously.

"Don't worry, Smitty, old boy. He'll turn up."

"I know, but it *looks* so odd——"

"He's probably got stage fright."

The Registrar's blue eyes, enlarged behind thick lens, looked puzzled. "Stage fright," he said: "why?"

"Take a look." Captain Lloyd indicated a group of young women, the daughters of Linfield's gentry, who, in printed linen and Joyce sandals, were gazing about them with an air of bright expectation. "The local floozies waiting to give him the works," he said.

"I thought he looked a bit queer at lunch——"

"He's probably locked himself in his room at the mess. Unless he's hiding behind Matron's skirts——"

"I doubt if he'd go there for sanctuary," said the poker-faced Major McRae: he was the hospital pathologist.

"I wonder if—I know there was something——" Major Smith checked himself. Aware that the others were watching him with interest, he changed the subject hurriedly. "It's the prizes," he said; "if he's not here when they give out the prizes—— It's not fair to Lady Brent——"

"Excuse me, sir," Burke, the six-foot R.S.M. intervened respectfully. "What do you think, sir? Would it be possible to have the hundred yards now, and leave the obstacle race until more people have arrived?"

"Very well," Smith said, consulting his list.

"It's nearly time, sir. Will you——"

Smith lifted the megaphone. He cleared his throat. "Ladies *and* gentlemen." Inflated, his voice boomed forth. "The next event will be the hundred yards! Take your places for the hundred yards race, *if* you please!" He lowered the megaphone, took a large khaki handkerchief out of his pocket, and patted his chin. Already, the more athletic members of the staff were standing by, in running shorts, bare arms folded protectively across their chests. A number of the orderlies were preparing to compete, shirt-sleeved, in braces and sand-shoes. Sunlight flashing on white teeth, on Brylcremed hair, they flexed their muscles, mock-sparred among themselves, as they waited. Sister Blair and Sister McDonald, inseparable as usual, watched this display of manly form from behind the ropes.

Nigger-dark legs emerging from snowy aprons, their bony Scottish wrists framed in starched cuffs, they stood side by side, glances darting here, there and everywhere; conversing together, exchanging queries and comments, without for a moment relinquishing the scene with their eyes, or ceasing to offer to all concerned a bright unvarying smile. "What's the matter with Captain Carmichael?" one of them said. "He looks like a cat on hot bricks."

"He's been like that all the afternoon."

"Is his wife here?"

Sister McDonald turned her head this way and that, searching the faces of the new-comers. "No, I don't think so. Not yet."

"I don't believe I've ever seen her," the other said thoughtfully, "What's she like?"

"She keeps herself to herself."

"Stuck up?"

"No. Shy, I fancy." The Sister's shrewd northern eyes rested on Colin. "I shouldn't think he's a particularly easy man to live with," she said.

"I don't know," said the other. "He's good fun, when there's company." She was a dark, vivacious girl.

"Look out—here he comes."

Colin came up to the ropes. "Enjoying yourselves?" he asked.

"Why not?" The smiles became adjusted, focused. Sister Blair admired the waspish cut of Captain Carmichael's tunic; the rakish pallor of his tie. "Aren't you competing?" she said.

"Certainly I am—Just before the tea interval."

"You know who'll walk away with all the prizes, don't you?"

"Who?" said Colin, self-conscious.

"Why—the Commando, Captain Herriot, of course! Linfield Park will have to look to its laurels."

"It doesn't follow——" Colin began.

"Doesn't it . . . ! You know how fit these fellows have to be—the training they go through: why, it'll be child's play, to him."

Sister McDonald intervened. "I had a look at the prizes before I came down," she said. "Did my eyes deceive me, or was there a bottle of whisky on the table?"

Colin nodded. "Lady Brent gave that," he said.

The Sister grinned. "For the toddlers' race, I suppose?"

"The topers' race, more likely," said Sister Blair. She gave a high startling laugh. "Ha! Ha!"

Colin turned his head. He took a quick surreptitious look around the grounds. A moment later, he turned again; this time, to watch a car coming up the drive. Sister Blair misinterpreted his anxiety. "Is Mrs. Carmichael coming?" she asked. Speaking of Colin's wife, she found herself affecting a genteel southern accent. . . .

"She will, I expect. If she can leave the baby."

Sister McDonald smiled. "I saw him in his pram outside the post office yesterday," she said. "Isn't he getting bonny!"

"The image of his father, what?" Sister Blair cocked a dark eyebrow.

Colin smiled vaguely. Once more, he turned and looked at the drive. Abruptly, "Have you seen the C.O.?" he asked.

"He's not here yet."

"I know that." Colin was impatient. "I thought you might have——"

Sister Blair screwed up her forehead. "Didn't he go into Cirencester, after lunch?" she said. "Now I come to think of it, I believe I saw the truck go by——"

"The truck," Colin said sharply. "What time was that?"

"Oh, I couldn't say, exactly. I *think* it was just after lunch —I'm not absolutely sure——"

Colin paused. "Was he alone?" he asked.

"Now, was he, or wasn't he?" Finger raised, she
affected to search her memory. "I didn't really notice——"

Colin dropped his eyes to the ground. He could not
look at Sister Blair. He felt a cold destructive anger
towards her. A silence fell between the three of them.
Colin broke it. "See you later," he said abruptly. Without
further ado, he turned away and left them.

> "Three little sisters, three little sisters!
> One loved a soldier, one loved a sailor,
> And one loved a man in the Marines!"

Snatching the microphone to him, the lance-corporal
mouthed the words, his eyes rolling. The pianist's thick-
set fingers flew over the keys. Alternating his instruments,
the drummer beat, clanged, and rattled: a fixed grin on
his face. But something was lacking. The players themselves felt it. They were not getting results. The open air,
like a vast bell of glass, clamped down over them, muffling
the volume, reducing the impact and precision of their
notes: for all its ardour, the Linfield Rhythm Quartette
remained a background noise only; an accompaniment
to the talk, the laughter, the sudden shouts and hand-
clappings. The children, however, were an attentive
audience: they gathered about the dais, staring, with the
open-eyed yet wary curiosity of animals, ready to spring
away at an unexpected gesture. The small boys stood
together, with knobby knee-joints and hanging hands;
fresh from the village barber, but for a ceremonial plume
of hair at the crown, their heads were as bare as the heart
of a globe artichoke. The little girls wore their Sunday
best; pink or blue taffeta, with gold lockets chained
about their necks. Under the brim of daisy-bound straw
hats they watched the drummer, the crooner; they gazed
forth, rapt; moist eyes shining; the pious ghost-like breath
going softly in and out of the naïvely opened mouths. . . .

"So said my soldier, so said my sailor,
And so said my man in the Marines!"

The earnest, nasal voice floated out across the air,
mingling with the talk and laughter. Absently, the village
girls tapped their feet to the rhythm. To-night in Cirencester, or at the village hall, they would dance to the
same tune. Wearing on their breast various forms of love
token, Air Force wings, or the R.A.M.C. twisted serpent,
they stood talking to the orderlies; their hair, bright with
henna or peroxide, curled about their ears; their bare
legs stained, unevenly, with a pinky-brown cosmetic.
Mouths painted, lids oiled, they looked like film stars:
when they smiled, the disguise cracked apart, and you
saw (as at the pantomime: a glimpse of the human face
under the animal's head) the homely girl beneath. . . .

"Who," said Captain Lloyd in an awe-struck voice
"is that peacherino I see under the tree, there?" He indicated a blonde with a close-fitting sweater and coloured
slides in her hair, who was gazing about her with the air,
radiant, and yet curiously blind, which an inner obsession
with the details of their own physical appearance gives,
at times, to certain young women. "I've seen her before
somewhere—I'll swear I have."

Major McRae turned his long sunless face to look.
"That?" he said, surprised. "You know who that is,
don't you? It's Ginger Rogers."

"Ginger Rogers!" Dick Lloyd looked closer. His face
lit up. "Why, so it is." Ginger Rogers was the name
given to Ivy, the girl in the local post office. "I must be
getting near-sighted, or something."

"Possibly," suggested Major McRae, "you find it
difficult to recognize a girl you've never seen below the
waist? . . ."

Captain Lloyd ignored this. "I know what it is, of
course. I've always seen her behind bars, before. It gives

one rather a shock, to see her wandering about loose. . . ."
He looked across at her, a glint in those marmalade-
coloured eyes of his. "Take a deck at that pair of gams,"
he said.

"Pardon? My French is very rusty——"

"Her legs. It's a crime to keep legs like that behind a
counter." He watched Ivy King walking, languid and
self-conscious, among the rose-bushes. "Is being in the
post office a reserved occupation, do you know? he said
suddenly.

"I rather think," Major McRae said, with a glimmering
smile, "you'll find that it is, in Miss King's case. . . ."

Colin joined them. He was taking part in the next race.
He had been up to the hospital, to change. He wore a
white vest and dark blue trunks, with white braid up the
sides. His legs were bleached-looking; the calves small
and knotty. With the tunic of his uniform slung across
his shoulders, a college scarf knotted at his throat, he
looked less like an athlete stripped for action than a
bather coming down, unwilling, to the water's edge.
The others glanced at him and then looked away. They
were uneasy in his presence; wishing that he would not,
with such flamboyance, expose himself to a failure that
they would be compelled to witness and therefore, in
some degree, to share. . . . He folded his slender arms
about his chest. "Lady Brent has arrived," he told
them.

"Already! Poor Smitty. He must be in a stew."

"*No* one seems to know where Mayne is. They've been
on the phone to the Trout—to the George, at Cirencester—to Oxford, even——"

There was a pause. "Has any one seen Captain
Herriot?" the pathologist asked gently.

"No," Lloyd glanced quickly at him. "He's not here,
either."

"He was going to compete, wasn't he?"

"Compete? He was going to wipe the floor with the lot of us——"

"Was that his declared intention?" McRae lifted his forked eyebrows.

"Well, not exactly. But it's what every one expected—the girls included. That's what they've all been waiting for."

"Do you know," said Major McRae thoughtfully, "I sometimes think that there's something just a little queer about that fellow. . . ."

"What do you mean?" Lloyd said swiftly. The two young men looked attentively at McRae. He waved a lean indeterminate hand. "I don't know. It's hard to put into words. It's not himself, exactly: it's the effect he has on other people." He said nothing further: he had no wish to discuss Mayne with his junior officers. He looked vaguely about him. "Well," he said. "I suppose I'd better go and give poor Smitty a hand. A little moral support, don't you know——"

"Queer stick, old Mac," Colin said. He looked after the departing Scot.

"He's right about Herriot," Lloyd said. "He does have a queer effect on people. He took a few of us out, the other evening, we landed up in a flat, somewhere in Oxford——" He stopped short. Colin listened, ears pricked: rumours of this adventure had, of course, already reached him. The fact that he had not been asked to participate rankled still; it had the effect, moreover, of making him take up a censorious stand-offish attitude towards the whole affair. He said coolly "You overestimate the man, I think. He strikes me as a thoroughly trivial sort of person. Rather objectionable, if anything."

"What I can't understand," Lloyd said, "is the effect he's had on Mayne. Mayne of *all* people! Remember him when he first took over here? A stickler for routine—considerate, conscientious—*too* conscientious, if anything

—worked till all hours, never spared himself, always ready
to listen to anybody—— And now—— Well, here you are
—to-day's an example." He shrugged his shoulders. "You
wouldn't think it's the same man. It's *not* the same
man!"

"'The fault, dear Brutus, lies not in our stars, but in
ourselves,'" quoted Colin.

"I don't follow. What's that *à propos* of?"

"Wasn't it in the Barrie play that people got a chance
to live their lives all over again? But you don't have to
double back on your tracks to do that—all you need do,
is switch over onto another track——"

"Meaning what?"

"Meaning that Herriot, or any one else, can't make a
man what he isn't. Perhaps *this* is the real Mayne we're
seeing, now."

"The real Mayne?" Lloyd exclaimed. "Rubbish."
Colin saw to his surprise that the young man was angry.
"The real Mayne," he repeated: "you know the real
Mayne as well as I do." Under the gingery poll of hair,
his light complexion was suffused suddenly, with colour.
"A decent, honourable person—one of the finest men I've
ever had the luck to meet——"

"If that's the case, how do you account for——"

"Quite easily." Lloyd cut him short. His voice was
rapid, emphatic. "It's a temporary thing—a sort of dis-
figurement, like an illness. It might happen to anybody.
You can no more pretend to see the real Mayne in it
than you can tell a person's true complexion when they're
suffering from a skin disease."

There was a pause. "Look," Colin said suddenly. He
gripped the captain's elbow. "There—isn't that——"
Lloyd swung round. He was in time to catch a glimpse of
the hospital's small utility truck bowling lightly up the
drive. He whistled softly between his teeth. "Well,
well——" Colin said nothing. They watched the small

hooded car thread its way through the laurustinus; it disappeared in the sudden dip in front of the Superintendent's house, reappeared again before the cowled air-raid shelters, swung left to take the short cut between the sergeants' mess and the Poison Gas Contaminated Persons (Male) Cleansing Station: and reappeared finally, in the open parking space in front of the hospital's main doors. Here it slowed down: it drew up, it came to rest with a short jerk, on the near side of a waiting ambulance. There was a pause. Then one of the doors swung open. A figure got out onto the asphalt. At that distance it was not possible to distinguish features, but even without the coloured band of authority, the manner of standing, the mature stooping gait, were unmistakable. It was Colonel Mayne. "The C.O.," Lloyd murmured. And the same thought flashed into both their minds. Alone . . . ?

The door on the opposite side of the truck was flung open. Two legs shot forth. A man ducked forward beneath the hood of the car and then stood upright. A tall man; taller than the Colonel. He wore battle-dress; and, tilted to one side of his head, a green beret. . . . Without turning, casually, with the crook of his elbow, he knocked the car door to behind him. It slammed shut. The noise echoed faintly down the slope.

". . . . So, can I, Mummy? Can I have it? Please, can I, Mummy, please?" Presently she looked down at him. "What is it, Peter?" He was frowning. "You don't *listen!*"

"I'm listening now."

"Well, then, can I?"

"Can you, what?"

"Can I have an ice-cream? Can I, Mummy? Please, can I? Can I, Mummy, please?"

"Ice-cream," Honor said vaguely. "Yes, of course you

can have ice-cream. If there is any." She looked about her.
I should have worn my other dress after all, she thought,
seeing the elderly ladies in straw hats adorned with
chiffon roses, the young women in printed linen, in
bright American cottons, with intricately plaited red and
blue suède sandals. But Colin said, for heaven's sake
don't wear anything fussy. He hates that. He doesn't
want me to be conspicuous. . . .

A whistle shrilled briefly through the air. "There's
Daddy down there," Peter said suddenly.

"Where?"

"There. Where those men are running." He clutched
her arm. "Look, can't you see! There he is. He's running
—look, quick—quick——!"

"I see him." She looked eagerly down the slope at the
race-track, at the white-clad figures fanning out against
the green. She heard the cries from the ropes. "Come on,
Tom. . . . Shorty! Shorty . . . !" Craning her head, she
watched the progress of the race, her under-lip caught up
between her teeth. . . . After a moment, she turned her
head away. "Let's go and get tea," she said.

Peter looked at her. "Daddy didn't win, did he?"

"No, not this time." She hesitated. "It doesn't matter.
We won't say anything about it, will we. . . ."

"All right," He dropped his eyes. To her surprise, she
saw a deep flush come up over his face and neck.

The tent was crowded already. A low hum, a mild
benevolent roar of voices, mingled with the cackling
reverberation of china. The latter was constant: cups
rose and fell, striking the saucer, teaspoons rotated,
minute clappers inside the bell of every cup. Now and
again, swift, irresistible, outstripping the other noises, a
burst of laughter went off like a rocket. The striped
canvas sloping overhead cast a tawny light on all the

faces. Between the drum-taut walls, a buffet had been
erected; a series of trestle tables swathed in white. A tall
silver-plate epergne which presided at all the hospital's
festivities stood in the centre, dressed with fern, gypso-
phila and roses. On either side were the urns, ready to
gush forth either tea or coffee from a small knuckled
spout. There was a smell of sugar, of steam, of trampled
grass. Neatly spaced about the table were the plates of
food: sandwiches, sweet or savoury, the moist triangles of
bread sealed with jam or with a smoky-tasting paste;
plump tapering bridge rolls; sausage rolls sprouting
parsley; penny buns in their ripe glazed skins; lemon
tartlets bright with a vaseline-like curd; stiff downy
sponge cake; canary-yellow slab cake; fruit cake mottled
with raisins; biscuits of various sorts; the blunt sallow
shortbread; the crackled ginger-snap; the scalloped
Marie, or paper-sweet wafer. And beyond, in goffered
cardboard dishes, stood the Naafi sweets: trifles in which
a single *glacé* cherry bulged like an eye out of a pall of
congealed custard; multi-coloured jellies, red and green
and orange, with a bland elastic surface, velvet-cool.

Lady Brent stood by the table, sipping lemon-juice,
and talking to Smitty and the Matron. A tall straw hat
like an old-fashioned beehive shaded her happy foolish
face. A large woman, she had elected to confide her
figure to the mould of an earlier generation; with the
result that, tightly laced, the displaced contours had no
resource but to billow forth tumultuously at the corset's
brim, thereby giving her (appropriately perhaps in one
so bountiful) something of the appearance of a human
cornucopia. She turned to the table. "I'm going to make a
pig of myself, and have another cake," she said. Under
the beehive, she glanced archly at Major Smith.
Advancing age had restored to Lady Brent a privilege
forfeit on leaving childhood: that of uncontrolled exhi-

bitionism. A wheel had come full circle. Fifty years ago, the grown-ups about her had smiled to hear the poly-syllabic words on childish lips: to-day, she discovered, they were equally indulgent towards the lispings of child-hood in a sexagenarian. The *enfant terrible* had become the *grand'mère terrible*, a phenomenon, in all English-speaking countries, tolerated, encouraged and respected.

"Mummy—can I have ice-cream?" Peter demanded. The Naafi girl heard him. "No ice-cream," she said. She was busy passing across the table cups of greyish-looking tea or coffee made with chlorinated water; pouring into tall glasses the coloured fruit drinks that hissed briefly, and then subsided for ever. "Have a jam sandwich," Honor suggested. He asked for lemonade: it came in a tall glass with a straw. Cautiously, before drinking, he sniffed: the liquid had a faint waxy flavour, reminiscent, he thought, of furniture polish. He bubbled surreptitiously through the straw, which presently became limp, and folded in two.

Honor felt a slight touch on her shoulder. "Thought I'd find you here!" She turned. It was Claudia. At once, her face lit up. "You're early," she said.

"I came direct from the station." Claudia had her jacket across one arm, a small attaché-case in the other hand. Under the brim of the severe straw hat her face looked drawn, a little sallow. Glancing at her, Honor thought suddenly, It's time Claudia was married. What are she and Andrew waiting for . . . ? Her eye fell on the attaché-case. "Let me take it." In one of those quick protective gestures of hers, she put out her hand to relieve Claudia of her burden. Claudia stepped back: "No, no. It's all right, I can manage. . . ." She looked down. Peter was still drooling happily into his glass. "Well, young man?" Summonsed, he gave her a guarded look. "You're making a pretty mess of yourself, aren't you?" Claudia meant to be friendly, that much was apparent; as usual, and this was equally apparent, something intervened: even friendliness, it seemed, had to be expressed in a sharp, jocular, almost agressive form. This was becoming more marked of late. It was as if the real, the instinctive matter of Claudia's personality was perishing under the veneer of that acquired manner: as if a process akin to a slow calcification threatened to imprison her in what was at the same time a semblance to and a caricature of her own original form.

Honor gazed at her sister, absently, it seemed; her brown eyes soft and dilated. With Honor, the act of looking at something could scarcely be called a positive activity: on the contrary in that momentary relationship it was the thing seen that proved the active force, invading, printing itself upon the area of sensitivity exposed. . . . Claudia grew restless under that glance. "What's the matter—is there a smut on my nose?" she said sharply. Honor did not reply. Claudia took her elbow and shook it slightly. "Wake up," she said. "Snap out of it. I hate to say it, darling, but you do look quite gaga, at times."

"I'm sorry," Honor said, confused. "I thought—that you—that you and I——"

Claudia put her case down. "I'm dying for a cup of tea," she said. She turned to the buffet. "Tea?" said a voice. Before she had time to speak, a khaki-clad arm held a brimming cup towards her. "How's that, umpire?" Startled, she turned. She saw above her the swarthy face, the gleaming toothy smile of Captain Herriot.

They looked at each other for a moment. "Hallo," she said.

"Hallo." There was a pause. He looked down at the cup. "Aren't you going to relieve me of this?" he asked.

"Oh, yes. Thank you." Belatedly, she took the cup of tea from him. To her own surprise, she found that her heart was beating quickly. She averted her eyes from that dark troubling face. "I wonder if they've put sugar in it," she said. Under his gaze, she bent her head and sipped from the brim of the cup. Tasting chlorine, she made a grimace. "What's the matter?" he asked.

"They've emptied the operating-room slops into this."

"I know," he said "—it's an old R.A.M.C. custom."

Claudia accepted a sandwich from the plate he offered her. Did she imagine it, or was there a faint flavour of alcohol on his breath? She glanced quickly at him. She had not noticed before, or she had forgotten, that there was this reddish haze in his brown eyes. She bit the edge off her sandwich. "Well," she said "I suppose I must congratulate you. You've carried off all the prizes, I presume?"

"Me?" he said. "But I'm not competing. Don't you see?"

"See what?" She turned her head. "Oh——" She looked in surprise at the heavy stick, on which, unnoticed by her, he had all the while been leaning. "What's wrong?" she asked quickly.

"You haven't heard? It happened the day before yesterday. I ricked my ankle, going over the assault course with the candidates."

"What bad luck!" Claudia was aware of an obscure feeling of disappointment. A momentary vexation, even, that surprised her. What, then, had she hoped for? What vindication was there to have been for her to-day in this man's avowed triumph over others?

"Is it bad?" she asked, looking down at his foot.

"Not that bad. I can get along, limping a bit." He shrugged his shoulders. "Pretty silly, really, to come through Vaagso and Dieppe without a scratch, and then do a fool thing like this on a molehill in Gloucestershire."

Claudia listened to what he said. What was there, she wondered, about the way he said "Vaagso" and

"Dieppe," that gave her a momentary discomfort, almost uneasiness? The impression was gone before she had time to fix it. Unbuttoning the pocket of his battle-dress, he drew out a cigarette-case. Under the pressure of a lean up-curling thumb, the two wings flew apart. "Smoke?" he said. He presented the case to her.

"In a moment, if I may. I'll drink this tea, first." There was an inscription inside the case. Her eye caught the words "To Neil. . . ." She could not see the rest. From Mary, was it . . . ? He withdrew the case. She drank her tea.

Herriot picked out a cigarette from the elastic band. He put it between his lips; struck by a sudden thought, he withdrew it again, unlit, and looked about him expectantly. "Andrew's not here, is he?" he said.

Claudia's eyebrows went up steeply. Andrew indeed. . . . "I didn't know that you knew my fiancé," she said frostily.

His answer surprised her. "Oh yes," he said. He smiled pleasantly down at her. "I met him the other day in Cirencester." He paused. "Didn't he tell you?" he asked.

Claudia too paused. "No," she said.

Herriot laughed. "Didn't think it worth mentioning, I expect."

"As a matter of fact," Claudia said, "I've not seen him since the week-end."

"That accounts for it, perhaps." He clicked rapidly at his lighter without producing a flame. "A very remarkable man, I thought."

"He is, in many ways."

"They say he's first-rate at his job." An ear of flame sprang up on the lighter: frowning, he lit his cigarette. "I can well believe it. I'd rather have him on my side than against me, any day."

"In court, you mean?"

"What else—?"

There was a pause. Claudia looked curiously at Herriot. She had the impression that he had discovered in the encounter with Andrew some sort of challenge to himself which disturbed him, and which he could not ignore. His next words confirmed the idea. Tapping shut the cap on his lighter, he said to her abruptly, "Well—now that we're all acquainted—you must come, both of you, and have dinner with me at the George one evening."

"Thank you," Claudia said. She hesitated, and then wondered why. She felt compelled to explain. "We'd like to come," she said. "Only—Andrew doesn't go out very much, these days—he's been very ill, recently——"

"Invalided out of the army. Yes, so I heard. Tough luck." He saw that her cup was empty. He took it away from her, and put it down on the table. "Now have a cigarette," he said. She accepted one of his Gold Flakes. He wrestled with the lighter again. "There's a big do— a dance, probably, on here next week. Are you coming to it?" he asked.

"A dance?" Claudia was surprised. "I haven't heard anything about it," she said.

"Mayne told me. A sort of unofficial farewell party."

"A what?" she said, startled.

"Oh, nothing," Herriot said quickly. "I'm talking out of turn, as usual. . . . Probably got it all wrong." He gave her a light for her cigarette, and then put the lighter away in his pocket, buttoning it carefully, his fingers under the flap.

"There was some talk of a dance at the sergeants' mess—would that be it?" Claudia asked, frowning slightly.

"Probably. I get things mixed up. Anyway—if there is a show of sorts, I hope you're coming. You can't leave me to dance with Sister McDonald."

"But your ankle——"

"Oh, that'll be as right as rain, by then." He was

silent for a moment, drawing quickly on his cigarette. He looked at her, under those hooded lids of his. "Come out and have dinner with me somewhere, first," he said.

"I told you," Claudia began, "I don't think Andrew——"

He cut her short. "You, I meant. The two of us."

There was a sudden silence.

"No," she said.

A smile lit Herriot's face. "I'm flattered."

"Flattered?" She stared at him.

"That you should think it necessary to refuse."

She was equal to this. "You made it necessary—by the way you asked me."

"I beg your pardon," he said then. "Would you have preferred a formal invitation?"

"Yes," she said. "I'm rather a formal sort of person."

He put out a hand and touched her quickly, caressingly, on the back of her arm. "That's what you think," he said.

Claudia drew away a step. But when she spoke, no trace, either of anger or excitement, was apparent in her voice. "I'm a very conventional person," she repeated; "and if you want to know why, I'll tell you. Because I happen to believe in those conventions."

"Even when they prevent you doing what you really want to do?"

"Even when they prevent me doing what I want to, as you say."

"My poor girl, you must live in a state of perpetual civil war——"

"Not at all. I'm perfectly content to be ruled by principles that I agree are right."

"Whi-ew!..." He gave a low brief whistle. Then, changing the subject, apparently: "Tell me," he said abruptly, "I've often wanted to ask you. What exactly do you do, at that school of yours?"

"I teach history."

"You——?" At that, Captain Herriot threw back his head and laughed. "You do," he said. "You do. . . . But not in the way you think!"

> "Praise the Lord, and pass the ammunition,
> Praise the Lord, and pass the ammunition!"

Alternately inflated or diminished by the breeze, the lance-corporal's voice came lowing through the microphone as full of ardour and synthetic vowels, he put over this, the final number in his repertoire. Already people were streaming down the banks, taking up their positions around the semicircle of chairs, the big wooden table, from which the prizes were to be distributed: the patients, their scarlet ties vivid under lean-drawn faces, hopping along on crutches or making their way with rigid gait, plaster-bound under the blue; the ambulance drivers; the sergeant-cooks; the orderlies; the Naafi girls: and mingling with them, diffidence long ago thawed out by strong tea and warm sunshine, the men and women and children of the neighbourhood. Laughing, talking and chaffing, they edged their way into position along the banks. The circle of chairs, too, was filling up: the Matron, the officers' wives, the Sisters, the posse of local ladies whose self-appointed task it was to distribute library books to the patients, filed into place one by one; sat, with crossed legs and smiling faces, awaiting the ceremony to come. A certain subdued excitement was perceptible in all of them. Now that the moment for the prize distribution had actually arrived, many who had neglected to compete or done so in a facetious inconclusive fashion, wished secretly that they had exerted themselves to more purpose; that they were in consequence eligible for one of the prizes, cigarette-cases, writing-pads, or pen-knives which, lying there awaiting the winners, had acquired a desirability and significance quite out of proportion to their own real value.

"Here they are!" The whisper ran through the crowd. Heads were turned. Lady Brent was coming down the steps, escorted by Colonel Mayne. A bouquet of flowers had been presented to her, mauve and pink sweet-peas: she carried them clasped before her, the stems sheathed in silver paper. Under her tall straw hat, she kept glancing at the Colonel, smiling and talking, while a rosy flush, sprung from some still untarried source of youthful emotion mantled her long cheeks. Lady Brent was a very susceptible woman. She was moved by the Colonel's proximity, by his good looks, his attentiveness; by the way, whenever she spoke, he bent forward to hear what she had to say, his blue eyes fixed upon her, his small mouth set in a steady, contained smile. It was not perceptible to Lady Brent, walking along at his side, that at the same time on the back of his neck which bulged slightly over his collar, the short-cut hairs bristled and stood out like the hackles of an angry animal.

There was a burst of clapping. The Colonel looked round a little irritably: he gave a quick signal to Major Smith, who understood what was wanted: he stepped forward, list in hand, and the proceedings began without any further preliminaries. "The three-legged race. Sister Fitt and Mr Hewitt!" The routine was simple. Major Smith stood ready to pass the appropriate wallet, cigarette-case, or pen-knife to Lady Brent, who shook hands with the contestants as they came up, spoke a few words to them, before presenting to each the prize he or she had won. Major Smith took advantage of the clapping, the good-humoured cheers and barracking that greeted the first couple, to glance surreptitiously at the Colonel. Under the peaked cap, the older man's face had that peculiar clay-like pallor which, in him, permitted a series of thread-

fine veins to inflame the surface of the skin. Smith could
see the effort it cost him to be amiable to Lady Brent: as
soon as he had finished speaking he seemed to relapse
into himself; the mouth became pinched, the handsome
eyes glazed over, and he sat staring before him with a set
and lifeless expression. It was most unusual to see Mayne
looking as he did at this hour of the day. The Registrar
frowned. Behind the thick lenses his eyes had a troubled
look. Smith was a painstaking and conscientious man:
the atmosphere in which he lived of late was becoming
increasingly distasteful to him. He had the impression at
times, both in his work at the hospital and in his relationship with the people about him, that he was up against
something retrograde; some force, a sort of languorous
but powerful current to which the others seemed more
than half inclined to resign themselves, and which he
alone, as a result of early upbringing, or through some
temperamental disinclination, was impelled tenaciously,
and with a fierce concealed anger, to resist.

"The high jump. First prize: Sergeant Dyson!" The
muscular little sergeant, who had all his front teeth
missing, came up, grinning, to shake hands with Lady
Brent. The applause rose to a crescendo: Dyson was a
popular figure in the hospital. He came back to his place,
examining his prize, a tin of cigarettes, with a disgruntled
and comical air. Colin, standing near, caught his expression. He too smiled. "Tough luck," he said. "What's
the matter?" Honor asked. "They've given him cigarettes and he doesn't smoke—"

Peter tugged at his arm. "Daddy—I can't see."

"Can't you?" Colin looked down at his son with an
air of tolerant amusement. "Here," he said. He bent
down: catching the small boy under the armpits, he
hauled him up, and sat him precariously on his right
shoulder. "That better?" he asked. Peter nodded, he
sat there, legs dangling, clasping his father diffidently

round the neck with a thin sunburnt arm. He could see everything now: the people standing all round him; the table; the white- or khaki-clad figures going up to take their prizes: most novel of all, the top of his father's head; to the small boy, an astonishing and unfamiliar sight. He kept glancing down at it: there, very close to him, so close that the oily fragrance of hair was in his nostrils, was that unknown head: examining it, he could see the side parting, carefully ruled, the way the hair, like his own, went into a small ruffled whorl at the crown. He was aware of something new: a sense of kinship with his father; and mingled with it, strangely disturbing to the child, a sudden, inexplicable feeling of pity.

"The Sisters' race. First Prize—Sister Thomas!" A storm of applause greeted the prettiest of the Sisters, with her fair downy face and twinkling black legs. Colin, grasping Peter by a knee and one ankle, was unable to clap. He waited until she came by "Attagirl," he called out. She smiled and waved her hand at him. Colin was happy. Released from the tension that Mayne's absence always caused in him he experienced a sense of tranquillity and well-being: he had but to turn his head slightly to know where Mayne was, what he was doing, to whom he spoke. Indeed now that he had the older man under his eyes and therefore to a certain extent in his power, it seemed to him that his feeling for him diminished along with the anxiety; that, relieved of the aforementioned anxiety he was also to a large degree relieved of his obsession: and though he knew this to be but a temporary respite, yet he was glad to accept it for what it was worth: playing with the fantasy (which he knew, all the while, to be but fantasy) that Mayne had lost the power to disturb him; that he himself, released from his thraldom, was a new man, free, powerful and indifferent.

Honor looked at her husband; at the boy perched on his shoulder, one arm round his father's neck. A secretive smile touched her lips. Colin felt her gaze upon him, unexpectedly he turned his head and smiled back at her. Her eyes shone. She felt herself, for a moment, back in the very early days of her marriage, her first pregnancy, when Colin had seemed absorbed and satisfied in her alone; full of a simple curiosity and tenderness; and gentle, always so deft and circumspect and gentle, in his treatment of her. That was another Colin, the Colin of the early Worthing days, black-coated, pin-striped, the rising youg doctor.... What had happened since then?

She looked at him standing there in his khaki tunic, neatly belted and buttoned. It was the uniform, she felt suddenly, that had changed him. It was as if the anonymity conferred on him by uniform gave him a new sense of freedom and irresponsibility: as if he were masked, and, being masked, privileged, in a sort of carnival spirit, to conduct himself in a manner wholly alien to his normal way of life. The discipline of military life did nothing to correct this: on the contrary: being an imposed discipline, to be accepted whole and without question, it seemed to permit, in compensation, the relaxation of those personal standards, self-imposed and self-maintained, by which up till now as a private citizen he had chosen to live.

"There's Aunt Claudia," Peter announced.

"Where?" Honor turned her head. At the same moment, she saw her. She was on the bank opposite, a little way away from the rest of the crowd, standing on a seat with Captain Herriot. Although they had climbed onto this seat with the overt intention of watching the prize-giving, it was obvious that neither of them paid it more than a cursory attention. They were talking. She saw the Captain's dark face, his persistent smile; and Claudia looking down, pensive, it seemed, at the ground and nodding at intervals. Something in her pose, irresolute, half reluctant, struck Honor. She looked attentively at the couple. What were they talking about, she wondered. Suddenly Claudia lifted her head, she said something to Captain Herriot and then turning, stepped down from the seat and walked off alone in the direction of the spectators. Herriot looked after her, the smile still on his face. After a moment he followed her, descending from the seat in a calm unhurried fashion, he walked after her down the slope, swishing at the grass with his stick as he went. Honor watched him. A look of surprise appeared on her face. She turned to Colin. "I thought Captain Herriot had hurt his ankle," she said.

"So he did. That's why he didn't compete—fortunately for all of us."

"But I saw him walking past just now. He didn't seem to be limping."

Colin looked sharply at her. "You must be mistaken," he said. "He's been hobbling round on a stick, all day." He paused. "Are you sure?" he asked.

"Well, I think so. He had a stick, all right—but he certainly wasn't hobbling."

There was another pause. "That's strange," Colin said. He frowned. "What do you make of it?" he asked.

"I don't know," Honor said. They looked at each other. The incident made a queer disturbing impression on both of them.

"I wonder——" Colin began. He did not finish: at that moment he caught sight of Dick Lloyd, making his way towards him through the crowd. Something in the way the young man was walking, pushing his way hurriedly, without ceremony, past men and women alike, struck Colin: he knew at once that Lloyd was seeking him out, that he had something of importance to say to him. His hand, on Peter's ankle, tightened suddenly so that the child perched on his shoulder turned his head in surprise.

Lloyd came straight up to them. His face was flushed,

the roots of his hair dark with perspiration. He fixed his glance on Colin, ignoring the presence of Honor and Peter, and said without preamble "I suppose you've heard?"

Colin raised his eyebrows. "Heard?"

"I've just been talking to Neil Herriot."

"So what?"

Lloyd stared at him suspiciously. "Haven't you heard what he's been saying?"

"About his ankle, you mean?"

It was Lloyd's turn to look puzzled. "His ankle? What about his ankle?"

Colin glanced at Honor. "He sprained it on the assault-course, or something."

"We know that," Lloyd said, impatiently.

"Well, what do *you* mean, then?"

The young man ran a hand through his vivid disorderly hair. "He stopped me just now: we got talking. He told me—in strict confidence of course, as he always does——" Lloyd scratched his head irritably "——and, as he always does, he seems to have told everyone, already——"

"Told everyone *what*?"

Captain Lloyd turned his head away. He fixed his eyes on the clock-tower of the hospital, which seemed to lean, to reel slightly, against the vacant blue sky. In a hard, indifferent voice "Mayne is going," he said.

There was a pause. Colin did not move. "What did you say?" he asked quietly.

"Mayne's leaving us." Lloyd repeated his former statement. "He's being sent overseas. He's taking a B.E.F. hospital to Egypt. He'll be going almost immediately."

In the silence, Colin put up his arms. He lifted Peter from his shoulder, and set him down, carefully, on the ground.

CHAPTER SEVEN

A CHANGE IN THE WEATHER

THE next day, the weather changed. It was threatening rain when Claudia left for the station; and later, when Colin was ready to set out for the hospital, rain had already begun to fall. He looked up briefly at the low-hanging sky and went round the side of the house, to fetch his bike out of the garage. He pushed apart the green-painted doors. It was cool and gloomy in here. Disused gardening instruments leaned against the walls: the shelves were lined with empty jam-jars. In the middle of the oil-stained floor the Hadley-Stuarts' two cars hibernated, shrouded and tyreless, for the duration. Colin picked up his bike, disentangling it with a familiar morning irritation from the baby's perambulator and the wheels of Peter's tricycle. He slammed the doors behind him and made his way round to the front of the house. The mingled odours and reminiscences of a domestic morning seemed to float about him still: the smell of his own pyjamas, sleep-creased; the sourness on the baby's bib; the bland fresh smell of *The Times* lying folded on his plate. He heard the sound of a window-sash being raised. Honor leaned out of a window on the first floor. There was a white flannel apron round her waist: she was in the baby's room getting ready to wash and feed him. "Colin— it's raining," she called down to him. "You'd better take your mac."

Colin kicked down the pedal of his bike. The chain whirred. "No need," he said. "It won't be much."

Honor knew from his tone that she must not insist. "Will you be late?" she asked.

"Couldn't say."

"Well . . . bye-bye, then!"

"Good-bye." He flung one leg astride the bike: the gravel crisped sharply under the spinning tyres. "Good-bye, Daddy," called a high-pitched voice. He raised one hand in acknowledgment; without turning his head, he pedalled down the small curved drive and disappeared. Honor, from the first floor window, Peter, through the panes of the conservatory, watched him go. "Daddy's gone," Peter told Edith, who had come in, with her tray, to clear the breakfast table. Edith nodded. A quietness seemed to fall on the house; a sense of domestic peace and leisureliness. Edith, stacking up cups, began to hum to herself.

Colin pedalled moodily along the small winding lane. Rain was falling silently through the air. He could feel the drops softly blistering upon his face as he went. A stony smell rose out of the earth: the dusty leaves along the bottom of the hedge grew bold and lustrous. In the field on either side, Jersey cows cropped the fresh-dyed grass. Above, on the knoll, the trees seemed to stand very still, experiencing the sensation of rain on their foliage. Colin pedalled on, the faint squeaking of the chain accompanying him as he went. The rain puttered softly, sibilantly, about him.

He turned the corner into the village. The grey stone houses faced each other, darkening in hue as the rain continued to fall. A smell of dust haunted the gutters and cobble-stones. The High Street was almost deserted: one or two bicycles leaned their pedals on the kerb opposite the post office: a woman hurried past, a mackintosh thrown over her cotton frock, a string shopping bag in her hand. Colin looked at this scene. Under the peaked cap, his face, newly shaved, the tender skin inflamed, was set in an expression of grim unhappiness. He was seeing Linfield at that moment, not as it appeared to him, but as he imagined it must look to Mayne, now that the Colonel knew that at any moment he would be leaving it for ever. It was a peculiarity of Colin's nature (since earliest childhood, when the departure for the summer holidays provoked this feeling in him) that as soon as a journey was proposed his surroundings, which up till that moment had seemed quite normal and desirable, underwent a sudden depreciation: they became meaningless to him, as drab and dusty in his estimation as the surroundings he anticipated were brilliant and desirable. So Linfield, he imagined, suffered as a result of this prospective departure. It was as if, overnight, it had been blighted; it had shrivelled; and now, all sap and virtue run out of it, it stood there under the morning rain, small and petty and depressing beyond endurance.

His tyres hissed on the wet surface of the road. He turned the corner, past the Blue Trout, and cycled over the bridge. The sluggish stream was fretted with raindrops; above it the hoop of the bridge showed dark. There was a rumble at his back: the Cirencester bus overtook him, gleaming, blue and silver, in the wet. Women sitting, sheltered, within, their shopping baskets on their knees, looked at him as they went past. He reached the big metal gates of the former asylum and putting out his right hand in warning, swung inwards, past the lodge. The close-set bushes on either side of the drive dripped water; now and then, a bird in the thicket gave a small oppressed cheep. Colin looked at the gloomy face of the hospital. His heart sank. It was as if, for him, the building held some menace which he must now face.

He walked down the long echoing corridor. As well as being barred, the windows of Linfield Park had been treated with an anti-blast solution that permanently vitiated the daylight. The walls were painted a deep ox-blood red; a colour, it seemed, considered sedative to mental trauma. On either side a series of mahogany doors opened off the corridor. As a precautionary measure, these doors had been so constructed as to lock automatically on closing: thereby proving in the early days of the hospital's establishment a source of combined irritation and hilarity to patients and staff alike, when the Sisters, or the medical officers, were continually locking themselves either in or out of their own and other people's rooms, with all the briskness and regularity of the best French farce.

A ward orderly passed carrying a scrubbing-brush and bucket. Seeing Colin he drew himself up and jerked his head smartly to one side. Colin acknowledged the salute. An odour of disinfectant rose out of the grey-scummed water in the bucket. There came a familiar clatter, clatter, as a trolley bearing enamel basins and instruments was wheeled hastily over a stone-floored passage. Colin remembered that he wanted to look through his case-sheets: he turned aside and made his way through an archway into the annexe which housed the Officers' Mess. The lounge, once the superintendent's billiard-room, was a long room with high bay windows at one end. Leather arm-chairs sagged about an empty fireplace. Tattered copies of *Esquire*, of *Redbook*, of *Lilliput* lay in a pile on the couch; while the *Lancet* and the *British Medical Journal* were spread decorously along with the daily papers on the big oak table in the centre of the room. Someone, in a self-conscious effort to impart what they imagined to be the correct Mess atmosphere, had pinned among the notices on the baize-covered board a page torn out of *Esquire*; a red-head wearing black lace panties and a black lace bow in her hair. A big radiogram stood in one corner of the room: switched on and forgotten, it was like a leaky tap, monotonously and persistently dribbling theatre-organ music into the room.

"Good morning!" Major Smith, who had been affixing a new notice to the board, turned round to greet the new-comer. "Ah, it's you," he said. "One of your patients tried to commit suicide during the night. I suppose you've heard."

Colin stopped short. "Tennant?" he said.

"That was the name, I believe. No—not dead. Just slashed about a bit."

"Where is he?" Colin said.

"Oh, they've carted him off already. You know we're not allowed to keep a suicide on the premises."

Colin strode over to the wireless and shut off the irritating dribble of sound. "Who was O.M.O. last night?" he demanded.

"Dickie. He dealt with the whole affair. He and Sister Brown, who was unlucky enough to be on night duty."

Colin frowned. "That man should never have been sent away. I wish I'd known. I believe I could have helped him——"

"Know why he did it? Dick couldn't get a word out of him."

"Someone wrote to him and said that his wife was carrying on with the lodger—the usual story. I knew he was very depressed—but I thought I could pull him through." Colin, who was apt to get involved in the lives of his patients (giving advice on their private affairs, intervening on their behalf for official concessions, a late pass, a grant of compassionate leave) frowned and bit his lip, concerned over what he could not help regarding as a failure on his part. Smith observed this. "It's not your fault," he said. "Your job was to cure him of jaundice. No one expected you to do more. You're not the trick-cyclist."[1] He changed the subject abruptly. "Been in to see the C.O. yet?" he asked. "I rather think he was looking for you."

There was a pause. "No," Colin said. "Not yet. . . ." He picked up a batch of case sheets and began glancing

[1] Army term = psychiatrist.

rapidly through them. "How is he?" he asked; casually.

"I've hardly seen him," Smith said. "He wasn't in to dinner last night."

"So I heard," Colin was busy with his papers. "Is it true he and Herriot took Ginger Rogers to Oxford?"

"Why ask me?" the Registrar said. "No one tells me anything." He pursed his lips. "I should think it very unlikely," he added. "Ginger Rogers, as you call her, happens to be an extremely respectable young woman."

Colin shrugged his shoulders. "'So are they all, all honourable men. . . .'"

Smith smiled. "You didn't by any chance do *Julius Caesar* for School Certificate, did you?" he asked. "I've suspected so for a long time."

"You're very cheerful this morning," Colin said. And as soon as he had spoken he was struck by the truth of his own words. The little Scotsman *was* very cheerful: quite restored, in fact, to his old form. Colin looked searchingly at him. Smith, embarrassed by the scrutiny, turned away. And it was then that Colin realized that Smith, far from sharing the general reaction to the news, was in fact secretly elated at the prospect of Mayne's departure. More, he was profoundly relieved and thankful. It was as if some pressure that was rapidly becoming intolerable, had suddenly and unexpectedly been eased. The forces of law and order had intervened on his behalf; he no longer had to hold the fort alone; from the outside, help had come; at the last moment, the siege had been raised. . . . Colin understood this, and a resentment he had not known that he harboured against the small hard-working little Scotsman, flared up in him suddenly. He looked at Smith, scarcely bothering to conceal his anger and contempt. "Always on the side of the angels, eh, Smith?" he said.

"What's that?" Smith looked at him in surprise.

"Never mind, never mind." Colin turned on his heel

and strode out of the room. He did not trust himself to say anything further. His anger was a complex one; based partly on fear. The fact was that, somewhere within him, Colin respected deeply all that Smith stood for (the sober and enduring values, the civic virtues), and wished to be identified with that aspect of life : at the same time he feared that by his own conduct he had prejudiced his right to do so; and it was this fear, combined with self-dissatisfaction and an envy of others, that was the inspiration of his anger at that moment.

In the corridor he ran into James McRae. The pathologist was shambling along as usual with his nose in the air and his eyes fixed on nothing in particular. He had a dirty rag in one hand and a bottle of Thawpit in the other : he had been endeavouring, with no conspicuous success, to remove some of the grease-stains from the front of his tunic. He stopped on seeing Colin. "Ah, good morning," he said. "The C.O. is looking for you."

"Yes, I know," Colin said with bad grace.

McRae did not take offence. A tall etiolated man, he was protected from animosity and ardour alike by that innate indifference to human affairs which he owed, in large measure, to the peculiarities of his own physique. Oddly enough, this indifference, which he never attempted to conceal, far from alienating others, attracted towards him their interest and goodwill : he was universally popular in the hospital where every one from the C.O. downwards confided in old Mac, who took no sides and repeated no gossip, merely gazing at the heated faces of those about him as Alice might have stared at the antics of the near-human creatures she discovered on the other side of the looking-glass. He looked at Colin now under those tufted sand-coloured brows of his. "Well," he said, referring at once to the subject uppermost in both their minds, "and how has Linfield taken the news? The village is fully informed, I imagine?"

"More fully than we are, it seems. . . . Is it true that Mayne is going to Cairo, that he will be a Brigadier?"

McRae, who was security officer for the hospital, raised one eyebrow. "Who told you that?" he asked.

"The milkman delivered the information with our morning milk."

"You don't say. The milkman, eh? Actually, the milkman . . . ?" He shook his head. "Talk of a whispering gallery——" In all this, as Colin noticed, he gave no indication of the way in which the impending change affected him personally, if indeed it did so at all. "Well," he said, "I must do some work, I suppose. You know how it is. The combined urine of the Western Command awaits my inspection. . . ." And off he went down the gloomy corridor with the floating, inconsequent gait of a man who is not altogether aware of, less, constricted in any way, by the limitations or peculiarities of his surroundings.

Colin turned right into the main building of the hospital. He crossed the big tessellated hall, with its pillars, its Dying Gauls, its convulsed Laocoöns; its ferns and palms locked in massive oaken tubs. A familiar rustle of starch reached his ears: he looked up: Sister Blair and Sister McDonald were ascending the flight of wide oaken steps leading to the first-floor wards. Unaware of Colin's presence in the hall below, they chatted together as they went. He saw the smiling animated faces inclined in conversation. "I wonder what the new man will be like, don't you?" he heard Sister Blair say.

The new man—Colin stopped dead in his stride. The new man: already they were speculating with curiosity and a certain excitement, as to the potentialities of Mayne's successor. It was then that Colin realized, in a moment of naïve astonishment, followed at once by anger and resentment, the change that had taken place in the hospital. Unaltered still, in form, Mayne's power (a power he owed, everyone had always agreed, not to his position but to his personality alone) that power had undergone a perceptible change: overnight it seemed the germ, the substance had gone out of it, leaving it lifeless. It was as if the hospital had become aware of the necessity of detaching its loyalty from one leader in order, the more fully, to accord it to another. This process had already begun. It was perceptible in the altered atmosphere of the place: in the searching glances exchanged, in the phrase begun and broken off: in the pervading air of subdued and almost guilty excitement. There was no denying the fact. Stealthily the hospital was withdrawing from Mayne its allegiance, an allegiance up till that moment, fully, warmly, and even fanatically accorded.

Colin felt a smack on his left shoulder-blade. He turned. It was Willy Wilson, the dentist: a thick-set young Yorkshireman with a perpetual grin. "C.O.'s looking for you," he said.

"I know, I know, I'm on my way there now." Wilson glanced with curiosity into Colin's sick-looking face. He opened his mouth to say something, changed his mind, smacked Colin again on the shoulder and then charged up the big flight of stairs three at a time. Colin walked slowly across the hall. Slowly and reluctantly he turned down a red-painted passage, mounted the small flight of stairs leading to the C.O.'s office. He wished that the C.O. had not sent for him. For the first time since he had come to Linfield Colin felt that he did not wish to see Mayne.

He stood hesitating outside the big panelled door. Before he could bring himself to knock the door was suddenly opened from within. Colonel Mayne appeared. "Ah, Colin, it's you. . . . Good morning." he said.

"Good morning, sir."

Mayne looked at the troubled face of his junior officer. He understood perfectly all that Colin was feeling. And because he did, there appeared about the firm, razed lips an enigmatic expression, in which it was possible to discern a certain contempt. "Come inside, will you?" he said abruptly. He turned away, Colin followed him into the room pausing to close the door carefully behind him. It was still raining: a grey light slanted through the tall window; fell across the bare walls of the room; the big littered desk. Outside on the rain-bitten tarmac the top of a waiting ambulance gleamed, sleek with water. Mayne sat down at the desk. He gestured Colin to be seated; and out of old habit Colin took his favourite seat: on the radiator under the window. For the first time he looked directly at Mayne. The Colonel was lighting up a new cigarette from the butt of an old one; with a steady wrist he matched the two ends and sipped rapidly, drawing fire. Colin saw then to his astonishment that there was no trace of dissipation or fatigue on Mayne's features. On the contrary. His eyes were sparkling, his complexion clear and ruddy. His whole manner, even sitting there at his desk, and in the trivial act of lighting a cigarette, spoke of an assurance and vigour that he exhibited only when at the very top of his form.

"Well, now——" The Colonel pulled a metal ash-tray towards him, and bent into it the butt of his cigarette. "About this unfortunate business last night——" he said.

"Yes, sir."

"It appears there was a constitutional factor involved. A whole dynasty of maternal aunts in Colney Hatch——"

Colin looked startled. "That's news to me. There was no mention of it in the case-history." Mayne said nothing, and Colin ventured on an analysis of his former patient's condition: while he was still speaking, he saw that the Colonel had begun to look about him in a manner vaguely irritated and distracted: a sign with him that the subject had ceased to hold his attention. Colin paused: he looked at Mayne, uncertain whether to proceed with the matter in hand, or discover a fresh topic of conversation. Mayne did nothing to help him out. A silence fell, Colin fidgeted restlessly on the radiator. Mayne observed his uneasiness. "Not in a hurry to run away, are you, Colin?" he asked, mildly.

"No, sir."

"Well, if you can spare me a few moments——" The young man looked up. Mayne was leaning back in his chair, his finger-tips joined, looking fixedly at him through the rising smoke of his cigarette. Colin saw the bold, pallid eyes, the brusque nose, the long upper lip, with its greying, closely razed moustache. The two men looked at each other for a moment. Then "I wanted to have a chat with you, Colin," the Colonel said quietly. "There's something I'd like to ask you——"

And at once, before anything else was said, Colin knew. He had guessed what was coming. His heart began to race; the blood flowed to his face and then receded; leaving him paler than before. He looked at Colonel Mayne and waited for him to speak.

CHAPTER EIGHT

MANY HAPPY RETURNS

ANDREW rang the bell. Through the glass panel of the door he peered into the wide, deserted hall. Rain was falling steadily, flawing the air about him, tapping, staccato, on the leaves of the big creeper; spitting into the stream of water that flowed, bubble-spangled, towards a gutter at the side of the house. He pressed the bell again: under the waterlogged brim of his hat, he approached his face to the glass. Presently, Edith appeared, crossing the hall and either tying or untying the strings of an apron about her waist. Smiling, she pulled open the door, and admitted the visitor. "Good evening, sir."

"Good evening." He stepped over the threshold, out of the falling rain into the sudden stillness, the smug and felt-like dryness of indoors. Plucking off his hat, he shook it, sprinkling the floor with drops. "Shall I take your coat into the kitchen, sir?" Edith enquired, looking at the dark-stained shoulders.

"I don't think that'll be necessary," Andrew hung it carefully over the back of a chair. Smoothing down his fair sparse hair he looked enquiringly about him. "This way, please, sir," Edith said. She opened a door on the right. Andrew walked past her into the big, old-fashioned room: that, too, was empty. "Madam isn't down yet," Edith said. "She's still feeding the baby."

"Yes, of course. Don't disturb her, I can wait." But Edith did not at once leave the room. She stooped and affected to pick up one of Peter's toys from the floor; busied herself gathering up and folding the day's newspapers scattered on the couch. Her small slant eyes (was there a cast in one of them?) kept glancing at Andrew with an expression which, as he detected it, filled him with uneasiness. He saw in it cunning, mingled, so it seemed to him, with a certain stealthy derision. It was as if the presence of this man, with his quiet voice and precise, controlled gestures, both fascinated her and at the same time roused in her an instinctive hostility, a will to destruction not unlike that which on other occasions drew her to the table on which Peter was skilfully erecting a tall brick house, and kept her standing there, awaiting the moment (which filled her, as it did the child, with horror and an obscure pleasure) when she would snap out a hand and send the whole carefully constructed edifice crashing in ruins to the floor.

Unexpectedly, she crossed the room: she came up close to him. Andrew moved back a step. Without speaking, she bent down then to pick up a sheet of paper from the floor. He was ashamed of that involuntary recoil and tried to address her in a normal voice. "Miss Abbott not back yet?" he asked.

"No, sir. She's always late of a Thursday."

"Ah, yes, so she is." There was a pause. He lifted one of the small marble ornaments on the mantelpiece, and put it down again. Her eyes were upon him. He did not turn his head or speak, and after a moment, to his relief, she left the room.

When the closing of the door had assured him of solitude, he turned and came away from the mantelpiece. Hands in his pockets, he strolled over to one of the big French windows and looked out at the garden, lying green and still under the rain. With the grass overgrown and the long beds high with weeds, there was something a little wild and melancholy about the place, entirely lacking in the days when Mr Hadley-Stuart had imposed his authoritative personality on house and garden. It was as if Weirfield now, was beginning to respond to another presence, to the personality of Honor, which, in its lethargy and benevolence alike, seemed to sanction a certain fertile disorder. As he was thinking thus the door behind him opened and Honor herself came into the room. He heard her voice. "Andrew dear—what a shame—leaving you alone like this——"

He turned. "Many happy returns of the day," he said to her.

"Thank you, Andrew—and—oh dear—I feel so old——" She broke off and looked enquiringly, like a child, at a parcel he had laid on the table. He picked it up. "Mother sent you these," he said.

"A present? How exciting." She undid the paper around the small wicker basket, and exclaimed at the sight of a dozen eggs, lying nested in straw. "Oh, lovely," she said. She looked at the smooth cold eggs, alike, and yet each one with its own personality; some blunt, some intelligently tapered; some freckled; some a pure dull white. She touched them lovingly. Andrew watched her. She was looking well, he thought. Her face, her neck, were flushed, and the hastily applied powder did little to dim the warm, almost tangible radiance of the woman who only a few moments before had worn a baby's mouth, like a carnation, at her breast.

There was a small silence. "Where's Colin?" Andrew asked.

"He's upstairs having a wash and brush-up. He won't be a moment." She fingered something at her throat. "See what he gave me," she said. Trying in vain to conceal the pleasure in her face, she held up towards him a small jade pendant on a silver chain. "Isn't it lovely?" she said. "I never expected——"

Andrew held it for a moment. "Is that mutton-fat jade?" The stone, which had lain on human flesh, was warm between his fingers: quickly, he relinquished it. "It reminds me of something," he said. He looked dreamily at it. "I know," he said. "The Backs, at Cambridge. The river's just that colour, in spring——"

"Is it?" Politely, Honor acknowledged the comment.

"Yes," he said, his eyes on the pendant. "It's the reflection you know—the grey stone, the green banks——" Honor nodded. He stopped. They waited for each other to speak. The silence grew. Once again, they realized, they had allowed the conversation to come to a standstill. . . . There existed between Andrew Peirse and his future sister-in-law a genuine affection and respect. Nevertheless, as these few moments proved, they had little to say to each other, and preferred for that reason not be be alone together. "Children all right?" Andrew said. "Quite, thank you." Another silence. They looked at each other, nonplussed. And then, even as they waited, the hoped-for reprieve came. There was the sound of the outer door opening and shutting, there were footsteps in the hall outside. "Claudia," Honor said gladly; at once discomfort vanished; it was as if Claudia were already in the room with them, they were absolved of responsibility towards each other. The door opened. And Claudia it was; in gum-boots, in a yellow oilskin coat glistening with moisture, a green oilskin square tied kerchief-wise under her chin.

"Hullo, everybody," Claudia said. Padding noise-lessly in her gum-boots, oilskins rustling, she came forward into the room. "What a day," she said, "what a day!" She undid the oilskin knot under her chin. Her forehead gleamed; there were beads of rain in her dark eyebrows. "Hullo, Andrew," she said; and then, as he leaned forward to kiss a rain-washed cheek, "Careful," she said, "I'm soaked." She began to undo the buttons of her coat, scattering a ring of drops on the faded carpet. "I missed the bus at the station and had to walk," she said. All the while she was looking about her, glancing sharply from one to the other, picking up a paper from the couch, laying it down again, acquainting hand and eye with the changes that had taken place during her absence from the house. "Anyone phone for me?" she asked. "Postman been?" she said. Her eyes searched along the mantelpiece for letters.

"There was nothing," Honor said. "Only a card for me." She pointed to the basket on the table. "Andrew brought me those."

"Eggs? oh, very nice," Claudia said, looking at them absently. A certain eagerness died out of her face. Honor saw it and wondered what it was, about her home-coming, that seemed of late to disappoint Claudia in this fashion. Claudia turned, she caught sight of the pendant. "What's that you've got round your neck?" she asked.

Honor had been waiting for this moment. She lifted her head. "It's a jade pendant," she said. "The chain's silver. Colin gave it to me."

Claudia stared. "Colin did!"

"Yes. Why not?"

Claudia gave a little laugh. "Why not? As a rule, he never even *remembers* your birthday, not to mind giving you jewellery!" She came over and looked closely at the pendant. "Real jade. Well, well. He must have a guilty conscience, or something."

The light went out of Honor's face. Claudia saw it. "Cheer up," she said angrily "I'm only joking. It's a lovely present." She forgot, time and again, that in thrusting at Colin she wounded not him but his wife: and it never failed to irritate her to discover anew that this was so. "Well," she said, "I can't stand here. I must go and·change. Though how on earth we're to get to Cirencester in this——"

"Colin ordered a car from Briggs."

"Yes," said Colin's voice in the hall outside "and it'll be here in precisely twelve minutes from now. Better make it snappy, Claudia." In he came. "Evening all," he said. He was wearing his best suit, newly back from the cleaners; his buttons glittered; his Sam Browne belt shone. Freshly shaven, his face had a youthful, rosy bloom. "Chosen a pretty day for our little jaunt, haven't we?" he said. He looked at the rain falling steadily past the long windows: even that did not daunt him. "Nice weather for ducks, what?" He polished his nails vigorously on the fatty cushion of his palm. "Fortunately Briggs had a car free," he said. "He's bringing us back too: we've nothing to worry about."

"I've given the baby a huge feed," Honor said. "Nearly eight ounces. He'll sleep till eleven, or half-past, I'm sure."

Unexpectedly, Colin put his arm around his wife's waist. "Well, well," he said, looking at her. He laughed.

"Thirty candles on the cake, eh?" He laughed again, seeming very pleased with himself. "All right," he said, "don't look embarrassed. Andrew knows the dark secret of our married life. . . . She's about six months older than me and doesn't like people to know it." He drew her up close to him and gave her a kiss. Andrew looked on in astonishment. It was perhaps the only time that he had seen Colin acknowledge his wife in this fashion. Honor however, received the attention calmly; a fact which suggested to Andrew that Colin was actually more affectionate in private life than anyone meeting him with his wife in a public place might be led to suppose. "Seen the necklace?" he said. "I picked it up in an antique shop in Oxford the other day. Nice, isn't it?" Then, before Andrew could answer: "What say—shall we have a drink now or wait till we get to the George?"

"Is that where we're going—the George?" Andrew asked.

"Yes. I've booked a table. Thought it best to make sure. It might be crowded—market-day, and all that." Andrew looked curiously at him. He had the impression that the excitement latent in Colin's manner was not connected with the occasion he spoke of; but that this occasion, created by him, was the means of giving incidental and legitimate outlet to a foreign emotion. Colin looked up. Finding Andrew's eyes upon him he smiled faintly as if acknowledging the truth of the other's intuition.

There was the brief bark of a motor-horn outside and then the slur of tyres across the wet gravel. "It's Briggs," Colin said. He started up. "Come on, the car is here. Claudia, where are you? Buck up, everybody. Briggs is waiting . . . !"

The big glazed door of the George Hotel revolved on its axis. They stood waiting their turn to step forward. "In you go." One after another, they slipped into the

moving files and were twirled away, translated; emerging
from the gloom, the rain-lanced evening, into a new
climate; softly lit, purged of all harshness; in which the
bland indoor air spoke in discreet gusts of spicy well-
cooked food; of cut flowers; of the presence of fashionable
women; of an order of things isolated from every-day
responsibility and dedicated wholly to the pleasure of the
moment.

Colin took his cap off. He looked about him: his eyes
brightened, he breathed in this atmosphere as if taking
the first sip of a revivifying wine. At his side "I'm going
to powder my nose," Claudia said. "I'm still only half
dressed. Come with me, Honor." They disappeared. Colin
and Andrew went on through the lounge to hang their
rain-spattered coats on a row of pegs along the wall. As
they did so Colin ran a swift glance over the greatcoats, the
caps on the other pegs. He liked the place to be full when
he visited it; he was disappointed if there was not a crowd.
It was as though he were coming to a theatre rather than
a restaurant: less to dine than to watch a performance,
into the drama of which he hoped secretly to find himself drawn. For him, it seemed, the impersonal background
of the public place permitted some fulfilment impossible
within the rigid confines, the destroying intimacy, of
private life.

The two men came back into the lounge. There was no
sign of Honor or Claudia. They sat down in the big plush
arm-chairs to wait. Andrew leaned back with a sigh. The
atmosphere of the hotel did not affect him as it did Colin;
indeed, that to which Colin was so notably subject, the
queer intoxication of the heart, was a thing unknown to
the young solicitor who at all times saw the world about
him accurately and without any colouring of enchantment. He leant his head and shoulders against the plush
back of the chair. He was tired after a long day's work
on a particularly intricate and harassing case. For a

moment he shut his eyes. One or two people, men and women alike, glanced at him; moved by the beauty in that fair, austere face; by a certain profound exhaustion, deeper than bodily fatigue, which the face revealed.

"I say." Andrew heard Colin's voice at his side. He opened his eyes. "Yes?" he said gently.

"Now that we're on our own—there's something I'd like to tell you—to ask you about——"

Andrew did not move. He looked at Colin out of those clear hollow eyes of his. "Yes?" he repeated. As if disturbed by the attention he had provoked, Colin turned away. He began to search, first in one pocket then the other, for something he had mislaid. Now that he had committed himself to a confidence he was, it seemed, reluctant to deliver it. He took out a packet of Players and held it in his hand uncertainly. At last with an air of taking the plunge "You've heard, I suppose, that the C.O. is leaving us—that he's going abroad?" he said.

Andrew nodded. "I did hear a rumour to that effect. . . . It's true, then?"

"It's true all right." Colin snapped open his cigarette-case, and busied himself lining the gilded panel with cigarettes. "He called me into his office yesterday. Said he wanted to speak to me. To tell you the truth—what with one thing and another—I wondered what was coming. . . ." He stopped. Andrew had the impression that the words Colin was now about to utter were fraught for him (Colin) with so much emotional content that he had to prepare himself, in some way, in order to pronounce them. His impression was confirmed a moment later by the manner in which Colin said, staring fixedly at the wall opposite "Well, he beat about the bush a bit, and then he came to the point. . . . He wanted to know what I thought of the idea of going overseas with him."

There was a pause. "Oh," Andrew said. He looked at Colin. "So that's it. He wants you to go with him, does he?"

"You see what it is," Colin said. He began now to speak very rapidly. "He'll be in charge of a big hospital, out there—much bigger than this potty little show. Eight hundred beds, at least. Very interesting work, too: *real* work at an important base hospital. Well, they're a man short, it seems: somebody cracked up at the last moment. He was asked to recommend someone in his place. . . . Nothing's decided yet, of course. He merely gave me first option, so to speak. . . ."

"I see," Andrew said. "So it's for you to decide."

"Yes, I suppose it is." He hesitated and looked uncertainly at Andrew. "Of course there are a lot of things to be considered. But I feel it's a great compliment, in a way, from a man like Colonel Mayne——"

"He must think well of your work," Andrew said, non-committal.

"Perhaps." Colin turned his head away. "Yes," he said; "yes he does, I suppose. . . . I don't know. . . ."

Andrew looked at him curiously. Unfamiliar with Colonel Mayne, and the effect he had on his junior officers, he did not know what to make of the mixture of elation and uneasiness that Colin's manner exhibited. "What have you decided to do?" he asked.

"Good heavens," the other said rapidly: "decided? I've not decided anything yet. I've—I've hardly thought about it."

"Honor won't like it," Andrew said.

Colin looked down at the carpet. "No, Honor won't like it," he said soberly.

"Have you spoken to her about it?"

He frowned. "No. No, of course not. There's no hurry. I don't want to distress her for nothing. . . ." He did not lift his eyes from the carpet. "Of course," he said suddenly, "it's a great opportunity, in a way. I mean, it won't happen again. The experience, and all that——"

"Yes—there's that side to it," Andrew said.

"On the other hand—it's perfectly true—there are certain drawbacks——"

"The risk, you mean?"

"The risk?" Colin looked at him in surprise. "Oh—that doesn't worry me," he said. It was obvious that he meant what he said. The element of danger involved was for him an integral part of the poetry surrounding the whole situation. Death, in the dramatic form permitted by war, was tolerable, not unattractive: something positive: a culmination, not a mere dissolution. "No," he said, "I was thinking of something else. After the armistice. It may take longer before one's demobilized. One's practice—what's left of it—may suffer——" And speaking of this his expression changed; something listless, apathetic, came into it. He sighed. It was not, Andrew perceived, the prospect of damage to his practice that he found depressing: on the contrary: it was the reminder of the fact that war could not last for ever: that, at some time in the future, this state of affairs, the soldiering, the freedom, the new uninhibited life, must come to an end like a curtain being rung down on a glittering and exciting show, and in its fall, returning actor and spectator alike to the greyness and uneventfulness of every-day life. . . .

Andrew was silent. He found nothing to say. We don't speak the same language, he thought; what's the use. . . . "Sh," Colin said at that moment - "here they are. Remember—not a word. We don't want to spoil Honor's birthday. . . ."

The shaded lamp threw a rosy glow over the cloth, over the faces gathered about the table. Knives and forks and spoons gleamed; wine-glasses gaped, frail and clear. In a silver-plate vase, a handful of florist's roses with long, sharp buds, were each one as tightly furled as a fashionable umbrella. "Good evening, sir. Good evening, *madame*." Small and sallow, the waiter hovered; pulled out chairs;

slid them neatly back under the haunches of the women
guests as they prepared to sit down. Another waiter hung
over them, card in hand. The party settled down; two
on each side of the table. Colin, the host, took possession
of the menu. "Now let me see." He scanned the small
typed card. "Soup," he said. "Soup, everybody? *Potage*
something or other——" The business of discussing, of
ordering a meal, began.

It was while they were thus occupied that Honor,
turning round to examine the other guests assembled in
the long dark-panelled room exclaimed suddenly "Look—
isn't that Captain Herriot over there?"

Unanimously, they turned to look. The Captain was
sitting by himself at a small table by the alcove; he had
apparently just finished a meal, and was slowly drinking
coffee and looking down at a letter laid out flat on the
table beside him. There was something unfamiliar about
him: for a moment they stared at him, puzzled. Then
they realized. It was his expression: the look he wore
when he imagined himself alone, eating alone amongst
strangers. He sat reading the letter, holding a coffee-cup
in one hand. There was a brooding look about the
lowered lids: his mouth was set in a hard thin line.

Suddenly, he looked up. He became aware, it seemed,
of the attention focused on him. He turned and saw them.
At once his face changed: he was familiar, recognizable
again. Smiling, he waved a hand to them; at the same
time, with the other hand, stuffing the letter away
hurriedly in his pocket. He signalled to them: should he
come over? Taking for granted their assent, he picked up
his coffee-cup and made his way towards them across the
dining-room. They watched him, silent. He came up to
their table and stood looking down at them. He was still
smiling. "Well, well," he said. "It's a small world, isn't
it?" He looked swiftly at the faces round the table. "Mind
if I join you?" he said.

"Do," Colin said in a detached voice. Herriot placed his cup down on the table. He reached out—"This free?—thank you," and drew up a chair from the adjoining table. There was a pause. He looked at Colin's resplendent tunic, at the women in their printed silk dresses. "You all look very festive," he said.

"It's my wife's birthday."

"Oh—really?" Herriot turned. "Many happy returns," he said to Honor. He paused. "I thought perhaps you were celebrating Colin's prospective departure East," he said.

There was a dead silence. Colin put down his spoon. "You've got it wrong, haven't you?" he said. "You mean Mayne's prospective departure."

"Oh," Herriot said. He looked from husband to wife. "Yes, I suppose I have," he said. "Sorry—all these comings and goings—one gets a bit confused——" He sipped at his coffee. "As a matter of fact—I shall probably be going myself, before long——"

"Going?" Claudia said sharply. "Where?"

Herriot looked at her. So did the others at the table. There was a short pause. Then Herriot smiled and shook his head. "Unfortunately, as they say in books, I'm not at liberty to tell you."

Andrew drank his soup. Without raising his eyes. "The Officer Selection job isn't permanent, then?" he asked.

Herriot flashed a look at him. "Oh, no; it was never intended to be. I was put on to it for a time—more as an experiment than anything. But there's some real work coming along shortly—a big show—we'll all be needed—every man of us—myself included." There was a slight silence. They looked respectfully at the Commando flash on his sleeve.

"When are you leaving?" Honor asked. She added quickly, "That is—if you can tell us."

"I can't say. It might be any day, now." They nodded, understanding the need for reticence. Andrew looked curiously at the Captain's face. For a moment, he had the impression that Herriot had succeeded in arousing this interest in his own movements merely in order to compensate himself for his exclusion from a gathering, to which, originally, he had not been invited. Then the impression faded. He must be mistaken, he thought. What need of reassurance of this sort had a man in military uniform, who publicly wore the badge of a hero on his sleeve . . . ?

The waiter removed soup-plates; proffered a basket of rolls. The wine-waiter brought the bottle of wine Colin had ordered. The second course arrived: they began to eat, a little incommoded by the presence at the same table of a man who did not eat with them, but only watched. There was duck; the flesh dark and succulent under a friable roasted skin; green peas, tender and sweet; and little slippery new potatoes. In sips, white wine refreshed the palate; astringent and warming. "Come on, Herriot—you must have a glass with us." It was necessary, by some token, to include him in the meal they partook of. He refused. "Don't bother about me," he said. "I'll smoke, if I may." He lit a cigarette, and sat with legs crossed, swaying a little, backward and forward, on his chair. "I've not seen you since the day of the sports, have I?" he said suddenly to Claudia.

"No, I suppose not."

"Not that I didn't try." He looked at Andrew, smiling. "I asked Miss Abbott to come out and have dinner with me and she refused. Showed not the slightest interest. In your place, I'd be flattered."

"On the contrary," Andrew said. "I should have been more flattered if she had accepted."

Herriot looked intently at him for a moment. Then he smiled again, showing his white teeth. "There you are," he said to Claudia. "What did I say?"

Andrew was busy finishing the remains of his duck. He said equably, "Claudia likes soldiers."

"I do?" Claudia raised her eyebrows.

"We all do. Otherwise there'd be no wars."

"What about pacifists? You can't say that they——"

"Oh, they're worse than anyone," Andrew said. "They love and venerate soldiers so much that they refuse point-blank to kill them."

"Now, Andrew, that's not fair," Claudia began. She laughed, but there was a note of vexation in her voice. "You will twist everything——"

"Everything *is* twisted," Andrew said, pausing to look at her over his fork. "That's the point. Every picture has its reverse side. Black becomes white, negative positive——"

Colin gave a deep exaggerated sigh. He turned to Herriot "Terrible, isn't it? They can go on like that for hours. These intellectuals!——"

The sallow waiter leaned over the table. "Cherry pie or prune mould?" he said briskly, with the air of one propounding a conundrum. He disappeared. Presently he brought to the table some faded cherries, custard-bound under a goffered wafer of pastry. "Prune mould, *madame*?"—he set in front of Honor a glass goblet filled with an autumnal-looking substance and decorated with a protuberant navel of *glacé* cherry. They lifted up their spoons. Colin glanced at his watch. "I don't want to hurry you, but we'd better not dawdle too long——"

Herriot looked at them. "You going somewhere?" he asked, through cigarette smoke.

"Yes; we thought we'd drop in to the pictures, to finish up the evening." Colin gave the information reluctantly; it was plain that on this occasion at least, he did not wish Herriot to join them. Herriot, however, smiled. Gently but deliberately he obstructed what he knew to be Colin's wishes. "Just what I was going to do," he said. "We must join forces——"

"Where were you going?" Honor said innocently. "We thought the Carlton——"

"That's right. Nothing else worth seeing. The big picture doesn't begin for another twenty minutes."

So that was settled. He was coming with them. A small silence fell about the table. It was broken by Herriot himself. He was looking at Andrew. There was something speculative, intent, in his expression. Suddenly and without any preamble "You're in a reserved occupation, I suppose?" he said.

"Mm?" Taken at a disadvantage, Andrew spat cherry stones into his spoon. Recovering, he laughed. The question amused him, it seemed. "Why am I not in khaki, you mean? That's quite simple. I was. For a short while, at all events. I've been invalided out."

"Oh——" Herriot screwed up his dark brows. "Yes, of course. I forgot. Tough luck." He smiled. "Or perhaps you don't consider it that.' It all depends on the way you look at it, doesn't it?"

"Yes," Andrew said. "It all depends on the way you— or other people—look at it."

"How did you enjoy your time in the army?" Herriot asked curiously. "Did you hate it?"

"By no means. It was quite a pleasant masquerade——"

"Masquerade?" Colin said sharply.

Andrew smiled at his future brother-in-law. "Well, I'm not a soldier—we're not soldiers, the majority of us. When the clock strikes midnight—when armistice is declared— the khaki will vanish, we'll be clothed in humble civilian tatters again——"

"They *will* be tatters, too," Honor said. "What with the moth and everything——"

Herriot reached out for the ash-tray and languidly tapped ash off his cigarette. "What will you be doing after the war, Colin?" he asked.

"Me? I'll go back to Worthing, I suppose. To my

practice. Surgery, visiting hours, the clinic—the old routine and grind——" He sighed. "Queer to think of it—seems so far away, so meaningless—— And you?"

"Oh, I've not thought about it much," Herriot replied. "Sufficient unto the day, you know. I have an idea I may go abroad—South America, or somewhere." He turned back to Andrew. "Now you——" he said. "You're all right. You'll be needed—you and your kind. You'll be right in the picture, then—helping to maintain law and order—keeping crime bottled up——"

"You have a strange conception of my job, haven't you?" Andrew said. "In the first place, I'm a solicitor, not a criminal lawyer. And secondly, if I were, it's not bottling I'd be doing but decanting."

"What do you mean," Herriot said, "decanting——?"

Andrew arranged cherry-stones in a pattern on the edge of his plate. "It's like this," he said. He contemplated the ring of denuded stones. "What I should like," he said, "is not to suppress crime, but to demand acknowledgment of the criminal in all of us. To lessen the distance between the judge and the man judged; between the man in the dock and the jury of his peers; a jury asked to condemn an act of which they themselves are equally capable, to hate that which secretly they love——" He paused. The faces of those sitting around the table expressed disagreement, even hostility. But no one spoke. It was as if, now that he had chosen to express himself, they had no alternative but to listen; they were powerless to move a muscle, utter a word of protest until he had finished what he had to say: a compulsion, Claudia knew, that he could exercise at moments without apparent effort or intention. "In other words," he said, "what I want to do is to provide a place for the antisocial impulse within the social framework itself. In the same way as an architect, say, plans to have parks and green trees inside the city—so that the city may breathe and not suffocate, so that the balance between oxygen and carbon dioxide, or whatever it is, be maintained as harmoniously as possible. Poison must be used to keep poison in suspense; otherwise, no health. And that's the lawyer's job, as I see it: not to segregate the ingredients as he's been doing, but to work out a better formula of collaboration. At the moment civilization is rather in the position of a person who refuses to be vaccinated, to be polluted with a mild dose of cowpox, and in consequence of his desire for purity, falls a victim to the foulest disease of all—to smallpox, or to world war——"

The waiter leaned over the table with his tray of coffee-cups. "Black or white?" he asked.

"Black or white," Andrew echoed smiling: "yes, that is the question. . . ."

Patiently, the waiter turned to the others. Metal pot lifted. "*Madame*——?"

"Black, please."

"White for me."

"Black——"

"I'll have mine half and half," Honor said.

"Bravo," Andrew said. "Very wise. No artificial distinctions: neither one thing nor the other. A sort of natural emulsion——"

"Stop it," Colin said. "I refuse to allow everything I eat or drink to be turned into a moral drama——"

"In any case," Claudia said, "I disagree, violently." She was talking to Andrew. "What you say is too dangerous. One *must* have standards——"

He raised his brows. "Must one? Even if acquiring them involves, say, world war?"

She hesitated, and looked away from him. "Yes," she said resolutely. "Even if acquiring them involves world war. Progress must be paid for——"

"And so must this dinner," Colin said: nothing, he was determined, should turn him from the role of cheerful extrovert that he had chosen to adopt for the occasion. He raised a hand. "Waiter—let's have the bill, may we? We're rather in a hurry."

"Yes, sir." The waiter brought it, folded, on a plate. Colin took out his pocket-book. The women were busy with their handbags; searching for powder, renewing lipstick: Herriot and Andrew stubbed out cigarettes in the saucer of a coffee cup. The dinner was at an end: the occasion over. The waiter came back with the change on a plate, after brief contemplation Colin selected the appropriate coins and waved the rest away. "Thank you, sir," the waiter said indifferently. Colin looked round. "Shall we go——?" They prepared to depart. Rising at the same moment, Andrew and Neil Herriot found themselves face to face across the narrow length of the table. Something passed between them, they looked at one another steadily without smiling, locked in some indefinable conflict of temperament: a conflict which because of its nature could find no overt expression, could only work itself out through the medium of a third, a separate personality.

CHAPTER NINE

WAR DANCE

THE saxophone uttered a wail, a tremolo of piercing sweetness, a bleat of pure agony. The drum throbbed steadily, drumstick rebounding from the taut-stretched surface. The fingers of the violinist sidled along the neck of his instrument as if taking its pulse: piano notes rattled like dice. And the lance-corporal, promoted to eminence for the evening, turning his back on the others,

clasped the microphone to him and confided to it words
of love; words that, mysteriously enlarged, buoyed up,
floated like bright soap bubbles over the heads of the
dancers beneath; of the spectators lining the dark-stained
walls of this ball-room built years before to cater to the
sad pleasures of the mentally deranged.

"You can't say no to a soldier,
   A sailor, or a handsome marine;
   He's got a right to romance, if you want him to win."

"Quite a good band," said the A.T.S. corporal, in the
arms of Staff-sergeant Owen.

"Good floor, don't you think?" Major Smith said to
Sister Fry. "Very," said Sister Fry. Her belted waist
creaked: her hand was dry and unsentimental in his.

"I always did like that tune," said Captain Lloyd: he
craned his neck to look into his partner's face. Ginger
Rogers said nothing: she gazed steadily at the row of
pips on his left shoulder. Under his hand, through a
crêpe de Chine blouse, he could feel the elastic of her
brassière. Her feet followed his, in and out, back and forth:
his right arm was clasped closely about her waist.

"Looks as if there's going to be a big crowd," Colin
said. All the while, his eyes darted here and there, searching the faces of new-comers. He danced accurately, in-
attentively; conscious of performing what was no more
than a social exercise. Honor's face was pale: there was
something about the eyes and lids which suggested recent
tears.

"'——You can't say no to a soldier——'" boomed
Willy Wilson, the dentist, in Claudia's ear. Energetically
he swung her about, showing a healthy independence
both of the rhythm and the proximity of other dancers.
"Smashing cricket-match on the green this afternoon,"
he said: "were you there?"

"I sometimes think," said Major McRae to Matron—
he danced or rather he walked, he ambled along, as if
instead of leading he were apologetically retreating from
the partner whose co-operation he had sought—"that
the whole human race is a little mad——"

The moon had not yet risen. Outside in the darkness,
people were still coming up the drive. The sound of
voices, of laughter, could be heard; the crackle of feet on
gravel. Here and there, a glowing cigarette-end punc-
tuated the obscurity; or the slatted headlight of a car,
creeping, cautious, up the drive, as if uneasy of the black-
out, of a potential charge of petrol-wastage. The hospital
itself was visible as a dark mass, darker than the darkness,
looming overhead as they approached. They turned a
corner: along the baffle-wall a line of paint gleamed,
phosphorescent. "This way," someone said. At the same
moment, as if the life pulsing within blinded walls were
perceptible to those who approached, the feverish beat
of jazz made itself heard. "Listen—they're dancing."
Overheard like that, through the mysterious stillness of
night, the music, a reminder both of pleasure to come and
of pleasure departed, gripped the heart with sudden
urgency. "Hurry," said a woman's voice, "come on—
hurry—we're missing it all——"

"Come and have a drink," Willy Wilson said to
Claudia. He took out a mud-coloured handkerchief and,
unabashed, wiped first one hand and then the other.
"Hot work, dancing," he said. He stuffed the handkerchief back in his pocket. They made their way across
the crowded floor to the alcove under the gallery where
a buffet had been erected. Before they could reach it
Claudia stopped. "Oh," she said in a startled voice: she
was looking at the door: "why, there's Andrew—I
didn't think—I must go and speak to him. Do you mind?"

"Not at all," Willy said. He relinquished her cheerfully and departed to look for other company.

Claudia turned. Andrew had not yet seen her. He was standing by the door, looking about him. He had obviously come straight on from Cirencester: his black jacket, pin-striped trousers, looked oddly formal among the khaki. Just as the austere face, the fine remote eyes set him apart in any crowd; and drew towards him the questioning, half-distrustful glances of others. Claudia went up to him. Smiling, she touched his arm. "Andrew, is it really you—you in the flesh——?"

"Me in as much flesh as I can muster," he said: "a bare quota, I fear. . . ." His eyes went quickly over her: examining the close-fitting red frock she was wearing. "You look very smart," he said. "All got up to kill— isn't that the expression?"

Claudia did not answer. Instead, she said impulsively: "I'm so glad you did come, after all! So *pleased*, Andrew! . . . . It'll do you all the good in the world, to get about again. It's no use shutting yourself away from people——"

"I may add," he said, "that Mother considers this night will be the death of me. I've strict orders under no circumstances to dance two dances running."

The animation went from Claudia's face. "Indeed?" she said. Up went her thinned-out eyebrows. . . . So she said that, did she? Her claims are becoming bolder, it seems. She wants now to control his actions even when he's out of sight. I knew that was coming. She wants to keep him an invalid. A child needing solicitude. And in that solicitude she'll imprison him, cut him off from me. . . . "Nonsense," she said. Her voice sounded brusque, unsympathetic. "What you've got to do is to forget all that and enjoy yourself naturally for a change." Andrew's face was impassive, he made no comment. Claudia hesitated. What if he *prefers* invalidism; not in itself, but as an excuse, a justification for some imagined failure?

On the platform, the lance-corporal tapped briefly with his baton: a pause: a moment of built-up silence: and then:

"She'll be coming round the mountain when she comes,
She'll be coming round the mountain,
Coming round the mountain,
She'll be coming round the mountain when she comes!"

From every corner of the room people came streaming back onto the floor. They met, they smiled, arms raised, they clasped their partners to them. The shuffle of feet was heard as once again the dancers revolved on their appointed treadmill. "Coming round the mountain ... !" Dancing, they joined in the chorus, drowning the voice of the lance-corporal at his microphone. Claudia's eyes brightened. She watched couple after couple whirl by, romping, caught up in the infectious rhythm. Her red-sandalled foot tapped the floor. Glancing at Andrew "Aren't you going to ask me to dance?" she said.

"Certainly, I am." Andrew took a newly laundered handkerchief out of his breast-pocket. He touched his lips briefly with it, and then replaced it. "But not this very moment. I've just walked up that never-ending drive——"

"Of course," Claudia said quickly. "Thoughtless of me. . . . Let's sit down for a bit." They made their way towards a row of chairs against the opposite wall. In silence, they sat there watching the dancers; nearly all hospital personnel: officers, Sisters, N.C.O.s and order-lies; with the visitors, men and women from Linfield and the neighbourhood, providing a leavening of mufti, of variegated colour, amid the prevailing khaki. Andrew looked attentively at the faces of the dancers as they passed. After a moment "Your boy friend not here yet?" he said to Claudia.

Claudia did not react. "Which one?" she said coolly.

"I was referring to the gallant Commando Captain——"

She thought: So you came here to meet him. You had to see him again, face to face. You too. . . . "I don't know," she said. "He may be. I've not seen him."

Andrew glanced at his watch. "It's a little early, perhaps. No doubt, as the star attraction, he likes to make an entrance——"

"I don't think," Claudia said, nettled, "that he studies his effects like that——"

"I'm not so sure," Andrew said. "I'm not so sure. . . . Though why he should feel the *need* to do so—that's what puzzles me: what I can't understand. It doesn't fit in, somehow——"

"You speak as if he should be perfect—a sort of superman," Claudia said angrily. "Why should you take up that attitude towards him?—*you*, with your brains—with everything you are——"

"Yes, I; what am I?" Andrew said gently. "I've never killed a man: slit no one's throat on a Norwegian beach; gouged no one's eyes out; broken no one's skull with my hob-nailed boots——" He laughed suddenly. "And we've got to take it on trust that *he* has. He pleads guilty to murder: but what if, on investigation, he proves innocent after all, and as such, unworthy of all this social adulation?"

"You distort things, as usual," Claudia said. "The plain fact remains that whatever else he is or isn't, he's a brave man who's volunteered for a dangerous job, and I don't think you've any right to—*belittle* him with your admiration."

"In unarmed combat," Andrew said, "there are no rules, save those of expediency. All sorts of underhand tricks are allowed, even encouraged——"

With a startling clash of cymbals, with the suddenness of a collision, the music came to an end. Concussed, the air tingled. For a moment, no one moved. And then, restored to life, the couples on the floor broke apart: so many Eves breaking from the rib of Adam; released to separate existence. Simultaneously, they turned towards the platform, clapping their hands; demanding renewal: but the clapping went unheeded: the dance was over: the musicians had abandoned their instruments; the lance-corporal was quietly drinking beer at the back of the platform.

"Colin's here, I see," Andrew said. Claudia turned her head. Colin was coming off the dance floor, with his arm about the waist of the small dark Sister with whom he had just been dancing. He stopped dead on seeing Andrew. "Well, for evermore!" he exclaimed.

"Good evening," Andrew said calmly.

"Didn't expect to see *you* here," Colin said. Remembering the young woman on his arm "This is Sister Blair—Miss Abbott—Mr Peirse," he said. Sister Blair smiled, a ready, open-mouthed smile; her skin was alight with healthy perspiration. Colin did not remove his arm from her waist: he looked down on Andrew with a face flushed still from the exertions of the dance. A warmth, a tangible radiance, emanated from him as from an iron newly removed from the forge, and glowing still with the heat of that imparted fire. He looked down at Andrew, sitting pale and collected on his chair. He had an impulse to bait him. "I thought you disapproved of this sort of thing," he said.

"What sort of thing?" Andrew asked.

"Dancing, drinking. All forms of escapism——"

"Escapism," Andrew said unmoved, "is a much abused term. Particularly as applied to things which help us to forget the so-called realities of war. The joke being, of course, that it's war itself which is the biggest piece of escapism of all—escapism *par excellence*—a flight from reason, from everyday duties and responsibilities——"

Colin did not wait to hear the rest. "Thanks a million," he said. "Now Sister Blair and I can dance the Hoki-Koki with an easy conscience!"

Slender, prematurely grey, the tall assistant matron came across the room. Years of authority had given her an upright carriage, a kindly expression. Her bust was austere, embalmed in starch; her legs surprisingly elegant. She smiled at Honor. "Good evening, Mrs Carmichael." Her smile had great charm with no real warmth; she was a woman who reserved herself, emotionally, for her duties. One was forced to respect the personality presented: to guess, only, at the reality behind the uniform; the transformation that privacy, and disrobement, must undoubtedly bring about.

"Good evening," Honor said. She moved gratefully into the other's orbit : abandoning the cup of half-cold coffee with which, a shield for her own conspicuous isolation, she had for the last ten minutes been rather desperately trifling. Matron glanced for a moment at the pale face, the swollen lids: at once, she looked away, and talked of other things. "Quite a crowd, this evening," she said. "I can't think where all the people come from."

"They all seem to be enjoying themselves," Honor said.

Matron nodded. And: "How're the children?" she asked.

"Very well, thank you."

"That's good."

Honor recognized that it was now her turn to say something; nothing apposite suggested itself, and she smiled vaguely. There was a pause. Then briskly Matron played her partner's hand for her. "Keep you pretty busy, don't they?" she prompted.

"Yes, they do, rather."

"You've got someone to help you with them, of course."

"Only Edith."

"Edith—hasn't she been called up, yet?"

"No; they won't have her. She's a bit queer, you know."

"Well, you're lucky to get any one at all, these days."

"That's true."

The orchestra was playing again. A slow foxtrot. With a minimum of delay, people sought out or accepted their new partners. Major Smith came towards them across the floor, a smile on his face. It was obvious that he was coming to ask one or other of them to dance. Aware that his intention was to separate them, the two women became watchful, uneasy; unable to continue a conversation which must, so soon, be interrupted by his presence. Up he came; glasses gleaming on the rounded brows. "Matron—may I have the pleasure?" he said.

Matron glanced apologetically at Honor; guilty at being the one chosen; at having, so summarily, to abandon a conversation newly begun. Honor smiled, releasing her from all obligation in this respect: Major Smith put a diffident hand on Matron's left clavicle; and off they went, sucked, it seemed irresistibly, into the tide of movement, of sound. Honor watched them go. At once, the dutiful smile died from her face. Her eyes went quickly, covertly round the room. Colin was nowhere to be seen. He was avoiding her; punishing her for the emotion that she was unable even now successfully to conceal. "*Honor—Mayne's asked me to go abroad with him.*" The words kept recurring in consciousness; and each time the impact was keener, more startling, gaining momentum in repetition. "*Mayne's asked me to go abroad with him.*" On first hearing them she had repeated the words after him, stupidly. She remembered then, Colin's anger "Don't look at me like that!" The way he had turned from her. Protecting himself by anger from her distress; keeping himself aloof, retreating from it as he might from a dangerous mælstrom, whose very impetus drew him unwilling to the brink; against whose unreasoning power he must fight to retain his own self-possession and free-will. . . .

She looked down into the empty cup between her hands. I needn't stay, she thought. I can go now, if I want to. I've always got the excuse that I have to feed the baby. And with that, a sudden yearning filled her. She thought of the quiet nursery; the gentle pulsing of the night-light in its saucer: of the physical presence of the child, so sweet, so infinitely consoling; the penetrating warmth of his being, the tender radiance of his breath upon her face. At once, her armpits, her breast, tingled; she felt the dawning irradiation, the sudden ripeness in each breast. It was time to go; she could stay no longer. She set the empty cup on a nearby window-sill; she turned to leave: too late, she saw that Colonel Mayne was standing in the doorway.

For a moment, neither of them spoke; startled by the suddenness of the encounter; trapped, each, in an unwanted proximity. Honor found herself staring at the Colonel, puzzled: there was something novel, unfamiliar about his appearance. The next moment, she realized what it was. He was in formal mess kit; and the dark overalls, red-piped, the high collar, long narrow trousers caught beneath the instep, the fact that he was smoking a cigar, all combined to lend him a curiously theatrical, Ouida-esque appearance, which confused her slightly and served, for some reason, to emphasize the distance between them; the gap that separated the two worlds they inhabited; worlds at present adjacent, seeming to overlap, but which were in fact altogether distant and incompatible. He faced her, blocking the doorway. His strong neck bulged slightly over the upstanding collar of the jacket; the cigar stuck out of his mouth at an angle, like a thermometer; he looked powerful, dangerous, amiable. Standing there so close to him, she sensed the power in him, experienced the full force of the man's personality as Colin might do; but unlike Colin she was not overborne, she did not succumb to the undoubted magnetism he exercised; on the contrary, she was deeply antagonized; repelled, without knowing why.

The Colonel spoke first. Politely, he plucked the cigar from his mouth. "Leaving us already?" he said. His lips smiled their tight-drawn smile. Above, the pallid eyes were as chilly, as unwavering, as eyes manufactured out of glass. Honor had endured this expression before: she had learned to expect it. It was as if, automatically, a protective glaze covered Colonel Mayne's vision in the presence of certain women. "Not going so soon, surely?" he insisted.

"Yes," Honor said, looking down at the ground. She became aware, as if he had pointed these things out to her, that her hair was dishevelled; that she perspired; that the front of her dress was stained: "I've got to— I'm sorry—I have to feed the baby——" But she no longer felt the fullness in her breasts; instead, there was a sensation of drought, of withering. It was as if the presence of this man could blight the sweetness within her: as if, voluntarily sterile himself, he had the power to create sterility about him; a power that he chose in full consciousness to exercise; withdrawing from the confusion of natural life and accepting in place of it the artifact not of a religious, but of a military order. For the first time Honor understood how deeply he must resent the presence, inevitable in war, of a bank-holiday crowd of pseudo-officers and their dependants, all sight-seeing within the very precincts, the closed exclusive quarters of that order under whose rule he had chosen to live and shelter.

"Feed the baby?" Mayne repeated the words, unsuspecting. Too late, he understood. "Ah, yes, of course."

And now his eyes could not rest on her at all; agonized, they flitted here, there and everywhere, to escape somehow the indecency her words suggested. "Of course," he repeated, "of course." He looked about him, seeking some means of escape. "Colin taking you home?" he asked.

"No," Honor said quickly. She did not want Colin to come with her. She knew that, as things were at the moment, her sudden absence from the room would weigh more with Colin than her continued presence there. The Colonel should not, by his intervention, deprive her of this small sorry advantage. "It's so early," she said. "There's no reason why he should go yet. I'll just slip away. . . ."

"Now, now." Mayne spoke with an appearance of cordiality. "We can't have attractive young women rambling about the countryside, unescorted. I'll send Colin to you."

"No," Honor said. "Please don't." She smiled wanly. "I've got to get used to doing without him, you know."

Mayne affected not to understand: "That's all very well," he said, determinedly jocose "but we musn't let him neglect you——"

There was a pause. Then Honor raised her eyes to his. She said simply, "Colonel Mayne—Colin's going abroad with you, isn't he?"

Mayne stiffened. He actually moved back a step. The smile, which he had forgotten, hung unhinged on his face. Honor understood that she had done something unforgivable: she had broken through the insulating veneer of politeness; she had obtruded herself as a human being; worse, as a human being pleading for some concession or enlightenment that he, it might be supposed in virtue of his official capacity, was in a position to accord. Mayne stared at her, as he might at a pickpocket whom he had surprised in the act of trying to steal his watch while his attention was momentarily distracted. He made no attempt to deal lightly or tactfully with the situation. He merely cut himself off from further contact with her. "Excuse me," he said abruptly: "I see I'm wanted." And without another word, he turned and left her.

"What's next, did he say? A Ladies' Excuse-me dance? Oh, goody. I'm going to ask that Commando fellow to dance with me."

"Hark at her!"

"She'll have to take her place in the queue with the rest of us——"

"He's not here yet, is he?"

"Yes, he is. He came in when I did—about ten o'clock."

"Where is he, then? I've not laid eyes on him."

"Do you know, it's a funny thing. You couldn't call him handsome, could you? And yet, there's something about him——"

"You're telling me!"

"Hetty Smith came into the shop yesterday. Wanted some new suspenders for her belt. While I was serving her, she told me Captain Herriot's going to be decorated, or something. For wiping out an enemy machine-gun nest. I think it was a machine-gun nest. . . . They say he killed five men, single-handed."

"Go on!"

"With the bayonet, Hetty said."

"The bayonet—makes you feel queer to think of it. . . ."

"They aim for the stomach, don't they?"

"They can kill a man instantly just by gripping hold of him in a certain way."

"Or by sticking something sharp into his ear-drums——"

"They black their faces, too. I've seen it on the pictures. Cor, fancy meeting one of them in the dark——"

"You're telling me!"

"I don't mean what you mean."

"Of course not."

"Girls, girls!"

"Well, talk of the devil! Just look at that, will you?"

"Well, I never——"

"So *that's* where he was all the time——"

"Would you believe it! And her as good as engaged to that nice young fellow out in Libya. . . ."

At the far end of the room, there was a side door that gave directly onto the hospital grounds. The frosted panel was pushed back and Captain Herriot appeared, with Linfield's Ginger Rogers on his arm. The young postmistress had lost nothing of her habitual poise; her hair was unruffled; the satin blouse as immaculate as ever: there was however, and this alone proved the betraying factor, something starry and unfocused about her look; coming into the lighted room she moved like a sleep-walker enamoured of her own dream, unwilling to wake. Herriot at her side, looked about him, smiling unconcerned: there was a long smear of lipstick under his left ear.

"There they are, now." Wordlessly, the signal ran through the room. The couple stood at the door; set apart, haloed, as it were, by the attention directed on to them; the close and watchful hostility of those whom they had chosen temporarily to exclude. As if they felt an actual resistance in their path, they looked about them in surprise and did not, at once, come forward. Then Herriot, with a laugh, said something to the girl; he put his hand on her arm. and without further ado led her off in the direction of the bar.

The orchestra broke into the first strains of a Palais Glide. A great sigh of release, of renewal, ran through the room. The old pattern was broken up, an original one substituted; once more, it was felt, anything might happen; the die was cast anew. They came streaming onto the floor eager to begin; to form up; to clasp hands, arms, waists. Linked, they could feel at once the human current running swifter than electricity between them; annealing one to the other; so that the individual could sunder neither mind nor body from the mind and body of his neighbour, but must move as he moved, feel as he felt, obedient to the strong impersonal will, the incalculable personality, which now controlled and animated them all. Locked together, moving all in unison, they swung past, men and women alike gazing before them with shining eyes, with fixed tranced smiles. The floor thundered beneath them: a wave of intense physical energy passed out from them, and, like something tangible, broke amongst the few spectators standing deprecatingly against the walls of the long room.

"You and I—we have our backs to the wall, as you might say," commented Andrew Peirse. He, of course, was not dancing; he stood with Claudia at his side, leaning negligently against the dark-panelled wall and watching the spectacle before him: isolated less by the limitations of his own physique than by a temperamental inability to abandon himself without self-consciousness to such innocent physical exhibitionism. He glanced at Claudia. She had not heard what he said. She was gazing fixedly at the dancers: her eyes shone, her lips were parted in a faint child-like smile. Andrew watched her for a moment. Then he leaned towards her. With his lips not far from her ear. "Why don't you join them?" he said.

Claudia started. She seemed annoyed at the interruption. She looked quickly at him, and then looked away again. "Because I don't want to," she said shortly.

Andrew laughed. "Ever seen a child looking into a

sweet-shop through a pane of glass——?" he said. Claudia did not answer. His eyes were still upon her. "Why don't you go in, and spend your tuppence?" he said softly. . . .

The Orderly Officer, a small reticent man called Creech, came in to inform Colonel Mayne that the red light had gone up on the internal air-raid warning system. The Colonel nodded: a few minutes later, faintly through the shuttered windows, the sirens could be heard, keening one to the other across the moonlit valley. The dancers coming off the floor either did not hear the sound or they ignored it. As always as soon as the music came to a stop there was an instantaneous surge towards the bar, at one end of the room, or the buffet at the other. At this All-Ranks dance there was no official separation of the sheep from the goats, but in virtue of the prices prevailing at each it was at the buffet that the N.C.O.s and order-lies entertained their friends; at the bar that officers replenished empty glasses with renewed doses of whisky or gin. Many, indeed, did not move from the immediate neighbourhood of the bar the entire evening; but, established, as Mayne himself was established, before small glass-topped tables or on the dusty wooden steps of the adjacent platform, sat there steadily hour after hour, as though unwilling to step outside the boundaries of the magic circle created about them by the mystery of alcohol. They were partnered there either by the more sociable of the Sisters or by young women from the neighbouring country houses: young women who were to be found in the same attitude and with the same smiles week after week in the local officers' club: a few of them on leave from civil defence services or the W.R.N.S.; others too young perhaps, or too frail, for national ser-vice; or technically protected from its demands by the presence of a baby sleeping in the pink and blue night nursery at home. A notable feature of the evening was the quantity of neat gin that, with a dazzling immunity, the majority of these young women, Sisters included, showed themselves capable of assimilating. At the other end of the room conditions were altogether different. Here, where refreshment was merely an interlude, and not an end in itself, excitement derived from a different source: it flashed wordlessly from eye to eye; whispered in the lisp of silk against khaki; spoke in the secrecy of a moist clasped palm. Here, hospitality took the form of coffee, of minerals, of sausage rolls. Offered a Goldflake, Edie, or Doris, or Marlene, in sky-blue marocain with velvet bows in her hair, picked one daintily out of the open packet, her stunted nails red-varnished: when she drank tea, her lower lip left in amorous signature a carmine "W" on the rim of her cup. Here, as in the *palais de danse*, the dance was the thing; and silence an interval to be endured until the clamour of brass summoned them once again to each other's arms, to the skilful execution of the latest routine in jazz. By this time the first bomb had fallen somewhere in the neighbourhood; and the familiar jar and vibration, over almost before it could be apprehended, had served as a reminder, or a first intimation, of what was going on outside. There was an imperceptible pause. "Jerry's about again." A laugh or two. Nothing more. Agitation, if any, was covert and displaced: to be detected presently in a gradual heightening of the excitement in the room, a phenomenon akin to the rise in temperature which, in fever, endeavours to match and subdue the alien germs at large in the system. Conversely, moral resistance was lowered, depreciating in ratio to the chances of self-preservation: it was as if the presence of an enemy bomber in the skies above changed all established values; as if under that menace only short-term values could prevail; and the girl, smiling intently into the man's eyes, was in a sense seduced, not by him but by the presence of danger, which, without striking, had already deflowered her.

> "I'll see you again
> Whenever spring comes round again. . . ."

Softly and sibilantly, the lance-corporal confided to the microphone the opening words of this ever-popular waltz. At the same time the lights were lowered; and a small glass-faceted globe, beginning to rotate, scattered about the floor and walls of the room moving flecks of light so that the room was filled, suddenly, with ghostly snowflakes that fell without settling or dissolving. At once, the floor was full of couples; turning, revolving; following the involute maze, the invisible text, of their own waltz-pattern. About them, the white flakes silently whirled; about them, each couple its pivot, the whole room revolved, turning faster and faster like a vast top stung by the lash of an irresistible rhythm.

Claudia knew that he would come for her. Although she could not see him, she knew that he would seek her out. During the whole evening he had avoided her, intentionally, perhaps: now, he would come. She sat beside Andrew looking straight before her: she did not speak: her heart was beating quickly.

He came at last. Without speaking, he stood over her. The moving lights dappled the tall form: cast fleeting shadows in which it was impossible to detect the expression on the long dark face. He stood there looking down, seeming to wait. Not a word was spoken, either by her or by Andrew, or by Captain Herriot himself. It was as if, in that involuntary silence, they acknowledged for the first time the nature of the situation between them: the pattern, the inner equation, concealed within the conventional outline of the so-called eternal triangle: that is to say, the polarity of the two men; the consequent tension between them: a tension that could only be resolved indirectly, through a medium distinct from and yet connected with them both: through the reactions, therefore, the decision, deliberate or unpremeditated, of Claudia Abbott.

"Will you dance?" Neil Herriot said. His voice sounded distant and withdrawn. Claudia got up. Without speaking, she laid her hand on his shoulder. Herriot lost no time. He encircled her with his arm. Gently, with the unmistakable authority of the experienced dancer, he drew her into the waltz rhythm, into his own personal measure. They mingled with, then disappeared amongst, the other dancers on the crowded floor. It was like being swept out to sea: at once the shore, its inhabitants, the life there, became remote: a horizon without imminence or importance. His right arm held her firmly against him, his hand was warm upon hers; dancing, she had no volition, she partnered his will, they glided and turned easily, swiftly, with a movement as of skating. All the while, the lights were muted, the impalpable snowflakes continued to fall. Seeing them fall across his face, his shoulders, she felt that he and she were hidden in a snowstorm; enclosed in one of these crystal globes that, when agitated, release a noiseless slow-settling shower of snow. . . .

Herriot laughed suddenly. He said, very quietly, "You are rather a darling, aren't you?" The comment reached her, flavoured with whisky. Claudia smiled dreamily. She accepted with a curious pleasure the banality of the remark; the second-hand mannerisms; the obviousness of his approach. And, of course, he had been drinking. Not that it mattered.

Presently, Herriot said, his breath warm against her ear "I asked you out to dinner once—do you remember?" He touched the rim of her ear with his lips. "I'd like to ask you again," he said.

"Why don't you?" Claudia heard herself say.

He raised his eyebrows at this. He laughed. "Well, you're such a peculiar young woman," he said. "You'd go and ask Andrew's permission, first." He looked down at her. "Wouldn't you . . . ?" Before she could answer, unexpectedly, his expression altered. He said to her, in quite a different voice: "Andrew doesn't approve of me, does he?"

Claudia was not listening. Languidly, she watched the snowflakes falling. "Who doesn't approve of you?" she said.

"Andrew."

"Andrew?" Claudia echoed. Not recognizing the anxiety, the motive underlying it, she was surprised at the question. "Why are we talking about Andrew?" she said.

"Why, indeed!" As if he had indirectly received the reassurance he needed, Herriot smiled. "You'll come, then," he said. It was a statement, not a question. His arm tightened about her. She became aware of the pattern of his body, imposed upon hers. She made no effort to withdraw or turn away: she made no effort of any sort: she accepted him, everything about him, his lack of principle, his irresponsibility, as an insomniac accepts sleep; accepts, after the weary self-imposed vigil, the peace of darkness.

On a high protracted note, the music suddenly ceased. The lights came on again, displacing the magic twilight, the hypnotic twirling snowflakes; revealing, without illusion, bald and platitudinous, the movements, faces, gestures, of the couples facing each other; marooned on what was all at once a derelict dance-floor. "Thank you," Herriot said to Claudia. He looked into her eyes for a moment, as if to remind her of a promise tacitly given. She said nothing. She left him and returned unaccompanied to Andrew, on the other side of the room.

He was as she had left him, still on his chair by the wall. He sat upright, his arms were folded across his chest: his lips had a calm and formal smile. Why, she thought, seeing the resemblance: why, he looks like his father; like the old man. . . . And she was disconcerted for a moment; as if a stranger judged her through his eyes. Then she smiled. "Hallo," she said. She sank into the chair at his side. She was warm; her eyes were glistening; her forehead, her palms, even the roots of her hair, were moist with sweat. Andrew, discerning the physical glow in her, saw that she was like wax, molten, receptive, ready for the seal: and he glanced stealthily at her as if he might read in her, already indelibly imprinted, the will and personality of another man.

Claudia laughed. "Heavens, I'm quite giddy. . . . It's ages since I danced the waltz."

"You both looked very expert, I thought."

"Oh," she said abruptly, not listening to him, fanning herself with her hand, "how hot it is in here. Can't they open a window, or something?"

"It is rather oppressive," Andrew said. "Let's go outside and get a breath of fresh air."

Suddenly, with alarming violence, the black-out shutters affixed to the long window rattled: the floor trembled: the lights flickered, went out, and then came up again. Claudia caught her breath. "That was a near one." She looked about the room. "Andrew—where's Honor?" she said sharply.

"Honor?" Andrew was surprised. "She went home some time ago. Didn't you see her?"

"No." Claudia frowned. "I hope she's all right," she said. "Honor's so nervous when there's a raid on." She paused. Then she went on, speaking rapidly, as if she could no longer trust to silence between them. "Or is it that we're all equally nervous, and won't admit it? All these people who seem so casual ... are they acting a lie, I wonder? Can people really be as unconcerned as they look?"

"I'm afraid they are," Andrew said. "And that's the trouble. That pukkha 'we can take it' attitude acts like morphia: it disguises the real meaning and message of danger. The spiritual warning—the reminder of the power of death. The siren should be like a tocsin; more compelling than church bells; a call to prayer, a reminder of our mortal state. Danger, in other words, should produce a spiritual renewal, not a social mannerism——"

Colin, who had been sitting at the bar with Colonel Mayne, rose suddenly and made his way towards them across the floor. "So there you are," he said. He spoke agressively, as if Claudia and Andrew had for some reason been concealing their presence from him. "What's become of Honor?" he demanded.

"Honor went home over an hour ago," Andrew said.

"Did she?" He frowned, squinting slightly. "Funny of her—to slip away like that—not say a word——" Colin had been drinking heavily. He was very pale, his hair was dishevelled, and his right eyelid drooped over the pupil in a sad and meaningless wink. Claudia, who disliked Colin when he was sober, averted her eyes from him, with the unwilling pity she felt for him now that drink, revealing him trivial and grotesque, unexpectedly exposed to her the defencelessness, the congenital innocence in all human nature. She turned away. "Come," she said to Andrew "Let's go outside, shall we?"

They crossed the room in silence. Then Claudia said: "Remember him as he used to be——?"

"Yes, I remember."

"It's unbelievable. The effect war has had on that man."

"Everyone has to seek out his salvation in his own way," was Andrew's comment.

"I should scarcely say it was salvation he was seeking——"

"Self-realization, then."

Claudia said nothing. As they passed the bar, the Colonel, who had not yet spoken to Claudia, lifted his head and looked attentively at her. He decided to recognize her. Smiling, he waved a thick-set hand in her direction. The Colonel's face was flushed, his eyes bright and injected: he was full, Claudia saw, of a dangerous, enveloping affability. She knew that affability; the power of it: she knew that Colonel Mayne could, if he so chose, draw her and Andrew too, unresisting, into his orbit: holding them there as long as the fancy took him, before suddenly, and with no perceptible reason or transition, losing interest in their company: at which point—with perhaps a cold glance, a sudden blankness—he would disavow the presence at his table of people he himself had invited to it. She skirted him therefore as she might the field of an enigmatic influence: distrustful of this man who used power over others to disguise a hidden weakness, the existence of which, in himself, he consistently refused to face or acknowledge.

Andrew opened the glass-panelled door: beyond it, a sort of booth made of plywood trapped the light. They stepped out onto the gravelled terrace. At once, the lighted room, the faces, the voices, were wiped from them: vanished, as if a slide had come down between them and even the recollection of such a room. The black-out preserved the frontier between the two worlds: divided, with a fanatical reticence, the light and animation on one side of the boundary from the calm and obscurity on the other. Not that it was altogether dark even here. Before them, the trees, the eccentric turrets, the sloping uneven grounds of the hospital stood, every contour intact, sealed within a moonlight sharp as frost. The moon itself, in full bloom, incomparably elevated and distant, lay. as if

tranced behind a veil of cloud, to the vaporous outline
of which it imparted a lambence soft and unstable as
mother-of-pearl.

A shadow fell upon the gravel at their feet. They looked
up. It was the Orderly Officer: the celibate Mr Creech:
standing not a yard away from them. They had not heard
him approach. He looked sideways at them under the
peaked cap, and in the moonlight Andrew observed
that the shape of the eye within the narrowed lids was
precisely that of a closed safety-pin. "Come out to see the
fire?" he asked them. They looked questioningly at him,
and Creech went on "Didn't you hear the crash just
now? A plane brought down—the Home Guard are
out——" He pointed. They turned. Behind them, a long
way away it seemed, a glow waxed and waned on the
horizon; growing taller, then seeming to shrink: an angry
inexplicable red: alien to the pervading moonlight.
"One of theirs?" Claudia said quickly.

"We don't know yet. I hope so." He looked from one
to the other. "But I musn't keep you," he said. And
before they could speak, as unobtrusively as he had come
Creech passed on: ostensibly to do a routine examination
of the hospital's black-out. "Queer fellow," Andrew said.
Claudia nodded. Side by side they leant on the long
balustrade: their arms on the grey stone; not touching.
Mysteriously adrift, the night air was clover-soft to the
senses. A bat swooped: came and went: startling as a
boomerang. They leant there, silent, not looking at each
other; waiting. Then Andrew said quietly, without
turning his head "Claudia—are you in love with
Herriot?"

There was a long pause: a pause neither of them
attempted to break: an acknowledged hiatus, the first, in
their relationship. Then Claudia spoke. Her voice was
unexpectedly sharp and high-pitched. "In love?" she
said. "How could I be in love with a man who stands for

everything I most dislike and disapprove of?" Andrew frowned: as if what she said had no bearing on the question he had asked her. "We were speaking just now of war giving people a chance to adjust——" he began.

"Yes?" She waited.

"But it sometimes happens that an individual may come along who seems to offer that chance in his own person." He paused. "It occurs to me that for you Herriot may be such a one——"

"No," Claudia interrupted, startled and hostile.

"Yes!" Andrew said sharply. Almost angrily, he overbore her resistance, her repudiation of the other man. "Claudia, don't fool yourself—or me. You've got to do this. It's vital for all of us that you should." He turned to her, then, and looked at her with a singular fixity. "You've got to find out who is the reality, as far as you're concerned —Herriot or me. Which is real to you—the life Herriot stands for—or the life I can offer you?" His face came close to hers; pale in the moonlight; the eyes wide and glittering. "I've got to know," he said. "You've got to find out, Claudia, and tell me. Do you understand? I've got to know."

She thought: It's as if he were trying to discover something, not about me, but about himself. ... And she reflected involuntarily that a year ago, before illness, affecting his heart, had tampered with the very mainspring of his existence, he would not perhaps have felt the need to ask her this question: to set her, to set himself, a challenge of this nature. She was silent, therefore: in that silence refusing to commit herself or jeopardize further her relationship with him. At the same moment the night air, shifting suddenly, brought to her nostrils, faint but unmistakable, the rankness of burning oil. She turned her head: on the horizon there still burned, remote and beautiful in the sky, the light of destruction.

CHAPTER TEN

THE ENEMY IN OUR MIDST

THE plane which was destroyed on the night of the dance was an enemy one. The crew baled out and were captured: later the pilot was found dead, furled in the silken shroud of his parachute. After a certain amount of delay and negotiation, the body was brought to the hospital; and it lay in the mortuary there for several days, a focus of intense, almost obsessive interest; until the parish of Linfield accepted the responsibility of burying it.

Edith, coming round the corner with the pram, the baby asleep on his sour-smelling pillow, Peter at her side, met the funeral procession in the High Street. Although neither the day nor the time of this event had been announced, for the past half-hour the pavements had been slowly filling in anticipation of it. Indeed, by now, everybody seemed to know exactly what the dead Nazi looked like; how old he was; where he came from; what he wore; what papers he carried: details of these— the photographs, letters, bread-tickets, identity cards— were a subject of open discussion not only in the hospital and the village but in the entire neighbourhood. The presence of the German airman in its midst had, in fact, a curious effect upon the community. As if reacting to the alien body it harboured, it broke out in certain very positive, albeit divergent reactions; it showed itself detached, non-committal: or full of angry resentment: or again of an almost feverish excitement and interest, which, by no means absent in men, was admittedly and demonstrably at its most acute in certain women.

"What is it, Edith? What is it?" Peter said, half frightened. Edith did not answer. Forgetful of the pram, of the presence of the children entrusted to her, of Mrs Carmichael's possible concern over the delay, she stood there: gazing not at the handful of men, constrained, in their official capacity to act as escort, but at the vivid red and black swastika; the enemy emblem draped over an unexpectedly small blunt coffin. The procession passed between the crowded pavements in absolute silence. Like Edith's, every eye was fixed in a look of mixed incredulity and fascination on the swastika. Here, tangible to them for the first time, was the enemy. Here were his emblems: here at last was his very body, which even in death had not lost the menace, the mysterious potency that enmity itself endowed it with. They gazed at the coffin; watched it pass along the High Street, and then across the big cobbled square. Rigid suddenly, no one moved: faces were set and impassive: there was an enforced suspension of all emotion, all judgment. Peter said nothing; he stared about him with wide frightened eyes. As for Edith, who knew no values, who, solitary, had nothing to lose or gain by the betrayal of her emotions, she gazed at the enemy coffin, at the strange device upon it; and as she did so there was in the glistening eyes, the uncouthly parted lips, unguardedly expressed, the very ecstasy of love itself.

Honor seized the small dangling acorn. She pulled the blind, transforming the room into an aquarium; full of green stilly light; of subdued reflections. Peter lay under the sheet in his shrunken pyjamas; his finger-nails raw from their weekly cutting; his hair damp still from the bath. "It's very late," Honor said. She bent to kiss him. "Good night." Mechanically she added "Be a dry boy, won't you." He watched her as she went towards the door. Livid as mercury in that half-light, his glance was erased, periodically, by rubber-soft lids. The door closed behind her. He sucked his thumb and plucked pieces of wool out of the blanket. Suddenly, he removed his thumb: he called out, softly but urgently "Mummy!" No one came. He sucked his thumb again and stared at the blind.

In her own room, untying the flannel apron from her waist, Honor gave a sigh of relief. She was finished, now, with the children until ten or eleven o'clock, when the baby would have to be fed again, and Peter lifted. The evening was before her: a few hours, if she was lucky, of relaxation with Colin. How she looked forward to this prospect: to the moment in which, whatever else may have absorbed him during the day, Colin's steps, his thoughts, oriented towards her, must in effect be homeward bound. She looked at herself in the mirror. Should she change her dress? She made no move to do so. The gesture was irrelevant. After seven years of married life, Honor no longer expected Colin to admire her; it was sufficient that in his own way and with no overt acknowledgment he needed her. . . . She went to the dressing-table and began to brush her hair. Slanting towards her in the big oval mirror she could see a picture of this room that she shared with him: the yellow carpet garlanded with roses; the marble wash-stand; the big old-fashioned bed with its claw feet, its ruched coverlet, its high-stacked pillows, that concealed, on the one side, her own night things, on the other, Colin's: his carefully chosen silk pyjamas, that she herself folded and put away every morning; in so doing, rediscovering, in a moment of dreamy pleasure, the evocative, highly individual smell of the night's intimacy.

Suddenly she stood motionless, the brush suspended in her hand. She stared into the sloping mirror. An image, not apparent in the mirror, had risen up to confront her. She saw the solitary bed; the wardrobe empty of Colin's suits; his brushes, combs and lotions gone from the dressing-table: the whole room, bereaved of his presence, standing blank and cold and numb. She caught her breath sharply. "No," she said, half aloud. Forcibly, before the suggestion had time to assert itself, she repulsed it; denying it even a foothold in her thoughts. This proposal that Colin should, at Mayne's instigation, leave her, go abroad for an indefinite period, was something that, after the first despairing outburst, Honor refused to talk, even to think about. She surprised everyone by the tenacity of her silence upon this subject. Even Colin failed to recognize the motive behind that fanatical reserve of hers. The fact was that Honor feared to admit even the possibility of such a thing taking place, because to admit it was to give that thing substance; to encourage about it the accretion of thoughts, plans, decisions which otherwise might well remain unformulated. In this she merely proved once again her innate distrust of the spoken word. This distrust was a characteristic thing with Honor. Meekly as she listened, for instance, to Claudia's advice about Colin, she never accepted it where it involved, as so much of Claudia's advice involved, challenge, mutual explanation. Her instinct here was perhaps a true one. So often, in an emotional relationship, to be articulate is to be in some degree destructive. If talking things over does, as Claudia liked to say, "clear the air," it also deprives it of a certain essential oxygen, and the final result may be not clarification alone, but impoverishment, resolution of conflict—no more than the calm of sterility achieved.

She put down the brush. Perfunctorily, she tidied the dressing-table and then the room itself; so as to give it, for Colin's benefit, an appearance at least, of order. She opened the door and listened: there was no sound from the children, asleep she hoped in their respective rooms. Downstairs, she could hear the faint tinkle as Edith in the kitchen washed the tea-things, or laid out on the trolley the knives and forks and spoons for the evening meal. Recalled to the subject of food, Honor frowned

slightly. Let me see, what was it we said . . . ? Oh yes:
macaroni cheese; then stewed cherries and custard. I
must remind her to brown the cheese well, he hates it
underdone. . . . See to that later. She went downstairs.
In the living-room, the french window stood open to the
calm evening. The scalloped roof of the veranda framed
a view so familiar to her senses that it seemed like part
of her own body. As always at this moment when the day
was preparing to relinquish its brightness, things seen had
a stereoscopic clarity: every blade of grass was distinct;
every outline (soon to be blurred and erased altogether)
vividly tattooed upon space. Never had the thorns looked
so sharp; the silhouette of leaves so emphatic; or colour
itself, decomposed by impending dusk, so sultry and yet
so fiery. It was as if an unseen hand had by twisting a
screw brought the whole scene, the imminence and
significance of matter, into sudden sharp focus. Honor
stood motionless; looking into the garden; lost in a deep
impersonal contemplation in which there was no longer
any known demarcation between her and the thing seen,
only a silent interchange in which her whole being was
gradually irrigated and renewed by the life of the leaves
and plants and grasses about her.

In the garden, something moved suddenly. There was a
flash of white; a rustle, rapid and furtive, in the bushes
by the summer-house. Honor started. What was that?
She turned her head. There was someone in the garden.
For a moment, she was irrationally frightened. Then,
before fear had time to take hold, she compelled herself
to investigate. Quickly, she went down the veranda
steps; with silent footsteps crossed the long overgrown
lawn. She reached the deserted chalet which served as a
summer-house. There was no one to be seen. She stood
still. "Who's there?" she called out. There was a pause.
Mastering her own fear "Who is it?" she repeated.

Close to her, the bushes rustled again: sharply she

turned her head. She saw Edith, standing motionless among the rose-trees at the side of the summer-house. Honor let her breath go in an involuntary exclamation: "Edith! Good heavens—how you frightened me, girl." She laughed at her own sense of relief. "What on earth are you doing there?" she said.

Edith did not answer. Across the small stunted rose-trees, she faced her employer with an expression which Honor had never seen in her face before: a look of anger, almost of hatred, as if Honor had practised upon her some intolerable intrusion. It was then that Honor noticed her attitude. All the while, Edith held one hand behind her back; stiffly, obstinately, as if she had in it something that must at all costs be concealed from view. "What's that?" Honor said brusquely. "What have you got there, Edith?"

There was a pause. Slowly, without speaking, Edith brought forth her hand from behind her. She was holding a small bunch of red and yellow rosebuds.

Honor was taken aback. "Roses?" she said. What she had expected, she did not know. "Aren't they pretty. . . ." Edith's expression changed. The rigidity of her pose was broken up; she muttered something and looked down at the ground at her feet. "What did you say?" Honor asked.

Edith's eyes were fixed on the ground. "He has no one to care about him," she said.

"Who?" Honor said, surprised.

Edith looked up. Her glance, meeting Honor's, became oblique, crafty, suddenly. "Him that was killed——"

"The airman?" Honor said, "You mean—the German——?"

"Yes."

"You want the flowers for him? For him, Edith——?"

"For his grave." Edith looked at the ground again. Her sallow face was slowly suffused with colour. Abruptly, she gave a deep hoarse sob.

Honor said quietly, "Of course, you can have the flowers, if you want them. Take as many as you like." It was she, now, who kept her eyes averted. She could not look at the roses in Edith's hand. Dedicated as they were, they represented a proliferation as pitiable as it was displeasing; a fungus growth of the emotions, uncouth, inexplicable. She said rapidly, and with the desire to absolve herself both of Edith's company and of all implication in the act she contemplated "You can have the evening off, if you like, Edith. Go to the pictures. There's nothing much to do: I can manage." As soon as she had spoken, she regretted her own offer. There—I've done it again. What if Colin wants to go out? Can't be helped, now. . . . She sighed, and went back slowly towards the house.

Colin hung his cap, his Sam Browne belt on the rack: from the table beneath, he picked up two circulars, re-addressed to him from Worthing; the familiar rolled baton of the *Lancet*. Irritably rubbing the imprint of his cap from his right eyebrow, he crossed the hall and pushed open the door of the living-room. "Good evening," he said.

Honor looked quickly at him. She could always tell (as she could tell, long before any one else, if Peter was about to be ill or not) what sort of day he had had at the hospital: what sort of evening, in consequence, she could expect to spend with him here at home. Of late, she knew, things had been going well with him: he had come back buoyant, full of elation, of a driving restlessness which he endeavoured, visibly, to temper by a solicitous and attentive manner towards his wife. This evening however, things were different. That much was obvious at once. There had been some change, some deterioration, some-where. Colin looked tired. His face was incongruously small and sensitive under the upstanding guardsman's

moustache that he had of late been cultivating. He made
no facetious comments, no jocular attempts to tease or
embrace her. Instead, he went to the sideboard, and,
frowning, started holding bottle after bottle up to the
light. "I thought we had some whisky left——"

"No," she said. "The other evening—don't you
remember?—they finished it——"

"Oh, yes," he said gruffly: "yes." He continued the
search, nevertheless. Over the big work-basket on her
knees, a familiar defensive position, a domestic strong-
point, she watched him without appearing to do so. "Had
a busy day?" she said tentatively.

"Fair." He poured himself out, without enthusiasm, a
glass of cooking sherry; all that now remained to them
of their original stock of wines. "The confounded funeral's
over, thank goodness. It's been getting on everybody's
nerves." He corked the bottle resentfully, with the flat
of his hand. "Couldn't keep people away from that
mortuary," he said. "Honestly—you'd think it was
Rudolph Valentino, or someone——"

Lowering her voice, Honor told him about Edith. He
looked at her, arrested. "How extraordinary," he said.
Although she waited upon him every day, he had never
before consciously considered the facts of Edith's existence.
He saw her face before him: that guarded evasive look
of hers. "It's a form of hate, really," he said: satisfied
at once with the truth of his own interpretation. "She
probably hates us all and feels the enemy is really her
ally."

"I don't see why she should hate us," Honor objected.
"We've always been good to her——"

"That's not the point." Colin sipped wryly at the
liquid in his glass. "It's much easier for some people to
love their enemies than their friends." He sighed, gloomy
again. "You've only got to read the daily papers to discover that peculiar fact about human nature."

Honor nodded, unperturbed. She looked round for her needle, her wool. Slipping the wooden mushroom into the heel of a sock, she began to darn; pricking the long needle in and out: resuming that essential maintenance and repair work, emotional no less than practical, which derives from the feminine desire to preserve at all costs the *status quo*. Colin, familiar with the sight of her thus engaged, and through familiarity no more conscious of her than of the reconstructive work of his own tissues, walked restlessly up and down the room. "That silly little twerp, Lloyd——" he said abruptly.

Honor looked surprised. "Lloyd?" she said. "Dick Lloyd? I thought you liked him."

"Oh, I *like* him, all right," Colin said irritably "I never said I didn't like him, did I? Only—he has his faults——"

"What's the matter with him all of a sudden?"

Colin turned. The light from the window fell on his face. In its pallor, there was a certain puttiness, unresistant, self-absorbed. "Oh, I don't know," he said. "The way he hangs round the C.O. for instance——"

"Yes?" Honor's voice was non-committal.

"Everyone notices it. It's positively sickening, at times. Always laughing at his jokes—sucking up to him——"

"Oh, yes," Honor said, mending steadily.

"How Mayne doesn't see through it, I don't know."

"Perhaps he does," Honor suggested.

"Well, it's about time he put him in his place, then."

Honor kept her eyes on the sock she was mending. "Does Mayne like him?" she asked.

Colin did not answer for a moment. Then, "He seems to," he said. "He's just taken him off with him to Oxford, for the evening."

"But I thought Mayne was taking *you* to Oxford, to-morrow——"

"So did I. But he's changed his mind, it seems."

"So suddenly?" Honor said. "Why?"

"You ask me that," Colin said bitterly. "Do you think I know? Do you think Mayne explains his real motives to any one?"

Honor repressed a faint sigh. Mayne, Mayne, always Mayne. . . . She reflected then that the position of a man placed in authority over others, over subordinates anxious to study his every whim and humour in order, in turn, to gain power over him, was not unlike that of a sheik with a harem of competitive wives: an unprogressive state of affairs, permitting, in default of exceptional integrity and will-power, a self-indulgence which in the end is destructive of that very power on which the relationship is based. Some men, it is true, are at their best in such service. Not so Colin. The emotional conditions governing the relationship had produced in him a rapid and unexpected deterioration: so that sometimes, hearing debated before her, for instance, the pros and cons of a State medical service (an idea with which she was otherwise in sympathy), she shuddered at the thought, after the war, of a renewal or prolongation of a situation tolerable to her only in virtue of its being a temporary one.

Colin walked up and down, biting his moustache. "They've gone to dinner somewhere, first," he said, "and then to that new show at the Playhouse——"

"How do you know?"

"Mayne was phoning up about it when I came into the office. He looked at me as if he had never seen me before, and wondered what I was doing in his room." His foot knocked against Peter's engine, sent it rolling noisily across the floor. He stared at it, frowning. "I sat next to him in the mess, to-day. He hardly said a civil word to me during lunch."

"It's just his manner. He doesn't mean anything by it." Honor spoke soothingly, like a wife consoling an errant husband for the infidelities of his mistress. . . . Except, she thought, that few women would dare reveal themselves, in the exercise of power over others, quite so capricious; in the demand for exclusive loyalty, so arbitrary. In that respect a commanding officer was to the average wife a rival whose range and scope, once recognized, she could not even aspire to emulate. . . .

There were footsteps in the hall outside, and then on the stairs. They heard a door open and shut. Honor raised her head. "Claudia's in," she remarked.

"She's late, isn't she?" Colin said without concern.

"She will be, all this week. End of term exams or something."

Presently, they heard her come downstairs again. The door opened and she came in. She had a letter in one hand; her attaché-case in the other. "Hallo," she said: she looked quickly from one to the other. Every evening, returning to the house, she expected to find in the situation between them a resolution of sorts; that Colin had admitted his desire for freedom; that Honor had finally accepted or rebelled against the prospect of his departure: instead, each time there was the same deadlock, the same tension, unrelieved and unexpressed: Colin's restlessness, Honor's silence and impassivity. It can't go on, she thought once again: it can't go on like this much longer. . . . Aloud, she said "This weather—the heat. I'm worn out." She put her case down on the table and examined curiously the letter she held in her hand. "Wonder who this is from," she said. She sat down and ripped open the envelope.

There was a silence. Honor, looking up, was startled by the expression on her sister's face. "What is it, Claudia?" she said quickly. Claudia did not answer. "Is anything the matter?" Colin raised his head, and looked enquiringly from one to the other.

Finding their eyes upon her, pinning her down as it were, Claudia gave a small deprecating laugh. Under the ochre face-powder she affected in summer, her face was a queer colour. "I don't know," she said "I don't know what to say, really. . . ." She looked at the letter in her hand. Visibly she hesitated, fearing perhaps for reasons of her own to invoke their judgment: then, with an air of embarassment she handed across the table a small sheet of note-paper "What do you make of this?" she said. Honor laid down her darning, she took the proffered letter. Colin came across the room to read it over his wife's shoulder. On a sheet of mauve lined note-paper in uneven, laboriously disguised handwriting were the words "Steer clear of a certain party, you know who, and maybe you know why." That was all: no address; no signature; no date.

For a moment, nothing was said. Then Honor folded the letter and handed it back to Claudia. Their eyes met. "What does it mean?" Honor said.

"I wish I knew."

"Let's see the envelope." Colin picked it up and examined it carefully. "Posted yesterday in Oxford," he said. "Who on earth——?" He did not finish. "You can always take it to the police, of course," he said. He looked curiously at her.

Claudia did not answer. She sat holding the letter before her; a brooding look on her face. "It gives one such an odd feeling," she said slowly. "Like being spied on in the bath, or something——"

Colin shrugged his shoulders. "You know what a village is—what *this* village in particular is—for gossip. You can't blow your nose without every one commenting on the fact."

"All the same, why should——? I don't understand——" Abruptly, Claudia tore the letter across. "Well, I'm not going to bother my head about it," she said decisively. "Let them gossip. I've other things to think about." Shifting the small locks under her thumb, she clicked open her attaché-case and drew out a pile of exam papers in a buff-coloured folder. She uncapped her red-ink fountain-pen. "The Main Causes of the Thirty Years War——" she read. Her attention wavered. Pen in hand, she sat gazing before her with a fixed and aimless expression. "Any one phone for me?" she asked suddenly.

"No," Honor said, "no one."

Claudia looked sharply at her. "Perhaps Edith took the message——?"

"No. I was here all the time." Honor did not raise her eyes from her mending. "Were you expecting something——?"

Claudia turned her head away. "No," she said. "No. Nothing. I just wondered, that's all." She sat digging the nib of her pen into a sheet of ink-speckled blotting-paper. Suddenly, she sighed deeply. "Oh dear—I wish I was a hundred miles from here," she said unexpectedly.

Honor paused, needle in hand. "Why?" she asked.

"Oh, I don't know——" Claudia did not look at her. "I believe the climate of Gloucestershire doesn't agree with me, or something." She sighed again. "I wish to goodness the war was over and the school would move back to London, and everything was normal again," she said.

"Don't we all?" Colin said.

There was another silence. Honor, with her small embroidery scissors, clipped the frayed edges from a patch she was inserting in Peter's trousers. Colin sat down in a corner and buried himself behind the evening paper. And Claudia, perforce, returned again to the causes of the Thirty Years War in Europe. Four or five times, without understanding it, she read the same phrase. There was it seemed a glaze on the familiar words, a treacherous surface on which attention skidded and could not grip. With a conscious effort, sharpening attention to a gimlet point, she managed at last to penetrate that glaze: to understand and assess what she was reading. But the process fatigued her. In the ordinary way, Claudia enjoyed teaching: she liked the desiccated, stimulating atmosphere of the class-room; the complete if temporary sequestration from the outside world: without altogether knowing it, she derived a certain strength and compensation from the artificial world created and maintained about adolescence; a world in which, with a minimum of resistance, she was able to impose upon others the characteristics of her own will and judgment. She disliked the process only at the end of term, during examination time; when, forced to examine, as she might a pile of negatives, the blurred imprint of her own teaching, she discovered in the slavish mimicry of her own phrase, her own point of view, not, as it might seem acquiescence and receptivity; but rejection, hostility, an occult and wholly intractable form of rebellion.

The phone began to ring. Claudia dropped her pen: involuntarily, she made as if to rise from the chair. But Colin had forestalled her. "I'll go," he said. Swiftly, he crossed the room. In the hall, the ringing stopped suddenly "Hullo . . . ?" They heard, through the closed door, the hope, the excitement in that query. Honor's needle flagged, she looked for a moment older, very tired. There was silence in the room. Then Colin reappeared. Both women looked expectantly at him. Aware of this scrutiny, Colin frowned. He advanced into the room, leaving the door open. Without turning to her, he said, in that tone of resentment with which people summon others to the telephone "It's for you, Claudia."

"For me?" Claudia pushed back her chair. "It's Andrew, I expect——"

"No," Colin said sullenly. "It's not Andrew."

Claudia got up without a word. As she left the room, she closed the door behind her, unobtrusively but firmly. Husband and wife glanced significantly at each other. "Herriot?" Honor said, lifting her brows. Colin shrugged his shoulders. "Very likely. I didn't stop to ask——"

"Hullo? Yes . . . ?" Through the door, they could hear her voice, sharp with what seemed unnecessary challenge. "Who . . . ? Who . . . ? No, I can't. I'm not good at guessing. . . . Oh, it's you, is it . . . ? That's funny. It didn't sound like you. . . ." Irritably, Colin rattled his newspaper, as if to disassociate himself from a conversation he could not help overhearing. "Me? So-so. . . . Well, not too good. . . . I don't know. Overworked, probably. . . ." There was a perceptible pause. "What, now? Now, you mean . . . ? No, I don't think I can. Not at a moment's notice, like this. . . ." Another pause. "Are you? So soon? I didn't know. . . ." In an altered voice. "But I don't understand. . . . Important . . . ? As important as all that . . . ? Oh, dear——" A deep harassed sigh. And then a sudden change of manner. "Very well, then. . . . Yes. Yes, I will. Yes, if you like. . . . I'll be there. . . . Right. . . ." The click of the receiver told the couple in the room that the conversation was at an end.

The door opened. Claudia came in. They were astonished at the change in her appearance. All trace of fatigue, of irritability, had gone. Her eye was alert, her step springy. It was as if she had recovered spontaneously from that state of indecision and inward confusion which, like a pernicious anæmia, had lately sapped all power to judge, to concentrate, to act. Without a word she went straight across to the table, and began putting her papers together. Gathering up the examination sheets quickly, methodically, she returned them to their buff-coloured folder. She replaced her books, pens, pencils, in the attaché-case and shutting the lid, snapped the locks to,

briskly, one after the other. Only then did she look up.
"I've got to go out," she said. "I won't be long. Not more
than half an hour, probably. Don't wait for me, if I'm
late...."

CHAPTER ELEVEN

OBSTACLE COURSE

HE sat waiting in the narrow window-seat. The bar
parlour was deserted. A long ray of evening sunlight, striking through the mullioned windows, flashed
brittle, on glasses and tankards standing empty on
window-ledges or tables; abandoned there when the
muffled booming of the gong eventually summoned
patrons to seek, in the hotel itself, or outside it, their
evening meal. He sat without moving, staring fixedly
before him. Out of the laden ash-tray on the table there
crawled, sluggish as thought, a slow blue smoke. On the
opposite wall, with pointed nose and snake-spotted belly,
the champion fish basked in his sealed tank. A wasp
seethed angrily, adrift in beer-dregs: above his head a
choir of flies occupied the low ceiling. From the whole
room, from the walls, the floor, the very chairs and
tables, there rose up a flavour of alcohol: as if through-
out the years they had been steeped in that element,
seasoned through and through in the persistent, the
recurring, emanations of beer and whisky and gin.

Without warning the metal rings over the door
rattled. He started. Claudia, drawing aside the heavy
curtain, met a glance so defensive and hostile that she
halted in the doorway, uncertain whether to advance or
retreat. Then she saw that it was not, as she had supposed,

directed at her. It was the glance of a man on the alert
for an enemy; and for an enemy whose face, for some
reason, has not yet been disclosed to him. "Hallo," she
said tentatively: with her smile, she introduced herself,
reassuring him as to her identity. The white teeth flashed:
a belated response. "Hallo," he said. He half rose in his
seat to greet her.

Reassured, she came forward. But when she sat down
beside him, leaning her arms on the table and glancing
expectantly at him, the smile died again from his face.
Under her scrutiny, he looked about him restlessly. She
had the impression that despite his pleasure at seeing her
he was uneasy, depressed; and this mood communicated
itself to her; damping the elation with which, succumbing
to an unusual impulse, she had come out to meet him.
"I can't stay long," she said, a little stiffly.

"All right." He did not look at her. "What'll you
drink?" he asked.

"Anything you like. Sherry, if there is any——"

He left her and went over to the counter. Mrs Stafford,
busy at that hour supervising the dinners in the dining-
room, looked in briefly to take his order. *Coiffure* high-
swept, emaciated body zipped-to in managerial satin, she
poured out sherry for Claudia and a double whisky for
Herriot. "See the funeral this afternoon?" she said. "To
think that we have to pollute our earth with the likes of
that . . . !" Herriot cleared his throat. "Yes, indeed," he
said. Claudia did not speak. The glasses clinked as, side
by side, Mrs Stafford pushed them across the counter.
"Well, I'll love you and leave you," she said. Her
colourless eyes darted from one to the other. "Be good,"
she said archly. And off she went. Her pointed heels
rattled as she hurried along the uneven passage leading to
the dining-room. A door opened. There was a sudden
clatter of forks and voices: a smell of mint sauce, of hotel
gravy. Then the door swung shut again, cutting off from

them the voices, the presence of other people. Claudia looked about her uneasily. It gave her a curious feeling of isolation to be sitting here in this fashion while other people, eating a meal at the accepted time, conforming to the normal pattern of existence, were linked in a solidarity she felt for the first time to be exclusive and condemning.

Herriot sipped at his whisky. The quietness of the room did not seem to oppress him. On the contrary. He became suddenly more cheerful. Turning to her, he put his arm over the back of her chair. His eyes, dark under the stained lids, looked into hers. "So you didn't mind me phoning you, then?" he said.

"No, of course not." She was afraid of that wheedling tone. "Is it true you're leaving?" she said.

"Quite true."

She twisted her glass about on its small pedestal. "Soon?" she managed to say.

Herriot looked indifferently at her. "To-night," he said.

"To-night . . . !" Her voice betrayed her, high-pitched. To her own vexation a wave of colour swept her face. Herriot seemed not to notice. "That's right," he said. "To-night's the night. I'm off. On the nine-twenty, to be exact."

"But I thought——" She hesitated, and looked away. "It's all very sudden, isn't it?" she said.

"Sudden? Not a bit. I've been expecting it for some time." He put down his glass. "Naturally, you understand, one can't publicize these things——"

"Naturally. All the same, I——"

He was not listening. "To tell you the truth," he said, "I'm not sorry to get away." He frowned at the brassy liquor encircled in his glass. "Between you and me and the lamp-post, I was getting a bit fed up with this job. Training to meet the enemy, talking of the enemy, thinking about the enemy—and never meeting him face to face—well, you rot. Either you begin to feel he doesn't exist at all—or he becomes such a powerful mysterious monster that your one fear in life is the prospect of having to meet him."

She raised her head. " *You* say that," she said, "*you*——" Accusingly, almost, she glanced at the flash on his sleeve.

He saw the direction of her glance. "That's just it," he said quickly. "All these fake obstacle courses—they get you down in the end. The make-believe assault courses pretending to be the real thing. And the testing—the continual testing. Takes it out of you. I'll be glad to see a spot of action again. The real thing." His voice changed, "Landing on enemy soil, forcing your way in, getting physically to grips with the enemy, feeling him, grappling with him, knowing him——" He laughed, a curious sound. "The relief of it. You can't imagine. The best, the simplest escape of all——"

"Escape?" she said sharply. "From what?"

He shrugged his shoulders. Claudia saw the gesture: quickly she lowered her eyes. There was a long pause. Somewhere in the hotel, a door opened and shut. "Tom!" called a voice, remote but peremptory. At an angle on the wall opposite, the evening sunlight hung like a faded poster. Flies skimmed the ceiling, tapping inconsequently at the discoloured plaster. Claudia lifted her head. She watched the light fretful minuet; the forked skirts, the hair-frail feet of the dancers. "Why did you ring me up this evening?" she asked suddenly.

In the act of raising his glass to his lips, Herriot paused. Without turning his head: "Because I wanted to see you," he said. "I had to see you again."

"You said it was important——"

He put the glass down. "I had to see you," he repeated. "Don't you understand? I couldn't go away unless I did."

She did not move. "Why?" she asked.

"Because," he said then—he spoke quickly, almost resentfully—"there are certain things that have got to be cleared up between us, and you know it."

Her eyelids flickered. "You've left it very late," she said.

He turned to her, at that. "So have you," he said. He sighed. Once more, his arm came over the back of her chair. "Why have we been avoiding each other like this?" he said.

"Have you been avoiding me?" She smiled, in spite of herself. "I hadn't noticed it."

"Yes," he said, "I've been avoiding you by trying to make love to you whenever we met. In other words, by treating you like everybody else."

"And now?" she said. She raised her long eyebrows. "Aren't you making love to me?"

"No," he replied. He removed his arm from the back of her chair. "I'm trying hard not to. It's my last chance. This time, I don't want it to come between us."

Claudia gazed at him. "Do you know," she said slowly, "you're an extraordinary person. I believe you're really very clever——"

"Me?" he ejaculated. "Heaven forbid! Don't you go accusing me of anything like that. I'm only a rough soldier."

She paused. "Are you?" she said, looking intently at him.

He bent towards her. "That's what you want me to be, isn't it?" he said.

There was a sudden silence. "Isn't it?" he repeated softly. His eyes measured her, tried to force from her an acknowledgment. And then he laughed. "Darling!" he said. "You are a funny girl, really you are. I've never met anybody so painfully respectable in all my life—— So afraid of yourself—and of everybody else——"

A car door slammed a yard from the window. Glad of

the diversion, Claudia turned her head. Between the small chintz curtains, she caught a glimpse of an elderly officer, thick-set, his cane cocked under one arm. The beaked nose, bright congested face were familiar. "Look who's here," she said.

At her bidding, Herriot turned. He glanced out of the window but made no comment. She was surprised at his lack of response. "Surely that's Colonel Llewellyn? Isn't he with you on the Officer Selection Board?" she said.

There was a slight pause. Then "Llewellyn it is," Herriot said rapidly, "and what's more, he's coming straight in here, the old toper." He drank up the remainder of his whisky. "Come on," he said. "We don't want him to corner us here. He'll stick with us the whole evening. Drink up—we'll go out by the side entrance."

Claudia hesitated. "It's late," she said, "I think I ought—they'll be expecting me——"

Without listening, Herriot took her hand. He drew her after him into the small white-washed passage. "We're going for a walk," was all he said. Claudia nodded. She followed him obediently.

In the meadow, a shire horse browsed, ponderously lifting its fringed hooves, rupturing the grass with great stained teeth; pausing occasionally with a patient tormented air to repel with a quick tremor of the sweat-glazed skin the Braille-like tracery of flies.

"Come," Herriot said. He extended his hand, and Claudia climbed over the wooden stile. Jumping, her heels sank into the uneven turf. The horse raised its head and gazed at them; dark hair hanging in ringlets between the pointed cornets of its ears; lip as long and cold and fringed as that of Abraham Lincoln. Beyond, the stream flowed dilatory between webbed reeds; between willows that trailed their branches to the water's edge, as if curious

to discover and assess the nature of their own reflection.
In the flaming sky, a company of rooks chattered for a
moment like castanets and then were gone. Gnats
danced in the air: flies, at their approach, rose, abuzz,
from horse-dung crusted in the grass. Noiseless, fish-
lips kissed the surface of the stream: a ring of water
dilated and vanished. The sun had set by now, but so
recently that there was a bloom still about the evening,
a heady glow, as if an etherous wine dazzled the senses.
For a timeless moment, the physical world stood revealed,
bathed in a glow from a sun already set: illumined, down
to the smallest detail, in breath-taking and melancholy
beauty, by a light from the past.

"What a lovely evening," Claudia said in a quiet
voice.

"Yes, isn't it?" Herriot glanced at the sky, then looked
away again, as if something about it, the very serenity
perhaps, unnerved him. With sudden anxiety, he tapped
at the face of his watch: held it to his ear. "Stopped," he
said, "what a nuisance. Musn't miss my train." He
sighed. "Time's getting short. . . ." Claudia glancing at
him saw that his face had fallen into heavy preoccupied
lines. How different he looks, she thought, startled.
Older. Much older. And tired. All the resilience gone.
Before this altered expression of his, she was aware of a
certain dismay: she looked diffidently at him and did not
know what to say. Silent, the two of them, they walked
along, watching the water flow, oil-slow, between its
banks. They came to a second stile. Herriot stopped.
"What, another?" he said. He grinned: all at once, the
heavy lines vanished, his face was restored to its old contours. "Can't get away from obstacle courses, it seems."
Cheerful, now, he gave her his hand. "Over you go," he
said. And "Steady does it." She jumped. "Nice going,"
he commented: "exhibits definite Officer Quality," He
looked banteringly at her. "You should be in the A.T.S.,

he said, "a girl like you. You've got the temperament—
and the figure." He approached his lips to her ear. "Why
don't you come out of that schoolroom of yours, and take
a look round? It's well worth doing, believe me. After
all, there may not be another war." Her hand was still
clasped in his: she made as if to withdraw it: he tightened
his grasp. "Oh, no you don't." he said: "Behave yourself." Unexpectedly, Claudia laughed. "That's better,"
he said. Hand in hand, they walked along the bank. They
had not gone very far however, when Claudia suddenly
stopped. "Look," she said in a voice of concern "Whatever's that?"

Herriot too stopped.   Before them, the grass was
scorched, plants and bushes withered and charred, the
very earth branded, the dust ashen. As far away as five
or six fields off, hedges were singed, the lower branches
of trees blackened, the topmost leaves hanging brown and
shrivelled as though a premature autumn had descended
to blight them. It was as if, by some ruthless surgery, the
earth had been cauterized, so that within that charred
and sterile dust the germ of life was now extinct for ever.

"What is it?" Claudia said, wide-eyed. "What
happened?"

"Why, the plane, you know," Herriot said. He stirred
a lump of charred wood with his toe, experimentally.
"This is where the Jerry plane crashed, the other night."

"Oh," Claudia said. Instinctively, she drew back. She
could not bring herself to step on that ashen dust. She
looked at Herriot. "They baled out, didn't they?" She
hesitated. "But the pilot—was it here——?" She stopped,
and looked with pinched brows at the desolation before
her; the signature of violence stamped into the mild
Gloucestershire earth. Herriot was watching her. "You
don't like to see that, do you?" he said suddenly.

"*Like* to see it? Of course not. No civilized person——"

"Quite," he said. "It stinks in your nostrils. And do

you know why?" He took her arm in his. "Because you're responsible for it. Yes, you, Claudia. You may not know it, but it's you, and people like you, who do all the damage."

"I?" Claudia said, stiff lipped. "I hate violence. I've always hated violence, in any form."

"Have you? Then why do violence to yourself, to your own nature, all the time?"

"I believe in self-control, if that's what you mean——"

He laughed. "And do you think self-control isn't a form of violence? The most destructive form of all, sometimes. As I know, to my cost. . . ." He turned away from her, and said in a low voice "Murder will out—don't forget that."

There was a silence. "Let's turn back," Claudia said. "I'm tired."

"Oh, no," Herriot said, sharply and resolutely. "You can't turn back now." Her arm was still linked in his. He tightened his grip, imprisoning her. "Let's go and sit down for a bit," he said. "I want to talk to you."

In silence, they settled themselves on the bank of the stream: scorched earth, charred sticks, on one side of them: on the other, green leaves, bright living grass. A cow stood in the stream, head bent, lipping the coldness; its udder hung beneath it, studded with teats: like a mine, Claudia thought. . . . At her side, Herriot flung pebbles into the stream: accurately, viciously: startling the cow. Claudia waited. Without preamble "I shan't be joining my unit at once," he said. "I'm going to Oxford first, and then to London for a few days."

"I see," Claudia said.

He held a stone in his right hand, weighing it. "If I asked you to join me—at an hotel in London, say—would you come?"

She did not move. "Is that what you're asking me to do?" she said.

"I'm suggesting it."

"Why?"

He turned to her. "Because we might as well settle this—this thing between us—once and for all."

"And Andrew," she said. "Aren't you forgetting him?"

He looked swiftly at her. "No," he said. A curious expression came into the dark eyes. "I'm not forgetting Andrew," he said. And a silence fell between them: a sudden inertia. Each waited for the other to speak. Herriot flung his stone into the stream. It sank with a faint gulp. Ripples ran widening to either bank. "Are you going to marry Andrew?" he said abruptly.

"You know I am."

He kept his eyes on the stream. "Are you living with him?" he asked.

She flushed. "You've no right to ask that."

He saw the flush. "What are you ashamed of?" he said roughly. "Of your own virginity?" Before she could answer, he gripped her arm. "Why do you want to marry him?" he said. "What can a marriage like that offer you? You know the truth of the situation. Why do you persist?" The grip tightened on her arm. With surprising vehemence: "What is it, then—what is it—this power he has over you?" he said.

"You're hurting my arm." Claudia spoke coldly. Herriot laughed. He released her. Calm again, leaning back on one elbow, he considered her. "Well?" he said. "Come on, let's have it. Explain the mystery." He raised his brows. "Or is it merely because he's a gentleman?" he said. "Is that it?" Claudia did not reply. He looked banteringly at her. "No? Because he has blue eyes, then. Or because he got a first in Greats. Ah, now we're on the right track. Of course. The marriage of true minds. The Intellectual's Love-call. The Highbrow yearning for its Mate. . . ." He gave a great guffaw of laughter. "Heaven preserve us!" he said. Sitting up, he stretched deeply:

drawing the air into his lungs: doubling his fists. "Seriously, Claudia, you're making a great mistake," he said. "You've got hold of the wrong end of the stick. Don't you know what sort of a world you're living in? The day of the intellectual is over——"

"Not over," she said. "Just beginning."

Herriot smiled. "Obstinate to the last." Lazily, he put his arm out and drew her to him. Claudia stiffened, but offered no other resistance. With a sort of desperation she accepted his embrace. For a moment he considered, detachedly, her closed eyes, tortured brows. Then he bent over her. Softly, tentatively, his mouth hovered upon hers; settled; opened with slow deliberation in the rite of a kiss. The resistance went out of her, momentarily he had her full weight on his arm. Then she broke away. She sat back in the grass and gazed at him. Her face, her whole expression, was transformed. Her mouth looked curiously swollen: the deep-set eyes were tawny with a colour he had never seen in them before.

Herriot said softly "So I was right. You are human after all. . . ." There was a note of self-congratulation in his voice. He had succeeded: he had proved something, if not to her, at least to himself. He smiled with satisfaction. And then, without perceptible transition, a light gradually fading, the triumph in his eyes was replaced by a look of aimlessness; of sudden lassitude. He stared at the blighted trees on the other side of the hedge. At the same time, vacantly, without knowing that he did so, he hummed to himself between his teeth "*You can't say no to a soldier.* . . ." Presently, he gave a sigh, and reaching out, took her hand in his. "You'll come to London with me darling, won't you?" He looked into her face, serious, unsmiling. Slowly, flexing his thumb, he caressed the smooth skin on the back of her palm. "You will come, won't you? Just the two of us. Away from everyone and everything. . . ."

Claudia did not answer. Lips parted, eyes fixed, she had the calm replete look of a sleeper. He insisted. "You'll come?" he said. "You'll come with me?" Claudia stirred. Belatedly, she discovered that her hand was locked in his. She looked down. Lying in her lap, covering hers, she saw the agile native-like hand: the wrist, emerging from the khaki cuff, covered with crisp dark hairs; the same hairs springing, dark, on the back of the hand, along each finger. Like an ape, she thought. And all at once, an expression of panic crossed her face. "No," she said. Blindly, she drew her hand out of his. "No," she said. "No, leave me alone."

Herriot was not disconcerted. "What's the matter?" he said. "Don't you want to come with me?"

"Go with you?"

"To London. . . . Or we'll stay in Oxford, if you prefer. Anywhere you like."

Claudia went suddenly pale. "You know very well I can't do that," she said.

He raised his eyebrows. "What's to stop you?"

For a moment she did not answer. Her head was averted. Then. "You're asking too much of me," she said. "Don't you realize? I hardly know you."

"You hardly know me," he said. "But that's not the point. Do you know yourself?" He leaned towards her. "Do you?" And then, as she did not answer "Isn't it about time you made your own acquaintance, Claudia?"

"No," she said. "Please. It's impossible. Don't say anything more about it."

He frowned. "I thought you had the courage of your own convictions——"

"I have. That's why I won't come."

"The courage of your own nature, then," he said in a low, caressing voice. "The courage to be yourself. Isn't that equally important?"

"No," she said. Lifting her head she spoke quickly,

emphatically. "It's not. On the contrary. We've got to learn how *not* to be ourselves—to have the courage, the strength to be something else. Otherwise there never *will* be any progress. I mean that with my whole heart," she added.

"So that's your philosophy of life, is it?" A curious smile, that she remembered later, crossed his face. "Well," he said, "I'm not sure that I don't agree with you. Why not? Why shouldn't life be a glorified fancy-dress ball?"

"That's not what I meant——"

He shrugged his shoulders. "Let's not waste time talking." He took her hand in his and endeavoured to draw her to him. Sharply, this time, she resisted him. After a moment he let her go. "All right," he said, "all right. I'm not insisting. . . ." He looked into her face and smiled. Slowly, nodding his head "I begin to understand," he said.

"What?" Claudia faced him, hostility in her eyes.

"I asked you just now why you wanted to marry Andrew Peirse," he said. "Remember? You wouldn't answer. Well, now I don't need to ask. I know." He grinned. "No one else can be relied upon to frustrate you quite so effectively——"

"You're talking nonsense," Claudia said, very angry. "You know nothing at all about Andrew."

"You're not trying to tell me that in private life this lawyer of yours is just a great big reckless cave-man——!"

"Please leave Andrew out of this."

He laughed. "Precisely what I'm trying to do," he said. "Fighting tooth and nail, in fact, to keep him out." The smile died from his face. "Seriously, Claudia," he said. "I like you. Let's put it no higher than that. I can't let you make a marriage like this. A girl like you." He stared at the singed trees; his brows drew together. "You don't realize what you're doing," he said. "Throwing yourself away. Turning your back on life. A marriage like that—what can it offer you? Security. But you can pay too much for security. Don't you understand? This marriage will be a sham—a charade—a pretty grim one, in the end. It'll get you down in time—like a wasting illness. Believe me, Claudia, you don't know what you're in for."

She looked curiously at him. "I've never asked you this," she said. "Are you married?"

"No," Herriot said. He paused: changed his mind, and said abruptly "That's to say, yes, I am in a way. Or rather I was. Once. For about six months. But that's a long time ago." He looked restlessly about him. "All over and done with, years ago."

"And the girl," Claudia ventured "is she——?"

"I told you," Herriot said angrily "That's all over and done with. She married someone else. I've never seen or heard of her, since."

"I'm sorry," she said then. "But don't you see? That's what I mean. I know so little about you——"

He raised his eyebrows. "I offered you the means of finding out more," he said. "But you turned it down." He darted a glance at her. "Didn't you?" he said.

Claudia looked at the ground. "Must you go to-night?" she said suddenly.

"I'm afraid I must." He gave an unexpected, biting laugh. "Circumstances over which I have no control——"

"You said you were having a few days leave, first."

"There's someone I must see in Oxford to-morrow morning. I'm sorry—I can't tell you more than that. You understand."

"Oh, yes," she said. "Of course." She paused. "And then?" she said.

"Oh, then I shall have lunch, and go up to town some time in the afternoon. Early enough to get dinner and do a show, probably." He looked slyly at her. "What would you like to see? Something rowdy, or a nice little drawing-room comedy?"

"No," Claudia said. "Don't. Not again. I told you once. It's impossible.

"Where there's a will there's a way, my dear."

"There *is* no way——"

"No will either?"

Claudia turned her head away. "Well," he said, shrugging his shoulders, "in that case—what's to be done?"

"Nothing," Claudia said in an unnatural voice. "Nothing. We must go our separate ways."

Herriot was silent for a moment. He looked quickly at her. "There *is* another alternative, of course," he said. An equivocal expression played about his lips. "I might have thought of it earlier."

"An alternative to what?"

"To your marrying the lawyer."

She looked up suspiciously. "What's that?" she said.

"You could marry me instead."

There was a prolonged silence. Herriot broke it. "Well, say something," he exclaimed. "React. You can't receive a proposition like that in stony silence." He laughed. "Aren't you at least a trifle flattered?" he said.

"No," Claudia said slowly. "But Andrew might be."

"*Andrew?*"

"That you were ready to go to such lengths to compete with him. . . ."

"To be honest," Herriot said rapidly, "the proposition is not quite as good as it sounds. I mean, of course, that as things are, I'll probably be killed within the next eight weeks, or so." He smiled. "Death permits of a certain irresponsibility. Even with regard to marriage. When it comes to the point—as the slogan says—I have nothing to lose but my chains!"

Claudia did not reply.

"Well," he said, looking at her. "What about it? The offer, though you may not think so, is quite as generous as Andrew's. Indeed it's very similar in some ways. Your situation as my wife, I admit, may leave something to be desired, but as my widow, it would be quite impeccable. I can do that, at least—make an honest widow of you." He grinned. "You might consider it. The position would have all the advantages of marriage to Andrew, and none of the drawbacks."

Uneasy, suddenly, Claudia looked about her. The sun had disappeared altogether. Light, fading from the sky, drew in its wake the long encroaching shadows. Perceptible, a silence began to settle; occupying the valley, the fields, even the tree-tops, where the high-pitched squealing of birds was all at once stilled. Claudia turned her head: there was no one to be seen: even the angler at the bend of the stream had disappeared. The sense of isolation that she had experienced in the parlour of the Trout returned to her intensified. "What time is it?" she asked abruptly.

"Time?" Herriot checked a movement of his wrist. "I don't know. My watch has stopped."

"It must be getting late."

"Does it matter?"

"Honor doesn't know—she'll be expecting me——"

"Right," Herriot said promptly. He rose: dusting the grass from his thighs, setting the green beret at its accustomed angle over his brow. He turned to her. "Come," he said. Lightly, grasping both her hands in his, he pulled her to her feet. "Ups-a-daisy," he said. For a moment they stood facing each other. Nothing was said. Then gently, Herriot drew her to him. "It's good-bye then, is it?" he said. He looked intently into her face. "Is it, Claudia?"

"I suppose so."

He gave a sudden robust laugh. "Did you think I'd give up so easily? . . ." She did not answer, and stooping, he put his lips to her right ear. "The Golden Shield Hotel, in Oxford," he said quickly and distinctly. "Join me there about four o'clock to-morrow afternoon, and we can have tea together before catching the train for London. . . ."

CHAPTER TWELVE

CHOICE

AT ten o'clock punctually the doors were thrown open. The small file of men, lounging in the passage outside and engaged in desultory talk, straightened their backs, abandoned the topic in hand, and began to move forward. The light from the big circular window above illumined the butcher blue of the jackets; the vivid red ties; the startling whiteness of a limb bandaged or in plaster. It played on the hollow cheerful faces; on ears pale or suffused, distinct on the close-cropped heads. Book in hand, each man made his way through the open doors into the room now set apart as a Red Cross library. Twice a week, on Wednesdays and Saturdays, this library was open to patients and staff. Lady Brent, and under her a rota of voluntary helpers, had undertaken the task of cataloguing and distributing the books allocated to the hospital. Prompt to time on those particular days, the young women concerned were to be seen cycling up the drive, one hand grasping the handlebars, the other modestly restraining the hem of a skirt over labouring knees. It was a spectacle that enlivened the convalescence of many: in particular, of the two wards, Kitchener and Timoshenko, that overlooked the hospital grounds. The overwhelming popularity of the library as an institution was not, however, to be attributed solely to such stimula-

tion: or even to the drawing power of literature itself.
That small sunny room, smelling of pasteboard, of
linoleum, of the presence of women, was for many something in the nature of an oasis: a temporary refuge from
authority; from the kindly or peremptory supervision of
others; from the hierarchy of military life itself, imposed
like a cumbrous splint on limbs numb with the desire
for spontaneous action. Hence, too, the popularity of
the librarians, of whatever age or aspect; the pleasure of
even a few minutes' conversation with one distinct from
the community she served; immune from its laws. This
did not, of course, apply in all cases. It was noticeable for
instance that on the days when his domain was invaded
in this manner, and under a guise that he was not at
liberty to resist, the C.O. secluded himself in his office,
from which, with a fanatical tenacity of purpose, he was
not to be lured until the sight of the same young women,
free-wheeling now down the drive, skirts briskly flutter-
ing, assured him that the *status quo* had, for the time
being at least, been restored.

Olivia, Lady Brent's niece, sat at the counter, horn-
rim glasses perched on a shallow nose; her fashionable
mauve lips pursed as she considered her card index
files: a system of classification which filled her, week
after week, with unconcealed dismay. "Sergeant Pye?
Now let me see. Your card, your card. . . . Where did I
put it . . . ? Oh, that's it, is it? I see—you're returning
The Rains Came, and taking out *Gone with the Wind,* is that
it . . . ? Right first time! Thank heavens for small
mercies. . . . Now, who's next . . . ? No, don't tell me, I
remember: Corporal Levy, You're taking out *Grey
Eminence: The Pool of Vishnu* too? No, you're *returning*
them—oh, *I* see. . . ." Frequently, the patients themselves
helped her out "in the other box, miss,"—glad to do
her a service, and rewarded by her humble "Oh, yes,
of course, how silly of me," her quick decorative smile.

The seven bracelets on her wrist jingled as she stamped the page with her little rubber stamp. "How's the foot, Corporal? No better . . . ? Ah, I know all about that. Broke a leg once, ski-ing. That plaster—doesn't it *itch*!"

Lieutenant Creech made his unobtrusive entrance. Without speaking to anyone, he sidled round the shelves, picking out a book and then quickly putting it back into place again. Finally, he came up to the counter with, *Of Guilt, Sin, and the Remission of Sin*; and waited in silence while Olivia entered and stamped it for him. Hastily, then, the musty purple-bound volume clipped protectively to his chest, he disappeared from the room. In the passage outside an airy whistling attracted his attention. He looked up. Colin Carmichael was strolling along, lips pursed as for a kiss, his hands tucked into the pockets of a pair of immaculate whipcord riding-breeches.

"Hallo, Creechy, old boy," Colin said. "Grand day, isn't it?"

"Very pleasant." Creech had a habit, when spoken to, of shrinking away, to stand with his back to the wall as if in need of protection. From that vantage point now, he surveyed Colin's legs. "Been out riding?" he said.

Colin paused. The question was not as innocent as it sounded. "No," he said. "Not to-day. Horse was lame, or something," Since, in the last resort, only the presence of a horse actual or implied, can justify the assumption of riding-breeches, Colin, who disliked animals, had latterly forced himself at certain intervals to mount and be seen in public in mastery of one of the local hacks. The ordeal by which he earned his spurs, so to speak, was not however a topic on which he chose to dwell. Evading it now he put out a hand. "What's that you're reading?" he said. He looked at the title. "Strewth," he said. "Well, there's no accounting for taste, I suppose. I prefer a good shocker, myself."

There were footsteps at the far end of the corridor.

Colin swung round quickly. He was in time to see a slight upright figure disappear into Mayne's office. Brief as the glimpse was, it permitted the recognition of red tabs; of the aura of authority, unmistakable even at that distance. Creech followed the direction of his glance. "The new C.O." he said. His snail-coloured eyes went slyly to Colin's face.

"Oh," Colin said. "That's him, is it." He showed neither hostility nor concern, only a mild curiosity. It was obvious that this indifference, surprising to Creech, was perfectly genuine. Colin jerked his head in the direction of the closed door. "Have you met him?" he asked.

"Yes. Mayne brought him into the mess last night."

"What's he like?" Colin asked.

"Well, you must judge for yourself. For one thing, he's Territorial——"

"——And likely, therefore, to be *plus royaliste que le roi,* eh?"

"At first, perhaps."

"Why only at first?" Creech did not answer, and after a quick glance Colin went on "Well, at all events, let's hope you find him congenial——"

Creech paused. "We?" he said. His eyelids narrowed. "What about you?"

Colin looked at the wall above the other's head and smiled faintly. "I don't know that the change of régime is going to affect me very much," he said.

Creech took this in. "Are you leaving us, then? he said.

"Ask me no questions and I'll tell you no lies!"

Involuntarily, Creech's glance turned in the direction of the C.O.'s door. "Mayne's not taking you with him, is he?" he asked.

"Well, if you must know, he did give me the option——"

"And you've accepted?"

"Not yet. I'm about to do so—when the Territorial gives me the chance."

Creech paused. "Haven't you left it rather late in the day?" he said.

Colin clapped him briskly on the shoulder. "Better late than never, they say." He grinned. "They likewise say that there's many a slip 'twixt the cup and the lip so oblige me, will you, by keeping what you've heard to yourself. For the time being, at any rate."

"I will," Creech said. He turned to go. Suddenly, changing his mind, he came after Colin in the corridor. He laid a hand on his elbow. "Your wife——" he began.

Colin looked round, startled. "What did you say?"

"Your wife," Creech repeated. "If you go—will your wife want to keep on the house? Because if not, I know someone who'd be glad to take it over——"

Colin's face altered. "I know nothing about that. We havn't discussed it yet," he said. "In any case," he added stiffly, "I doubt if we have the right to sub-let."

Creech disappeared. Colin walked on, frowning. The reminder of Honor at this juncture, when after so much delay and soul-searching he was on the point of accepting Mayne's proposal, waiting only for a convenient moment to do so, was inopportune. No use going into all that again. The die was cast, the decision taken. Deliberately he began to whistle again; and whistling, made his way through the open doors into the library.

"Good-morning, Captain Carmichael."

Colin looked up. "Olivia! A sight for sore eyes. What're you doing here on a Saturday morning?"

"I changed my day with Mrs Watling-Gore. She had to go to the hairdresser—it was the only time she could get an appointment with her own assistant. She's doing my day at the Canteen, instead."

"Life is very complicated." Colin leant on the counter. "You should always wear mauve," he said.

Olivia jangled her bracelets. "Do you want a book? Fiction this side, non-fiction that——"

"I promised to get something for Major McRae. He's the quiet sensitive type. What do you suggest? James Hadley Chase?"

"Don't ask me. I'm supposed to hand out books, not recommend then."

"True," Colin said. He detached himself regretfully from the counter. "Well, let's see what you have to offer." He went to the shelves, and made a pretence of examining the titles; head lowered; fingers slowly ruminating in the pockets of his breeches. It was pretence only, in fact his eyes ran unseeingly over the bulky spines, the titles, bright or faded, of pre-war books. He moved restlessly from shelf to shelf; and at last, wholly at random, picked out a volume which attracted his attention by its canary yellow binding. He brought it up to the counter. "Will this do, do you think?" he said. He waited while Olivia entered the book; looking, as she did so, and not without awe, at finger-nails that projected a good quarter of an inch beyond her natural finger-tips.

Sister Blair came in, followed by an orderly bearing a pile of books collected for exchange from the bed-ridden cases in her ward. She came up to the counter. "Good morning," she said briskly. She handed across a written list. "There you are," she said, "and they've all given a second *and* a third choice this time: so there'll be no running backwards and forwards." She looked with expressionless eyes at Olivia's blouse, on which was printed in recurring pattern a selection of victory slogans such as "*Careless talk costs lives*," and "*Is your journey really necessary?*"

"Oh," Olivia said, flurried, conscious of being judged; "now wait a minute. I'll just check this lot in, first." She turned the pages of her ledger. A note written in red attracted her attention. She looked up hopefully "Any sign of *The Madonna of the Sleeping Cars* yet?" she asked.

"No. We've searched the ward for it. Top to bottom. I'm sure we haven't got it."

"I can't think *what* can have become of it, then. It's extraordinary, the way books just vanish into thin air. Do you know, that's the *third*, this week. . . ."

Sister Blair turned to Colin, of whose presence, all the while, she had been conscious. "And how's Captain Carmichael, this morning?" she said brightly.

"Bearing up, Sister, bearing up."

Sister Blair's dark eyes looked him over. She observed the moustache newly trimmed; the lustrous Sam Browne belt emphasizing a narrow waist; the tunic on which two small buttons glittered like metallic nipples on either breast. Nor did his air of contained excitement escape her shrewd attention. "What's up with you?" she said. "You look as if you'd lost a sixpence and found a shilling." She grinned. "Or is it merely a case of 'Who's been at my Enos?'" she said.

"You wouldn't expect me to tell you if it were, would you? Or would you?"

Sister Blair glanced quickly to right and left of her. She moved a step nearer.

"I've got some news for you," she said, in a mysterious voice.

"Good," Colin said. Let's have it."

"You may not be seeing me much longer."

This was not what Colin had expected. "You," he said. "Why? You're not getting married on us, are you? For shame for you."

"No," she said. The broad white teeth flashed. "It's not that. Not yet, at least." She lowered her voice to say it. "I've put my name down for service overseas."

Colin paused. "Indeed," he said in an even voice. "And what made you do that, all of a sudden?"

"Oh, I've been thinking about it for ages. To tell you the truth, I've had about enough of this place. There's something about that village street—I don't know if you feel it—but it gets me *down*. . . . And I've always wanted to go abroad. I may not get the chance, later on. We're none of us getting any younger, you know."

"Perfectly true."

"I'd like to get to Cairo," the Sister said. "I believe they have a pretty good time there, from what I hear. Plenty of oranges and whisky. Going out on the ship too, a troopship with thousands of men on board—you hear some stories——"

"The true Florence Nightingale spirit," Colin said "I'm glad to see it, Sister." His face was impassive. "It's a good job I'll be there to keep an eye on you," he said.

Sister Blair laughed. "Remote control won't be much good, I fear," she said.

"It may not be so remote. The chances are that I'm going overseas myself——"

She opened dark eyes. "You?" she said.

"Why not me?"

"On the contrary," Sister Blair said "the more the merrier!" The white teeth glittered.

"We'll have to form an Old Linfieldians' Club, or something," she said. "Can't you just see us, raising Cain in the desert—you and Captain Lloyd and I——"

"Who?" Colin said sharply.

"Captain Lloyd."

"Lloyd," Colin said: "why Lloyd?"

"Why, because he'll be there, too, poor dear. Or not far off. You never know."

"Lloyd," Colin said slowly "is *he* going, then?"

Sister Blair looked at him in surprise. "Yes, of course. Didn't you know? He's going with the C.O.—with Colonel Mayne, I mean. It's confusing, having two C.O.'s about the place."

"Lloyd," Colin said. He stared straight before him. "*Lloyd.* . . ."

Sister Blair looked curiously at him. "Surely," she said, "you knew, didn't you?" She shrugged her shoulders. There was a faint crackle of starch. "This is a place," she said.

"No," Colin said, "I didn't know." He turned to her. His face looked small and pale suddenly. In a low voice "Where is he?" he said.

"Captain Lloyd? He left last night."

"Last night——?"

"To do his course of tropical medicine, in London."

"I see," Colin said. He added, after a silence: "It's definite, then."

"Oh, it's definite, all right. As far as anything can be called definite in the British army——"

"I knew nothing about it."

"We knew," Sister Blair said indifferently. "Quite a time ago. We had wind of it, at least. Soon after Colonel Mayne himself was posted. He called in Captain Lloyd, so I heard, and gave him the option of going with him, if he wanted to——"

"Claudia, where are you?" There was no reply. Honor turned in her chair. "Claudia!" Her voice rose. "Where have you got to?"

"Here I am," said Claudia's voice. She appeared at her bedroom window, dark hair overhanging her face. She looked down into the garden. "Do you want me?"

"It's so nice out here. Why don't you come out?"

"I'm washing my hair."

"Well, come and dry it in the sun. There's a deck chair, all put ready."

Claudia disappeared. Honor turned her attention to the garden. "Peter, don't put that thing in your mouth," she said "it's dirty." At her feet, the baby lay on a rug, his napkins undone to permit him to kick. The colour of the sky, a corner of his mother's skirt, her face, bending large above him: intermittently, all were reflected in the bright incurious bubbles of his eyes. Intermittently too, he crowed: he clasped his hands in sudden ecstasy, saliva leaked from the pouting incontinent mouth. Honor looked at him in idle appreciation of his existence. Behind her, a door slammed. Claudia came across the veranda and down into the garden. She had a towel about her shoulders and her hair hung in dark wisps about her neck, smelling of coal tar soap. About to adjust the rung of the deck chair, she glanced sharply at the baby. With a minimum of appreciation "Young exhibitionist," she said.

"He enjoys a good kick." It occurred to Honor that her sister did not like to see the baby in that state. "I'll cover him up," she said. "The sun is really rather strong. . . ."

Claudia sat down. The ends of her hair dripped with moisture, there was a bead of water on her brow. She buried her head in the folds of the towel and rubbed vigorously. Memories of schoolroom days returned to Honor: of faces bowed and roasting in front of a glowing gas-fire. She smiled. "Do you remember the time you dared me to put the end of my plait in the fire?"

Claudia whipped the towel from her head. "*I* did?"

"Yes," Honor smiled. "Yes, really you did, Claudia. You were always goading me on to do things, in those days. I don't know why."

"Jealousy, I expect." Claudia's face was hidden in the folds of the towel.

"Jealous? But you were always so much cleverer than me. Look at all the prizes you won. I never won anything in my life."

"That proves nothing."

"You had many more friends than I did, too. That proves something."

"It proves that I needed people." Claudia withdrew the towel, and shook back the damp hair from her eyes. "I wanted to live their lives, rather than my own. I used to wish secretly that some other family would adopt me——"

Honor looked at her, astonished. "You wished that——?"

"Other people's lives seemed—how can I explain it—*safer* than my own. Haven't you noticed—you often feel nervous when someone you know well is driving—and quite indifferent with a total stranger at the wheel——?"

"Peter," Honor called out: "put that *down*! How many more times must I speak——"

Claudia fingered her hair, compulsively twisting the ends over one finger. "Hear the planes last night?" she said.

"No," Honor said. "I slept like a log, I'm ashamed to say."

"They seemed to be going over all night."

Honor turned. "Didn't you sleep, then?"

"Not very well."

"Colin *said* he heard someone go downstairs in the night. Was it you?"

Claudia paused. She said in a curiously shamefaced fashion "Yes. I had an idea I'd left the side door open——"

This was not unfamiliar. Honor frowned. "Oh, dear," she said. "You're not starting another bout of that insomnia business, are you?"

"I hope not."

Honor looked quickly at her. Claudia was twisting a strand of hair between her fingers and staring fixedly before her. In a flash of understanding that did not reach the level of words, Honor saw a creature caught in the

trap of its own nature, hounded by impulses so contrary
that it took every available ounce of will-power and energy
to control them. She looked at her sister with pity, and
then a moment later with respect: with a dim recognition of the fact that, in accepting and enduring this
inward struggle, Claudia was no less a martyr to human
progress than the saint, the scientist, or in the last resort,
the soldier, doggedly holding a strong-point against all
comers. . . . Aloud, Honor said, "You'll be glad when
term is over, won't you?"

Claudia roused herself. "Very," she said. "I've had
just about enough of the British schoolgirl for the time
being. Let her parents cope with her, for a change."

"Parents are not very good at coping, these days."

"So I've noticed." Claudia frowned. "They accepted
discipline themselves, once—why are they so afraid of
imposing it in their turn?"

"Because they don't like being called Fascists. Peter
told Colin yesterday when he made him do something he
didn't want to, that he was as bad as Hitler."

"Charity isn't the only thing that begins at home,
apparently. So does world war." Claudia drew up her
fists and yawned. "Well," she said, rousing herself;
"talking won't buy the baby a bonnet. I must go and
set my hair——"

"Let me do it for you," Honor said at once. She loved
to handle human hair. "Here—sit here, on the rug."
Claudia obeyed, dropping to her knees. "Have you got
the pins?" Honor got to work: with the comb, parting
the sleek hair, and rolling it up into small flat curls. This
too, was like old times. "Modom needs a new perm," she
said. "And her neck, if I'm not mistaken, could do with
a wash——"

"That's a lie," Claudia said comfortably. She sat, head
bowed, looking at the baby on the rug beneath her:
soothed by the soft plucking at her hair, the persuasive

reiterated movement of the comb. "Why do children always look like their father and never like their mother?" she said. Honor did not answer. Deftly, her fingers twisted and pinned. Under the midday sunlight the garden was tranquil, domesticated. A line of napkins hung bleached, between two thorn bushes. Cautiously, one eye on his mother, Peter filled a rusty kettle with water from the tap, and bore it away to the end of the garden. From the house came the sudden tinkle of china, the dull thud of the oven door being slammed. Instructed by these sounds, Claudia raised her head "Are you having the joint to-day, then?" she said.

"Yes, We'll have cold to-morrow, when Edith's out. Keep still——"

But a restlessness had got into Claudia. With difficulty, she held her head in position while Honor adjusted a pin. "What time are you having lunch?" she said suddenly.

"As soon as Colin comes in."

"Will he be late?"

"I don't know. I shouldn't think so." She looked down at her sister. "Why—are you going out?"

Claudia did not answer at once. Then "I may be," she said briefly.

Honor's face changed. She inserted a pin into the final curl and said, casually "Are you meeting Andrew, then?"

"No," Claudia said. "Not to-day."

"But I thought you——"

"Oh, I don't know yet what I shall do," Claudia said, angrily twisting her head this way and that. "I shall probably go to bed and sleep for the rest of the day——" She put both hands to her temples. "If only I could," she said. "If only I could . . . !"

There was silence in the room. Honor glanced stealthily at the mantelpiece clock. She sighed, and looked away. A few minutes later she glanced at it again. This time she accepted its verdict: there was no point in waiting any longer. She put aside her knitting, and said with a false brightness that deceived no one "Well, we'd better begin, I suppose. It looks as if Colin's been delayed——"

Claudia dropped the *Educational Supplement*. "Why can't he phone you when he knows he's going to be late?" she said.

"He can't always tell." As usual, when Colin was under discussion, Honor was evasive both in her replies and her judgment. She said nothing further. They took their places at the table; round the bowl of over-ripe roses that for the past week had been its centre-piece; the glass water-jug in the handle of which lurked a rainbow; the loaf of bread resting, shorn, on its scarred board. Summoned by the sharp trill of the bell, which for over half an hour she had been awaiting, Edith pushed open the dining-room door and bore to the table the joint she had cooked: a half leg of lamb; the week's rations; heeled over and resting, as it seemed, on one oar. Above it, Edith's face was suffused from over-long communion with the electric oven and her own patience. "The potatoes are a bit overdone, mum——"

Honor did not look at her. "Never mind," she said. "They'll do. I'll carve it, Edith. Thank you."

Edith withdrew. Honor took up the carving knife and burnished it perfunctorily on the ribbed sharpener. "Now, then. . . ." The long slender knife slid noiselessly through crackling rind, through blanched fat, through the grey knitted fibres of meat. Peter watched apprehensively. "Don't give me much, Mummy. No fat—not fat——" He looked at his plate in terror.

"There's no fat *there*," Honor said. "Don't be tiresome, Peter. Ask Auntie to cut it up for you."

"I can cut up my own."

The assertion went unheeded. Claudia leant across and

dealt briskly with his plate and then stretched out to
receive her own. Honor looked swiftly round the table.
Everyone else was served: now she was free to eat herself.
She helped herself to a crisp burnished potato, to carrots,
to mint-sauce: her plate, green-freckled, was pungent
suddenly, with vinegar. Taking up her fork she ate
rapidly, indifferently; her eyes lowered, her brows fixed
in a slight frown. She no longer looked at the clock: for
now the passage of time, instead of increasing the likeli-
hood of Colin's arrival, steadily diminished it. The quiet
ironic ticking seemed to measure, to underline the quality
of his absence from the house. That absence became all
at once something positive: a leaden weight from the
oppression of which she did not know how to escape. It
was as if, through the deprivation she suffered, a paralysis
had descended upon her which left her unable to cope
except mechanically with the simplest task.

There was a sudden clatter. Claudia laid down her
knife and fork. "I'm sorry, Honor——"

Honor raised unfocused eyes. "What did you say?"
she said.

"I won't finish this, if you don't mind." Claudia
pushed her plate away from her. "I'm sorry," she
repeated. "I feel I can't face food, at the moment."

Honor looked at her in bewilderment. "What's the
matter?" she said. "Aren't you feeling well?"

"I'm all right." There was something evasive about
Claudia's manner which at another time Honor would
not have failed to perceive. "I've no appetite. It may be
the heat——" She stood up. "I think I'll go upstairs to my
room for a bit."

Honor looked at her helplessly. "A cup of tea,
perhaps——?"

"No, nothing thank you. Don't you bother about me."
Swiftly Claudia pushed her chair into the table, and left
the room.

There was a pause. "Auntie's gone," Peter said. Awed, he looked at her plate. "She's left all her dinner," he said. There was no reply. He looked about him at the empty chairs; the silent room. Suddenly he smiled radiantly at his mother. "Now there's only you and me," he said.

But Honor was unresponsive: too preoccupied to recognize in this form a declaration of love. Her eyes rested upon him without the light of intimacy which he had hoped to kindle there. "Have you eaten all your meat?" she said. "That's right. You can ring the bell, if you like. *Once*—that's enough——"

Edith appeared, tray in hand. She looked at Claudia's empty chair, at her untouched plate. Affronted by the sight of rejected food "Miss Abbott—didn't she——?"

"No. You can clear it all away." Honor made no attempt to explain.

Edith rattled plates and knives sullenly together. From the garden came a prolonged screech: repeated. Honor raised her head. "He's awake," she said. "Pick him up, Edith, will you? I'll feed him in a minute." Edith disappeared. Peter ate stewed rhubarb, the rosy fibres acid on the tongue, mollified by a bland velour-like custard. He glanced at his mother. She sat eating, eyes downcast. He endured for a while a silence which made no pretence of including him. Then, in a small voice "May we put the wireless on?" he said.

Honor looked up. "The wireless, Peter?" She saw his face. Contrite, suddenly, she hesitated; sought the means of making amends. "Would you like more glucose on your rhubarb?" she said. He recognized her intention and smiled. "Yes, please," he said. But before he could push his plate across to her, the door opened. Surprised, they turned their heads. It was Claudia. A different Claudia. She had changed her dress and made up her face. Under the powder, her cheeks were flushed: her eyes had a set determined look. Without a word or a glance in their direction she went straight across the room and began searching for something along the mantelpiece. Not finding what she wanted, impatient, she turned to the small desk in the corner and lifted up letters, books, papers, in the same quick intent manner. Honor watched her, spoon suspended. "Are you looking for something?" she ventured.

"Yes." Claudia spoke briskly. "The time-table," she said. "Have you seen it?"

"The buses, you mean? Over there, on the mantelpiece——"

"No, no. The trains."

"Oh, I don't know. Colin has it somewhere, I think. He may have taken it to hospital with him. What was it you wanted to know?"

Claudia turned. "The time of the next train to Oxford," she said.

Honor laid down her spoon. "The train to *Oxford*, Claudia?"

Claudia's expression did not change. "That's what I said, yes." The two sisters looked at each other. Claudia's face was hard. "You don't know, do you?" she said. "Very well, say so. I can easily find out. I'll phone the station."

"No. Wait. Claudia, wait——"

Claudia gave her a blind impatient look. She went to the door. "Claudia!" Open-eyed, Peter watched them both. And then before Claudia could reach it the door opened. Colin stood on the threshold. There was a moment of blank silence. The new-comer looked uncomprehendingly from one to the other. They waited for him to speak. Surprisingly, Colin did not do so. He neither spoke nor made any attempt to come forward. He stood there in his riding boots, his Sam Browne belt, his elegant tunic. He did not say a word. It was then that Honor saw his face. She forgot everything else. With an inarticulate

sound she got up and, knowing herself wanted, went
towards him.

CHAPTER THIRTEEN

FACE TO FACE

THE pavements were crowded. Long queues of people
stood at the bus stops: before the swing doors of
every tea-room: before the box-office of cinemas: before
fishmonger's slabs bearing in classical display their
stock of salted fillet and saffron-coloured fish-cake. It
was difficult to advance: every now and then Claudia
was forced to step off into the gutter, dodging bicycles,
R.A.F. lorries, despatch riders in domed helmets, top-
heavy buses that thundered along, crowded inside and
out. In both directions, defying the shins and elbows of
passers-by, women pushed their prams laden with children sucking the priority oranges that week allocated to
Oxford; and piled high with the week-end purchase of
potatoes, sausages, Madeira cake, watercress and Spam.
Soldiers and airmen, on leave or stationed close at hand,
and whose war so far retained a surprisingly domesticated
character, walked along with their wives helping to push
the pram or admonish an older child. Intermittently a
heavy plane roaring overhead added, if only by its noise,
to the prevalent traffic. The children raised critical
faces "A Halifax," they said, or "A Boeing", "A
Lancaster" like naturalists, accurately and without
excitement identifying the current phenomena of their
lives. And very occasionally, unheeded by the crowd—
in his plaid shirt and mangled flannels like a ghost, a
pale reminder of others who in years now gone had

walked these streets with assurance, with flamboyance—
a young man, very young, a war-time student, might be
seen book under arm making his way to college or digs;
unobtrusive, diffident: conscious of the fact which he
felt marked him for disregard, that his studies were of
life, of the long-term constructive values, while all about
him his contemporaries, acclaimed, were learning the
technique of destruction: training gaily for the death
that, graduating, they were either to inflict or receive.

Claudia turned a corner. She saw at the far end of the
street, suspended from its bracket, a heavy gilded shield.
At once, as if she had received a signal, her heart began to
beat. Set at an angle to the main road, the hotel seemed
to await her, to be conscious of her approach. Behind that
impassive façade, she felt, behind the long windows, the
flower-boxes, the fluted curtains, there were eyes that had
perhaps already detected her presence on the pavement.
She gave no sign that she felt this to be so, that she herself was in any way committed. It was casually, with-
holding her glance, that she turned aside a moment or
two later to step under the high archway: that, with the
sound of the traffic diminished in her ears, she crossed
the flagged courtyard with its small clipped trees locked
in green-painted tubs. And it was with the same detachment, but a detachment which concealed, now (and this
she could not control) the suddenly accelerated beating
of her heart, that she put her hand to the heavy glazed
door, and then, pushing it open, saw before her in actuality
the scene that she had so frequently and feverishly pictured
to herself during the past twenty-four hours: the big
sunken lounge-hall of the Golden Shield Hotel.

Anticlimax supervened. No one came forward to
greet her. No one advanced, smiling, with long intimate
grip to take her hand in his. She looked unbelievingly
about her. The lounge was empty. Neil Herriot was not
there. There was no one there at all. The big leather

arm-chairs, brass-studded, faced each other, vacant. On low tables, *Punch*, the *Illustrated London News*, lay as they had been flung, abandoned by visitors rising from the after-lunch cigar, the lethargic after-lunch gossip, to resume in the world outside other contacts and duties. Cold coffee lurked in discarded coffee-cups: from ashtrays full of splayed butts and blackened matches there rose, faint on the afternoon air, a stale ashen smell. Claudia saw at once that she had been mistaken: the hotel did not await her, it did not know or expect her; and now that she had chosen to intrude in this fashion, it was, she realized, in the person of an elderly clerk immured behind glass in his little office by the wall, gazing at her enquiringly; waiting for her to offer a convincing explanation of her presence and requirements.

"Yes, madam?" Above the polished mahogany counter he surveyed her: his ascetic face insulated from the rest of his body by the frontier of a peculiarly high stiff collar. Claudia came forward uncertainly. "Good afternoon." She smiled at him. "Is Captain Herriot in, do you happen to know?"

"Who, madam?"

Nervously, she repeated the name: "Herriot. Captain Herriot." There was a pause. The old man glanced down at a written page by his elbow. He shook his head. "There's no one of that name staying here," he said.

"No one? Oh, but surely——" She looked at him, bewildered. "This *is* the Golden Shield, isn't it—?"

"It is, madam."

"There must be some mistake," she said. "I know for a fact that Captain Herriot was to have arrived yesterday evening, some time——"

He shook his head, dispassionately refuting her. An idea seemed to strike him. He looked at his list again. Tentatively "There's a Major *Henty*——" he suggested.

"No," Claudia said. "No." And at the name, the

wrong, the meaningless name, a feeling of despair came upon her; the sense of impotence experienced in a dream when some mechanism by means of which one was either to be translated to a state of extreme felicity, or equally, rescued perhaps from great and imminent peril, fails to function: the aeroplane that will not at the crucial moment leave the ground: the train that does not depart, or, departing, arrives at a destination recognized only too soon to be its own starting-point. "No," she said. "There's been a mistake, obviously. I'm sorry to have troubled you. Thank you very much." She turned away from the desk.

Under his eyes, she crossed the red-carpeted lounge. Mechanically, she pushed open the heavy glazed door: mechanically, walked across the paved courtyard with its clipped trees in tubs. Once more she found herself in the busy street. She heard the buses thundering by: saw the women returning home, their net shopping-bags sagging with the day's varied catch. Turning to the right, she walked along quickly, intently: as if she had an appointment that must at all costs not be missed. Her face was burning, her lips dry. Well, that's that, she said to herself: that's that. Presently she was able to distinguish, amid the pressure of other emotions, a faint feeling of relief; as if she had at the last moment been granted exemption from a test that might have proved too rigorous for her powers. That's that, she repeated. Finished. Over and done with. Now to forget. . . . She put the palm of her hand, in an unconscious gesture, to one cheek; trying to cool the shame that still burned there.

The traffic lights went green: cars and buses surged forward: she waited on the edge of the kerb to cross. And it was at that moment, on the opposite kerb, also waiting to cross the road, that with a painful leap of the heart she saw the khaki-clad figure, the green beret, the long saturnine face of Neil Herriot.

They looked at each other intently across the intervening traffic. For a moment, neither moved or made any sign: startled, they seemed each to recognize in the other the hidden nature of their association: not, as might appear, spontaneous and creative, but on the contrary, will-bound, mutually destructive. That queer revealing moment passed: the lights flashed to red: reined in, forcibly arrested, the traffic came to a halt and Herriot, smiling broadly, waving his arm, came towards her with big strides across the road.

"Claudia!" He caught her by the elbow: stood looking down, smiling, into her face. His next words were surprising. "What are you doing here?" he said.

She thought she had not heard aright. "What am I——?"

He laughed. "I don't mean what are you doing in Oxford," he said. Lightly, in token of his full appreciation of the meaning of her presence there, he caressed, for a moment, the back of her arm. "I mean, what are you doing, chasing off in this direction? The hotel is the other way."

"I've just been there. They told me they knew nothing at all about you."

"That's not surprising," he said. He grinned. "Darling, why should they know anything about me? I'm not staying there."

"Oh," she said. "But you told me——"

"I said we'd *meet* there. Remember? It seemed as good a place as any. Quiet, not too many people——"

"Yes, I see." She looked quickly at him. "What hotel *are* you staying at, then?"

He met her glance. "I'm not staying at a hotel, as it happens. A friend of mine has rooms here—he put me up for the night. That was why—you understand—we couldn't very well meet there——"

"No, of course not." There was a pause. He took her arm again. "Well—we don't want to stand on the street

corner——" They began to walk along in the direction
from which she had just come. Claudia was silent. Was
it by design, she wondered, that he so persistently denied
her a glimpse of his background and associations? And
if so what was there about himself, his own origin, that
he wished to conceal from her? As if he had sensed what
was going on in her mind, Herriot bent towards her. His
dark eyes searched her face. "You don't trust me, do
you?" he said.

Claudia gave a wry smile. "It seems that I do," she
said.

He pinched her arm. "You shouldn't," he said. "I've
never given you any reason to—don't forget that."

"I don't forget it," she said quickly. She averted her
eyes. "I know what it means. We're under no obligation
to each other."

Herriot looked at her, surprised. "You have more
courage than I thought," he said.

They walked along the crowded pavement. Claudia
became aware, as she had been made aware before, of
the reaction of other people to Herriot's presence. It was
not the uniform only: something about his height, his
darkness, something perhaps in the quality of his glance,
bright and unsettling, rendered him conspicuous. It did
not need a small boy's sibilant "Cor, look Bill—a
Commando . . . !" Even privates, domestically involved,
and as such, allergic to pips, released smartly the handle
of a perambulator in order to salute : in order to receive,
in return, Herriot's off-hand acknowledgement of the
gesture. Women (immature girls; a wife on the arm of
her husband; a middle-aged matron), recognizing the
shoulder-flash, glanced boldly into his face. How different,
thought Claudia involuntarily, how different the atmosphere when she appeared with Andrew in public : Andrew
in his civilian jacket, his civilian hat, ignored by the
crowd, belittled by the glances of women : Andrew the

civilian, the intellectual: branded by the violence not committed: by the brutality not perpetrated; the ignominious innocence of hands that have never shed blood. Different, indeed, the acclaim that greets the man who bears, in symbol, the mark of Cain. . . . In a moment of self-revelation: we are not outraged at the murder of Abel, she thought. On the contrary. We hate Abel, the guiltless man, the victim: it's Cain we love: Cain, the killer. And we permit war in order to justify that love in our hearts.

"Penny for your thoughts," Herriot said slyly.

She lifted her head. "I was just wondering what I'm doing here—why I'm here with you," she said.

"Indeed," Herriot said. "And did you come to any conclusion on the matter?"

"Yes," she said, sombre "I think I did."

Herriot paused. "You think too much," he said. "You should give up Thinking for a bit. It's a bad habit. Worse than tobacco. Impairs the digestion, promotes neuralgia, giddiness and lassitude——"

She smiled. "Give me the prescription, then," she said. "A remedy for the Prevention and Cure of Thought. . . ."

He glanced ironically at her. "Is that what you've come to me for?"

Claudia was silent. They reached the courtyard of the Golden Shield Hotel. Herriot made as if to turn in there, but Claudia, understanding his intention, resisted him. "No," she said. "Not again. Don't let's go there. Isn't there anywhere else?"

"Anywhere you like," Herriot said. He turned his head. "There's a tea-room of sorts over there. Will that do?"

Once more, they crossed the road. Anne's Pantry, the place was called. There was pottery in the window, and a wire tray displaying some small blanched scones. Inside (when finally after waiting their turn, they got inside; they secured a table) there were green wicker arm-chairs, green china rabbits, and curtains whose modernism was already more dated than the sentimental designs which they had displaced. There were no hired waitresses: only two middle-aged ladies whose flowered smocks, shielding in such an environment neither pregnancy nor an artistic temperament, were a guarantee of genteel origins and natural inefficiency. Herriot looked about him, distrustful, a little irritated. But to Claudia, familiar with the atmosphere of the mistresses' common-room, the place, if not exactly congenial, was at least fully within the range of her own experience. She understood only too well its aspirations, its evasions: the courage of this fanatical genteelity which held at bay, with paintings of hollyhocks and home-made cakes and clay rabbits and bright ladylike voices, so many ugly and terrifying aspects of reality.

They sat at a round wicker table in the window. Claudia poured out tea into conical cups decorated boldly in green and orange. She split a small damp tea-cake and spread it with margarine, with a thin layer of apricot jam. Herriot declined to eat: he lit a cigarette and sipped at his tea. Now and then he glanced at her, frowning. Suddenly he put his cup down and turned to the clock over the door. He studied it critically. "The train goes in precisely forty minutes from now," he said.

"I know." Claudia poured more hot water into the teapot.

"Time flies, they say." He glanced at her. "We might as well say good-bye here," he said.

She went cold. "Good-bye?" she said.

"Well, there's no point your coming to the station."

She stared at him. "No point—? But I—I——"

He leant across and took her hand in his, disregarding interested glances from crowded tables on either side. "Darling," he said "why fool yourself—and me? Be honest. You've never had the slightest intention of coming with me."

She withdrew her hand from his. "You're wrong," she said.

"Am I?" He smiled. "Then why, my sweet, take such good care to turn up without even a suitcase? How did you think you were going to manage for a toothbrush, for instance?"

"Oh," she said. Her face cleared. "Is that it!" The tension went out of her. She laughed. "My suitcase?" she said. "I left it at the station, of course. You didn't expect me to carry it around with me, did you?"

Herriot looked at her. Suddenly he leant across the table. In an altered voice "You mean—you will come?" he said. He seemed to hold his breath as he awaited her reply.

"Yes," Claudia said. "I will."

There was another silence. And then Herriot laughed: relaxed, sitting back in his chair again. "I apologize," he said. "I doubted you. I thought all along you were fooling. I couldn't believe that I really meant anything to you—that as things were, you had it in you to accept such a challenge——"

Claudia too smiled. "Let's call it an invitation, not a challenge," she said.

He drew quickly on his cigarette. Without looking at her, abruptly "You stand to lose a lot by coming with me," he said.

She raised her eyebrows. "Are you trying to discourage me?" she said.

"I'm in duty bound to make some sort of attempt——"

"You needn't bother. I know what the odds are."

He gave her a level glance. "No," he said. "You don't."

"I shall find out, in that case."

"You may not relish the process."

"I'm not afraid."

He laughed. "I wish I could say the same," he said....

They were in a taxi. In front of them, unseasonable, dim with dust, three Haig poppies in a metal vase quivered with the motion of the engine. A must of stale tobacco-smoke rose from the flabby upholstery. Herriot's arm was about her: she felt on her cheek the now familiar roughness of the khaki blouse. He put his hand under her chin and turned her face to him. Ignored, the crowded pavements slid by on either side. She accepted his kiss. Under indolent lids his dark eyes gazed, wide open, into hers. Suddenly, he released her. "You can still change your mind," he said. "There's time yet. You haven't quite burned your boats."

Claudia rearranged her hair. "You're being very conscientious," she said.

He was appalled at her composure. "Remember," he said. "I did my best to discourage you."

"I'll remember."

He took her hand. Insistent "Promise?" he said.

She smiled. "I promise."

He turned her hand towards him and breathed kisses into the palm. "You'll forgive me?" he said, strangely. "You won't pursue me with your regrets?" A lingering kiss. "You won't destroy me with your anger?"

She was startled. "Why should I do that?"

"You're a woman," he said.

Claudia was silent. After a moment, Herriot removed his arm. Sitting up, he fumbled in the pocket of his blouse and brought out a cigarette case. "Smoke?" he said casually. She shook her head. He selected a cigarette and tapped it briskly against the lid of the case. "Well, now," he said. His voice changed. "To get down to practical details——"

She turned. "Yes?" she said.

"I don't know what sort of thing you had in mind," he said. "But I thought we'd avoid the bigger hotels. In the circumstances."

"Yes, yes, of course," she said. She looked out of the taxi window.

He lit his cigarette and flung away the match. "There's a small place near Victoria where I sometimes stay," he said. "It's not much cop—compared with the swagger hotels, I mean—but it's comfortable and it's quiet. We wouldn't be much bothered there——"

Inexplicably, Claudia's heart sank. "Whatever you think best," she said.

He flashed a look at her. "It's not as if I'd had all that much experience——"

"I didn't say you had."

"We can always find something better, later on. Not that the surroundings matter much——"

"No," she said.

There was a silence. Claudia continued to gaze out of the window. Suddenly, she stiffened. She craned her neck. "Where is he taking us?" she said. "This isn't the way to the station."

"It's not," Herriot said. "I told him to go this way. I want to pick up my bag——"

"Where is it?"

"At my friend's place. I'll just dash in and get it. You wait in the taxi for me. I won't be many minutes."

"Very well," Claudia said. She looked with curiosity at the shabby streets through which the taxi was cruising. Suddenly, Herriot leaned forward and rapped on the glass. The driver inclined his head. "This'll do," Herriot said peremptorily. "Stop here."

"This isn't Crescent road, sir."

"Never mind. It's close enough. Wait here till I get back."

Claudia thought: a subterfuge. He doesn't want me to

know where he spent the night. She understood that he did not trust her. There was no rancour in the thought. She accepted, without surprise, the values of the unknown world into which she was venturing. Herriot stepped down onto the pavement. He slammed the door shut, imprisoning her. Through the lowered pane of glass he smiled in at her. "I won't be a moment," he said.

He disappeared. The driver kept his engine running. She looked out into the narrow street. At his wheel, the driver took out a copy of the sporting edition and studied it indolently. Children were playing on the crowded pavement: women sat, bare-armed, in doorways and at first floor windows. What was Herriot doing in this neighbourhood? Who was his friend, if indeed, there was a friend at all? Soon, she realized, she would know: that and more: subterfuge would no longer avail: in the last resort he would be 'exposed, defenceless, as she to him: a state he had anticipated, she recollected, with misgiving. The engine continued to purr: the poppies in their vase quivered. From a near-by church a clock chimed the quarter. There was no sign of Herriot. Anxiety possessed her. What if he were late—if they were to miss the train?

"Here I am," Herriot said. He smiled in at her through the window of the cab: he had come up unseen from another direction. He glanced at her face. "Sorry to have been so long," he said. He wrenched open the door and slung onto the floor at her feet a very new-looking suitcase, without label or initials. "There we are," he said. He climbed in beside her and slammed the door. "Now we're all set to go." At the wheel, the driver folded away his newspaper. He turned his head. "Where to, sir?" he said.

Herriot put his arm around Claudia. "Station," he said briskly. "The London side. And as fast as you can make it."

There was six minutes to go. She stood on guard over

the two suitcases while Herriot, wallet in hand, waited his turn in the slow-shuffling queue at the booking-office. The edge of one of the suitcases pressed against her knee: she shifted her position, her heart hammering uneasily. She looked again at the clock. As if importuned by her glance the long hand clicked forward: five minutes, now. The people in the queue seemed interminably dilatory in their negotiations over tickets, change. The bustle of the station, the long whistling of engines, the periodic thunder of a train passing along the line, inspired in her a sense of urgency mingled with apprehension. She stood there in the centre of the busy crowd, soldiers, civilians, children, airmen, hauling kit-bags, perambulators, rifles, suitcases, respirators, all passing ceaselessly backwards and forwards about her, and felt herself, in the midst of so many people, peculiarly, painfully, exposed. She longed for the shelter of the train, of the small secluded carriage: the compartment suspended magically between station and station; between one destiny and another: between the act and its consequence. . . . If only she were in the train: once there, she felt everything would be all right. Hurry, she thought; oh, hurry. . . . The hand of the clock clicked forward: snipped off, neatly pruned, another minute dropped like a dead twig at her feet. And then, at the last moment, she felt, Herriot in his turn reached the booking-office. She saw him stoop at the small window. She saw him slip across a note, receive, after a small interminable delay, the appropriate tickets and change. He put forth his hand and in a single gesture swept it all up, tickets, silver, coppers: then, stepping aside to accord another the place he had occupied, holding the tickets in one hand, shoving his change back into his pocket with the other, he turned, ready at last, and came towards her.

It was then that it happened. Suddenly, and for no apparent reason, Neil Herriot stopped dead in his stride. His face altered. He stared, not at her, but at someone or something over her shoulder. Looking at him, Claudia caught her breath. She saw before her the face of a man who, day after day, has awaited some inevitable encounter, only to find himself at last, and at a moment when he least expects to do so, face to face with the enemy. The enemy? Claudia swung round quickly. She had time to wonder what there was in the aspect, quiet and unaggressive, of this middle-aged man, an army officer, that might be capable of inspiring such fear, before she caught sight, and in a flash realized the connection between the two, of the red caps of a couple of military policemen who with an air of detachment, chatting together, were standing one at each side of the entrance to the station.

The officer came forward through the crowd. He was thick-set and grey-haired, wearing above the pocket of his tunic the ribbons of the last war. He went up to Herriot who stood, tickets in hand, motionless, awaiting him. There was a moment in which not a word was spoken by either man: in which the other's glance ran quickly, impersonally, over Herriot's face; his shoulder-flash, badges. And then the new-comer spoke. In a quiet pleasant voice: "Captain Herriot?" he said.

"Yes," Herriot said.

"Would you be good enough," said the older man, still in that unemphatic voice of his "to let me see your military identity card?"

"My identity card?" Herriot said. "Oh yes, of course . . ." He put his hand towards his breast pocket. And then his expression changed. He let his hand drop to his side, empty. "I can't do that, I'm afraid," he said.

The other looked sharply at him. "You haven't got it?"

"No," Herriot said.

"Can you produce it?"

"No, sir."

"In that case," said the officer, and while his voice was no less pleasant there was now an overtone of briskness in his manner "I must ask you to be good enough to come along with me."

Herriot turned his eyes away. A look of great lassitude came into his face. "Yes," he said. "I understand."

Claudia stared hypnotized at the two men. The foregoing conversation had taken place so quietly and with such mutual absence of excitement, that the people all around, busy with their own concerns, were unaware of what was going on: that in full view of the public, and with little attempt at concealment, the Assistant Provost Marshal was in the act of arresting an army officer. In the same moment the two men turned towards her. For the first time, Herriot let his eyes rest on Claudia, standing, white-faced, by her suitcase. His expression did not alter. He looked blankly at her and blankly turned his eyes away again. It was impossible to say whether he resented her presence, or whether on the contrary his intention was, in as far as it lay in his power to do so, to protect her. To protect her, she realized a moment later: for as the two men stood there, she saw what the A.P.M. did not see, that Herriot, a hand behind his back, let slip from his fingers one of the tickets he had just purchased, retaining the other as if to give the impression that he had been setting out on his journey alone. Repudiation, Claudia understood, was all he could now offer her. . . .

"Coming?" Opposite him, the A.P.M. raised his eyebrows slightly.

"Yes," Herriot said. He paused. "I'll just get my suitcase," he said. He looked about him, as if wondering where he had left it. "Oh, there it is," he said. Claudia stood inert. He came forward. Without looking at her "Excuse me," he said. Stooping, he rescued the suitcase from what appeared to be its accidental proximity to hers. Then he straightened himself, suitcase in hand. For a moment, face to face, their glances met. Quickly, he turned his head away from her. And then without another

word or gesture, under escort, the Commando Captain
left the station.

CHAPTER FOURTEEN

THE INSOMNIACS

THE decorations in the ballroom were modernistic in
character. There was a good deal of chromium, of
incised glass, of the type of lighting known as concealed:
in effect, both evasive and curiously dazzling. At the far
end of the room on a platform banked with fern and
hydrangea, members of the orchestra wearing coloured
waistcoats and big frilled sleeves sat plucking idly at their
instruments and turning over sheets of music. All around
the long floor that gleamed invitingly under its polish
stood tables for two, for four, for eight: each bearing a ring
of cups and saucers, a small three-tiered cake-stand
holding scones, sandwiches and pastries, laid out in that
order with calculating precision. The cups were empty:
tea had not yet been served: the waitresses stood in a
line, their backs to the wall: elderly women in black,
with big starched aprons: for, despite the modernism of
its ballroom and bar, the Court Royal Hotel, now the
headquarters of the local Officers' Club, was a singularly
sober, well-nigh Victorian establishment, a fact perceptible at once in its drawing-rooms and lounges, in which,
against richly crocheted antimacassars, with a formidable
display of breeding, the permanent visitors outstared
the incautious intruder.

"We're a bit early," Colin said, looking about him
quickly. He was disappointed that there were not more
people present. He had come here to escape an atmosphere

he dreaded: that of the domestic Sunday afternoon: and he was visibly apprehensive that any waft of the same slow contagion might succeed, despite air-conditioning and artificial lighting, in percolating even into this chromium-plated refuge from boredom. "Let's get a decent table," he said. "It's sure to fill up, later on."

He selected a table on the edge of the dance-floor. At the same time the orchestra, rallying suddenly, brought forth the first tender wail, the measured beat, of a tango. Without wasting any time, seizing the opportunity for isolated performance, a flight-lieutenant from the neighbouring aerodrome stepped onto the floor with an emaciated blonde. He was followed by a portly major from one of the anti-aircraft batteries on the hill who, succumbing to the rhythm, rocked placidly back and forth in the arms of a Waaf officer. Colin watched both couples attentively. Honor, looking at him, knew (so susceptible, for all his apparent cynicism, was the nature of this man) that he was disturbed, personally affected, by the emotion latent between the men and women he saw linked before him on the ballroom floor. He sat silent, one elbow on the table leaning forward a little, intent. Honor said, to divert her sister's attention from that absorbed face "I like the blue dress, don't you?"

Claudia turned her head. "The blue?" She surveyed it critically. "Too skimpy—I prefer the silk jersey affair, there."

Fragments of this conversation reached Colin's ear. He moved restlessly: the domestic atmosphere he had come here to escape was permeating even this stronghold: his own fault so to speak for bringing the Trojan horse with him. He looked about him, frowning. "It'll liven up soon," he said, as if someone had complained "it's always a bit slow at the outset——"

With petunia and gilt-piped sandals, a flimsy petunia-coloured dress, with antique bracelet locked about her hollow arms, Olivia, looking amiably around her out of

big short-sighted eyes, crossed the floor on the arm of a
naval officer. Colin caught sight of her "Why, look who's
here!" Pleased and excited, he waved. Olivia turned her
face away with no acknowledgement of the gesture: at
that distance Colin was to her a mere blur on the horizon.
Unaware of this fact, Colin looked in silence from her to
her escort: a large, sunburnt man with a fully matured
black beard. At the same moment "Just look at that
naval officer," Honor said. "Have you ever seen anything
quite so magnificent!"

"Very impressive," Claudia agreed.

Colin said nothing. Claudia grinned. "And to think,"
she said, "that before the war a beard was considered a
sign of effeminacy . . . !"

Honor looked quickly at her sister. She thought of
something Colin had privately said to her, two days
after Claudia's return from Oxford. Claudia, he said, is
her old self again, only more so. . . . It was a fact that
nothing in Claudia's manner betrayed her own feelings,
either over her abortive attempt to accompany Herriot
to London, of which she alone knew, or over Herriot's
arrest, which was by now common knowledge in the
village and county. This composure of hers, like an
involuntary shortening of the lines, enabled her to conserve
her strength, to discover within herself a new and more
rigid integration; defensive in purpose; harder to break
down or demoralize. It was in the vehemence put into
intellectual concepts, into ideas, that in future could be
divined the force of an emotion now recalled, to be expended no more, or expended vicariously under a
régime in which the will was in supreme command: a
death which, as it happens, is not without its own victories.

Colin, whose thoughts had, perhaps, followed something of the same channels, said suddenly "Claudia—do
you remember that anonymous letter you got last week?"

Claudia turned her head. "Yes," she said, "What about
it?"

"You didn't by any chance keep it, did you?"

"No, of course not. I tore it up."

"Pity," Colin said. He paused. "You don't happen to remember what the notepaper was like, do you? Was it pale blue by any chance?"

Claudia looked at her brother-in-law. "Yes," she said. "It was. A narrow blue sheet, with lines."

"Ah" Colin said, triumphant. He leant across the table. In a conspiratorial voice "It may be pure coincidence, of course——" The two sisters looked sharply at him. "This morning," he said, lowering his voice "in the mess—I happened to see a packet of notepaper—exactly like that—lying among the case-sheets of—of——" he hesitated "——of one of our officers at the hospital."

Neither woman respected this half-hearted attempt at reticence. "Who was it?" Claudia demanded instantly. "Come on," Honor said "don't be cagey. Tell us."

Colin lifted his eyebrows. "Who do you think?" he said.

"I haven't the faintest idea," Claudia said. "Unless you're trying to tell me it was a *billet-doux* from Colonel Mayne."

Colin ignored this. Lowering his voice still further "It was Lieutenant Creech," he said.

"Creech?" Claudia said, astonished. "*Creech?* But I hardly know the man. Why on earth should he——?"

Colin shrugged his shoulders. "*There are more things in heaven and earth, Horatio*——"

"In any case," Honor pointed out "it proves nothing. Anyone can buy notepaper."

Claudia gave a deep sigh. "Well!" she said. "There's one thing at least, this war has taught me. I used to think it was only women who were gossipy and jealous and hysterical—I know better now. Heaven preserve us from a community of men——!"

On a long-drawn-out flattened note, the music came to an end. There was some peremptory clapping, which the

orchestra smilingly ignored. Drained of music the dance-
floor lay flat and arid: a shore without a tide. Self-
conscious, the couples picked their way across it. More and
more people meanwhile were coming through the big
double doors at the other end of the room: the best tables
on either side of the floor were occupied already. With
each new-comer the temperature of the room, seeming
to rise, to become more buoyant, consumed rapidly the
apathy of the previous half hour. The waitresses reappeared, tray in hand: they began to serve tea, bending
over the tables with teapots and cream-jugs, with tiny
frilled paper-cases holding each a teaspoonful of sugar.
"I'll serve out," Honor said: pleased to resume a familiar
occupation. She raised the teapot over a cup. In that
attitude, she paused. She looked across Colin's shoulder
to the door. "Look," she said. "Just coming in. Isn't
that——?"

Colin swung round quickly. There by the door, in the
act of giving up his ticket to the attendant, was a slight
khaki-clad figure: a figure that for all its physical
insignificance was remarkable already to a certain
group of people; bearing, visible especially perhaps to
those who were subject to it, the caste-mark, distinctive
and inspiring, of authority. Colonel F. E. C. Calthrop,
O.B.E., M.C., successor to Mayne, and newly appointed
commanding officer of Linfield's Military Hospital, gave
up his ticket and, glancing curiously about him, came
forward into the peach-coloured electric light.

"Heaven help us," said Colin "the whole ruddy
mess——!" Honor turned. She saw Smith, the registrar;
McRae, Willy Wilson, young Waterhouse (newly
posted to Linfield to replace Dick Lloyd) and (surprisingly
in such surroundings) Creech. "I didn't know they were
coming this afternoon," Colin said: he was offended, it
seemed, that they had composed their plans without
consulting or including him. Honor did not answer. Her
eyes were fixed on the slight figure of the new C.O. She

was aware of a vague feeling of reassurance. He looks very quiet, she thought. . . .

The party made their way, Indian file, to a long table which had been reserved for them in a corner of the room. They settled themselves down on gilded cane chairs, crossed their legs, lit cigarettes and looked about them. Colin, whose table in the corner they had not yet seen, was on tenterhooks: in the effort to attract their attention he turned his head this way and that, he lifted his chin, he half rose in his chair and shamefacedly sat down again. Claudia and Honor ate tomato sandwiches. Suddenly (like a sailor on a raft who has been sighted by a destroyer, thought Claudia) "They've seen us!" he exclaimed, thankful. He smiled, he waved. "They want us to join them," he said. "Shall we . . . ?"

Half an hour later, Honor found herself sitting in unexpected prominence at Colonel Calthrop's side. She was maintaining with him, to her own astonishment and despite all her efforts to steer away from a topic so indiscreet, a conversation about the ages and idiosyncrasies of her two children. The efforts she made were unsuccessful and in any case unnecessary: the C.O., it appeared, was the father of two daughters, one of whom, married to a surgeon-lieutenant, was expecting her third child, and in the intricacies of babycraft and child guidance the Colonel took an expert, well-nigh maternal interest. "A good many breast-fed babies won't take the bottle after the nipple: the smell of rubber, I often think, puts them off," he said. Claudia, at the other side of the table, inadvertently overhearing this statement, raised startled eyebrows which her sister saw, but did not trust herself to acknowledge.

The orchestra broke into a foxtrot. Major Smith was sitting next to Claudia. "Come and dance," he said dutifully.

Claudia hesitated. "Don't be so energetic," she said. To dance with Major Smith, to hurry up and down the room pinioned to that resilient waistband, was an experience, she knew, unrewarding on all levels save that of pure exercise. Exonerating herself "I've just had my tea," she said, smiling at him.

Mr Waterhouse leaned across the table. "*Johnny Zero is a hero to-day*," he said.

"I *beg* your pardon?"

"The band. That's what they're playing," Waterhouse said. His fair classical face flushed, unexpectedly, with colour.

"Are those the words?" McRae said, interested. He repeated the line to himself. "It takes a popular song to state a truth so frankly," he said.

Major Smith was watching a group of new-comers. "Look at all those Poles," he said. He screwed up his eyes. "I wonder what they think of the set-up here."

McRae turned his head. "Oh, I don't know," he said mildly. "It may be that Linfield is more like Poland than we think."

Willy Wilson sighed. "At all events," he said, "the bar will soon be open," and with that comment, in the general reaction to it, it became apparent that the animation hitherto displayed by the party, like an overdraft of nervous energy, was an expenditure based largely on account, as it were, of the alcohol to come. "*Now they still call him Johnny Zero*——" sang Willy: he clicked with his tongue against his teeth; agile, one foot tapped the floor beneath the table. Colonel Calthrop glanced at him for a moment; then he turned to Honor. "I don't dance," he said, "so I mustn't monopolize you——" He looked again at the exuberant Captain Wilson. "William here shall deputize for me," he said. Gratified, a little surprised, Wilson stumbled to his feet. "Acquit yourself well on my behalf," said Calthrop, as Willy, beaming his big gold-studded smile, took Honor with a certain deference onto the crowded dance-floor.

Claudia, who had watched this manœuvre, found herself admiring the ease with which the Colonel, having done his duty by Captain Carmichael's wife, relinquished first her company and then any further obligation towards her. He turned to the rest of the party, whom Honor's presence had hitherto obliged him—unwillingly, he now let it appear—to neglect. For a moment his eyes rested upon the fair youthful features of the new-comer, Water-house. The young man, unconsciously neglecting the demand laid upon him, sat with averted profile. The Colonel sighed faintly. His eyes went to McRae: to Creech: to Colin; passing from face to face with a gentle, curiously uncertain expression. Claudia was struck by the contrast between that fugitive expression, which seemed to demand of his subordinates not respect, but a measure of sympathy and support, and the passivity of a face which an effort of will alone, she intuitively felt, maintained in the clipped formality of the military mould. Involuntarily, she found herself contrasting this man with his predecessor: with Colonel Mayne. The thought crossed her mind: was this to be, perhaps, and in an even more tortuous form, a case of out of the frying pan——? She looked up. Colonel Calthrop was speaking to Colin. Colin, leaning eagerly forward, one elbow on the table, listened smiling. . . .

Six o'clock was striking as the blue and silver bus ground to a standstill in the cobbled square in front of the Blue Trout. Claudia alighted and after her, Honor. Claudia heard the chimes. "Just in time," she said. Honor nodded without speaking. The two sisters turned, and made their way along the small High Street in the direction of Weirfield. Honor, who had left the party at the Officers' Club in order to feed her baby, had done so with the promise extorted from her by the Colonel, that she would be back within the hour: a stratagem which permitted Colin, after accompanying her to the gates, to return to the ballroom with an easy conscience, knowing at the same time, as Honor did, the Colonel too, that the promise elicited was not intended to be binding.

They crossed the common with its trampled grass, its tired-looking chestnut trees. The sisters were silent: occupied each with their own thoughts. Claudia said abruptly "Is Edith going out this evening?"

"Yes," Honor said. She looked apologetically at Claudia. "There's only the remains of the joint for supper," she said. "I hope Andrew won't mind."

Claudia said shortly "He won't mind."

Honor paused. "It seems a long time since he came round to see us," she said.

"He's very busy, these days."

"Yes, I suppose so." They walked on: Honor looked at the rusty cannon on the edge of the common. Unexpectedly she said "I'm very fond of Andrew." Claudia turned, surprised; and she went on, resolute, a little confused: "You know what I mean. There's something about him—I don't know what it is—but you feel you can *rely* on him. I sometimes wish I weren't so tongue-tied in his presence."

Claudia looked down at the ground. "He likes you, too," she said. She gave a faint sigh. How easy to like those we need not love: the friendly neutrals, with no stake in the game, aloof from the battle. In silence, they turned into the lane: saw the white gate of Weirfield pinned back against the sharp tricorne-like leaves of the holly. Impervious to sunlight, the yew-tree stood sentinel above; its long branches furred with darkness. They walked up the drive: the gravel tingled, dry underfoot. From the house, there came a sudden cat-like wail. "Oh— he's crying," Honor felt the familiar tightening in the muscles about each armpit: unconsciously she quickened her footsteps. The glass doors were open: in the late sunlight, the hall with its untidy hallstand, its neglected brass urns, had a faded look. The sisters separated: Honor went upstairs: Claudia, with a preoccupied expression, turned towards the living-room. She opened the door. There was a movement on the veranda beyond: quickly, she lifted her head: Andrew Peirse rose out of a chair, and smiling his detached smile came forward to greet her.

The house was very quiet. It was as if the focus of peace that was Honor with the child at her breast, deepening, permeated the whole house: as if from her body there radiated a beneficent influence which, in the silent household, in the stillness of evening, was detected by senses that were incapable at the same time of recognizing its source. Claudia let her head rest against the cushion on the back of her chair: the faint fretful lines went from her eyes: she gazed out into the overgrown garden: saw the rose-bush: the smiling lips of flowers in bloom: beyond, a single pennant of sunlight, bright still on the topmost branches of the lime-tree.

Andrew sat in Honor's old rocking-chair and gently swayed backwards and forwards, controlling his movements with the ball of one foot. "The interesting thing about the whole affair," he said, "is of course the light it throws on one's own mentality." Claudia nodded without speaking and he went on, still swaying backwards and forwards in that gentle dreamy fashion. "It's an illustration of the sort of things we really want and expect. We create a fiction out of our own desires. The fiction in this case happened to be the Commando hero: the killer, tough, unscrupulous; outside the bounds of ordinary convention. A fiction so attractive to the law-abiding that we chose in its favour to ignore the reality: the fact that a Commando is a Commando precisely because he can be relied upon to conduct himself in a manner not less, but infinitely more disciplined and responsible than that of the average citizen. . . ."

Claudia said, without turning her head "You've seen him, then?"

"Yes."

She hesitated. "He's—— Of course, he's——"

"In prison, yes. He sent for me."

There was a pause. "He sent for you?" she said. "Why?"

Andrew smiled faintly. "He wants me to defend him."

"You?" Claudia controlled herself. She said in a detached voice "But you can't do that, can you? I mean, the army have their own people——"

"It's nothing to do with the army. He's being charged in a police court."

There was a pause. Claudia said in changed voice, "What's the charge?"

"Wearing without authority an army captain's uniform, for one thing."

"Without authority——?" She turned her head sharply. "You don't mean to say——" Andrew smiled, rocking backwards and forwards. "I do," he said. "The uniform was pure fancy-dress." The arm-chair creaked monotonously under his weight. "The Commando was not a Commando: he was not an officer: he was not even a soldier: he's never been in the army at all in fact, or in any combatant force. A perfect example of the tragedy of the Reserved Occupation——"

Claudia gazed out into the silent garden. "Tell me, then," she said, "who is he? What was he in real life?"

Andrew screwed himself round in his chair. "Give you three guesses," he said.

She took refuge in detachment. "I'm not good at parlour games. You'll have to tell me."

He smiled. "You'll be shocked, I'm afraid, when you hear——"

Claudia looked quickly at him. "I won't," she said. "I'm prepared for anything. What was it—commercial traveller, gigolo, swindler——?"

"Worse," Andrew said. "From our point of view— much worse than that."

She shrugged her shoulders. "Nazi spy, perhaps?"

"No," Andrew said. "Not a Nazi spy. Not a gigolo. Not a swindler." He paused. "A respectable middle-aged man," he said. Claudia looked blank. "A small-town bank manager with a career of unbroken integrity," he said. He looked at her. "A married man: the dutiful husband of a hard-working and capable housewife: the affectionate father of three boys attending the local Grammar School." There was another pause. "Shall I go on?" he said.

"Yes. Please do." Claudia did not turn her head.

"Town councillor and part-time A.R.P. official in a small county town which has never known a blitz. Which (all services exhaustively rehearsed and re-rehearsed) has waited night after night for the visitation that never came—not a stray H.E.—not even a small solitary incendiary——"

"Go on," Claudia said.

"A prominent member of the local Home Guard, of course. Always ready to turn out to parades, to manœuvres; childishly proud of real lethal weapons. . . . Only gradually, as the possibility of action seemed to dwindle, becoming more frustrated: more dissatisfied with fake attacks on a fake enemy: more sensitive about the H.G. flash on his shoulder; more uneasy in the presence of those he considered real soldiers——" Andrew's voice tailed off. "Need I go on?" he said gently.

"No," Claudia said. There was a silence. Suddenly, Claudia gave a deep sigh. "The wonder is that we didn't suspect it all along," she said.

Andrew glanced at her face. "We didn't suspect it because we didn't want to," he said. "We preferred the fairy-tale we ourselves had helped to create." Once again the rocking-chair began its motion. "A typical farce," he said "typical of our time. . . . The world is gradually growing colder, we're told. And the thin-skinned intellectuals, feeling the impotence, the death-like lethargy falling upon them, turn to violence as an escape. Only to find that on violence too the lethargy seems to be falling : that violence itself is a façade, a fake——"

Claudia said suddenly, "He asked you to defend him, you say. Are you going to do it?"

"To the best of my ability, yes."

"Why?" she said.

Andrew shrugged his shoulders. "Ever heard the fable of the jackdaw and the peacocks?" he said.

Claudia did not answer. She looked out into the still garden. "I was with him when he was arrested," she said.

The creaking of the rocking-chair ceased abruptly. "You——?"

"I was going with him to London."

Andrew said in his too judicial voice "The arrest was premature in that case."

Claudia did not move. "Yes," she said.

He paused. "You have the courage of your convictions," he said. "I'm glad of that."

Claudia smiled. Her face was wry, distorted. "No," she said. "You've got it wrong. It was my convictions I was fleeing from. Or trying to flee from——"

Unexpectedly, Andrew reached out and laid his hand over hers. At the contact her heart seemed oddly to shrink. "I know," he said. "I understand. Believe me, I know all about it. . . ." There was a pause. Her hand lay inert under his. He sighed faintly. "Well, there it is," he said. "We are as we are. No way out for us. Caught in the trap of our own reason. Like a rabbit with its paw in a gin. On the side of the angels, in fact, with a vengeance. . . ."

Claudia looked straight before her. "If only," she said in a flat voice, "one could sleep. Lose consciousness, a little——"

He glanced at her. "Sleeping badly again?"

"I hardly sleep at all." Claudia spoke in the same flat voice. She stared into the garden. "It's worse in the day-time," she said. She did not look at him. "Do you know

what I mean? To be conscious all the time—to get no
rest——" She stopped suddenly. "How can I explain?"
she said.

"Explain?" Andrew said. "To me?" He gave a faint
melancholy smile. "One's like a prisoner sitting under an
arc lamp in one of those unending third degree
interrogations you hear about——"

She looked intently at him. "That's it," she said. She
waited. "No cure for that, is there?"

"For Daytime Insomnia—none that I know of." His
hand still lay on hers. Glancing down, she saw the frail
wrist; the discriminating fingers. She was silent. The cool
nerveless contact was suddenly intolerable to her:
impulsively she drew her hand from his. Andrew turned
his head. Their glances met. It was a revealing moment.
A moment which defined all too clearly the boundaries
of future intimacy. Claudia saw the queer self-conscious
twist of Andrew's mouth. She averted her head. In a low
voice "Well, what happens now?" she said.

Andrew had control of himself again. When he spoke,
his voice was calm, almost contemptuous. "We've got
to accept each other as we are, it seems."

"Didn't we do that before?"

"Not altogether," he said.

"Very well," she said. She paused, weary. "For
better or for worse, then——"

"For better or for worse." There was a pause. He
smiled. "Meanwhile," he said, "I'm glad to think that
you made an honest attempt to break away: to escape the
doom of your own higher nature. . . . I made the attempt
too. I joined the army. We can at least respect in each
other a mutual failure."

Claudia was silent. "It seems an insufficient basis to
build on," she said.

"Not in our case," Andrew said. "Not in a marriage
such as ours. Don't you see what it is? Evolution's newest
romance: the union of insomniacs. An operation per-

formed without the anæsthetic of either infatuation or passion. Does the prospect alarm you?"

"No," she said. She spoke truly. In the very bleakness of what was offered her she discovered a certain reassurance. She recognized, as if for the first time, that she had found in Andrew, as he, it seemed, in her, the best protection against the impulses of her own nature. Implicated in the same temperamental defeat, he and she were already so closely knit that no one now could intervene between them.

In the house the telephone rang suddenly. "I'll go," Claudia said. Jumping up, she crossed the silent living-room; littered with the day's aftermath of abandoned toys, half-darned socks, dismembered newspapers. Like a nervous tic, the thought crossed her mind Why *can't* people tidy up after them. . . . Involuntarily, she sighed, as if the task, self-appointed, of maintaining order in her environment taxed the very depths of her nature. She lifted the receiver off its hook. "Hallo?" she said.

A voice, familiar but diminished, spoke her name. Her face changed. She listened without sympathy to the earnest croaking. "Oh," she said. The croaking continued. "Very well," she said. And again, impatient "Yes. All right. I understand. Yes, I will. Good-bye." She hung up. One of Peter's lead soldiers lay on the floor at her feet: she stooped to pick it up. It had been trodden on. She looked attentively for a moment at the tiny Guardsman, faceless, shouldering resolutely his damaged rifle. With a sigh, she set it down on the hall table and went upstairs.

She opened the door. The room smelt of bath-water, of scorched wool. Honor was sitting with the baby on her lap. She looked up as Claudia came in. "Wasn't that the phone?" she said.

"Yes," Claudia said. She stood at the door. Honor wore a flannel apron; her blouse was unbuttoned, one breast hanging disregarded, with its big blown nipple. Claudia averted her eyes. "It was Colin," she said.

Honor looked up quickly. "Colin?"

"He said to give you a message. The Colonel—Colonel Calthrop—wants to take him out to supper. He says he can't very well refuse. He said to tell you not to wait up. He'll probably be late."

There was a pause. "I see," Honor said. She sat with the baby in her lap, as if she did not know what to do with him. Then "All right," she said, turning away "thanks." Resolutely, she tied the tapes of the baby's nightgown: rolled him carefully in his white shawl. Claudia could not see her face. She rose finally, the baby in her arms. For a moment she looked broodingly into the small face: she had forgotten Claudia's presence, it seemed. With the look, at the same time absent and rapt, that at all times the physical nearness of her children could bring to her face, she pressed her lips to the rabbit-soft scalp. "Bed-time now," she murmured "bed-time, my little love. Time to go to sleep. Time to sleep. To sleep. . . ."

The house was silent. Doors and windows open to the summer evening, it stood there, absorbing the dusk. The hall was dimmer now: the glass eyes of fox and deer, bereft of kindling rays, extinct upon the walls. Claudia descended slowly. She was very tired: the dusk seemed to lap her about, compelling as sleep. Moving softly she crossed the hall. Andrew was sitting as she had left him, on the veranda. He heard her footsteps and turned his head. For a moment, they looked steadily at each other. Then he held out a hand towards her. "Come," he said. She tried, in response, to smile at him: unexpectedly, tears sprang to her eyes. . . .

Andrew gave her a glance full of affectionate irony.

The first Virago Modern Classic was published in London in 1978, launching a list dedicated to the celebration of women writers and to the rediscovery and reprinting of their works. While the series is called "Modern Classics" it is not true that these works of fiction are universally and equally considered "great," although that is often the case. Published with new critical and biographical introductions, books appear in the series for different reasons: sometimes for their importance in literary history; sometimes because they illuminate particular aspects of women's lives, both personal and public. They may be classics of comedy or storytelling; their interest can be historical, feminist, political, or literary. In any case, in their variety and richness they promise to confuse forever the question of what women's fiction is about, while at the same time affirming a true female tradition in literature.

Initially, the Virago Modern Classics concentrated on English novels and short stories published in the early decades of the century. As the series has grown, it has broadened to include works of fiction from different centuries and from different countries, cultures, and literary traditions; there are books written by black women, by Catholic and Jewish women, by women of almost every English-speaking country, and there are several relevant novels by men.

Nearly 200 Virago Modern Classics will have been published in England by the end of 1985. During that same year, Penguin Books began to publish Virago Modern Classics in the United States, with the expectation of having some 40 titles from the series available by the end of 1986. Some of the earlier books in the series were published in the United States by The Dial Press.